O Horrid Night

Chilling Holiday Tales for the Black-Hearted

A FunDead Publications Anthology

Edited by Amber Newberry & Laurie Moran

For the Ghosts of Christmas past.

CONTENTS

ACKNOWLEDGEMENTS

FunDead Publications would like to extend our sincere gratitude to the following local businesses for their amazing support:

Creative Salem
Wicked Good Books
The Black Veil Studio of Tattoo & Art

A GHOST STORY
Corinne Clark

"Well, have *you* got one?" The man called Jack spoke in the local dialect and wore the clothes of a sheep farmer: a flat, cloth cap pushed back on his head, a sagging overcoat, and trousers tucked into muddy boots. With his long, drooping face and oversized ears, he looked rather like a hound dog.

"What, a ghost story?"

Jack had spoken of nothing but spooks since my arrival; I took him to be simple-minded, though he was amiable enough.

"Aye," Jack's companion Edgar, said. Nursing a glass of whisky—his cheeks flushed red with intemperance—he lounged in a chair with the stuffing coming out of its cushions. "It's a Christmas tradition." His voice was deeper than I expected for someone so small in stature.

"Odd, for a Christmas tradition," I replied. Apparently, the innkeeper was superstitious rather than religious, for the only evidence of the sacred holiday was a bough of scrubby pine placed upon the mantelpiece and the remains of a sherry soaked fruitcake—heavy as a doorstop—still sitting between my ribs.

"Not round 'ere," the innkeeper said. "When a tall, dark stranger crosses th' doorstep on Christmas Eve, it means a spirit is coming." His expression was inscrutable; I suspected he was having a laugh at my expense. It was not lost on me that I was approaching six feet tall and had hair black as India ink.

Narrowing my eyes I said, "You made that up just now."

"I didn't." The innkeeper folded his meaty arms across his chest. "A spirit on Christmas Eve brings a death soon after."

"Rubbish," I scoffed. "You don't really believe that, do you?" I looked at the faces of the other men in the room. Clearly, they did. "The idea is ludicrous. I have not brought a spirit of any kind with me, nor will there be one coming along after me. You've been reading too much Dickens."

"If you give us a story," the innkeeper said, "a convincing one, mind, then I reckon the restless spirits 'ill think the inn's haunted already and pass us by."

"True enough." Edgar raised his glass as if toasting the innkeeper, then took a generous swallow of his scotch.

"Well, I'm sorry to let you all down," I said, "but I must push off. My wife's expecting me home. She's roasting a quail, promised me a figgy pudding. It's our first Christmas together as husband and wife, you see."

None of the men seemed moved by my sentiment. Retrieving my pocket watch I consulted the time: half-past four. Night was falling quickly. Christmas would be upon us in a few hours. I snapped the gold case shut and dropped the watch back into my pocket, just as the innkeeper lifted the curtain at the window. My heart sank. A sinister fog had descended on the countryside, obscuring everything from view.

I thought of Audrey sitting in the window of our cottage, with the gloom swallowing the light from her gas lamp, the darkness creeping in around her. She would have only our old dog Mix for company, his tail thumping on the rug as she scratched behind his ears.

"You can't go out in this." The innkeeper inclined his head toward the window.

"I'll set out on foot—a little weather never bothered me."

Edgar raised his woolly eyebrows. "You'll never make it," he said. "You can't see a blasted thing when that fog rolls in off the moors. Not even your own two feet, never mind the road beneath 'em."

"I reckon you'd fall into a ditch, or drown in the river. Freeze to death p'raps. Or go mad wanderin' the heath." Jack waggled his long fingers at me. His voice was a bit too dramatic for my liking.

"No one's leaving here tonight," the innkeeper said. "I'll not 'ave the death of a man on my hands." He gave me a pointed look. "You'll have t' stay put 'til the morning."

I stared at him in disbelief. He towered over me with a frown on his ruddy, pockmarked face, and I saw that he had the flattened nose and misshapen skull of a pugilist. I surmised he didn't have a wife to answer to.

"I've got plenty of empty rooms; you can have your pick of 'em." The innkeeper unstopped a bottle of lager, and with a *glug, glug,* filled my glass again.

"But it's Christmas Eve," I protested.

"You've got us to celebrate with." Jack offered me a lopsided grin. "And I can whistle any tune you can think of. How about 'God Rest Ye Merry Gentlemen'? That's a lively one." Without any encouragement, he puckered up his lips to produce a scratchy series of notes.

"He owes us a story first," Edgar said, cutting short Jack's performance.

Exchanging macabre stories with these bumpkins was not how I wanted to spend Christmas Eve, but perhaps if I shared a quick one with them the oppressive weather would lift by the time I reached the end of it. For now, I supposed I would have to make the best of my situation and beg Audrey's forgiveness upon my return home.

"Just one," I said, "and then no one will stop me from going out that door." I pointed to it for emphasis.

"Fair enough," the man introduced as Mr. Scott said, taking a white clay pipe from between his teeth and pointing its stem at me. "A man can't be saved from his own folly." He hadn't spoken much since my arrival. A long scar puckered the skin of his left cheek, with the corresponding eyelid drooping in a half-wink. I suspected he was more observant than was immediately apparent, as the quiet ones often are. He wore a sailor's cap, though he was so ancient it must have been an eternity since he'd been at sea. Tobacco smoke from his pipe curled into the air and lingered in a wreath around his head. Its woody, sweet fragrance drifted across the room, reminding me of my late father. Underneath it, I detected the sour smell of spilled beer and the mustiness of damp and decaying walls. I ignored his remark.

"But your story must be true," Jack said. "And spooky." He rubbed his hands together like a villain in a penny dreadful.

"It just so happens that I do have a few tales up my sleeve." I sipped some of my lager. "But only one of them is true."

"That's the one we want then," Mr. Scott said, puffing his pipe contentedly.

I lied when I said I had a story. I didn't, but I was adaptable and capable of making one up. I had been an actor, of sorts, when I was at university, and fancied myself skilled in the dramatic arts. So, if these men wanted a spine-tingling story, then by God I would give them one.

"Once, not so long ago, there was a tragic accident at the old Loyn Bridge." I tried to make my voice deeper than Edgar's.

"The bridge two miles hence?" Jack asked.

"The very one," I replied, relishing the worried look that passed over his face.

Edgar leaned forward in his chair, "Did you see a specter there?"

"Be patient man," I said, but I smiled. They were a keen audience, and I was warming to my narrative, though I didn't yet know where it would go.

"I must begin with the beautiful woman, newly married to a clever, charming doctor." I leaned forward in my chair, loosening my collar. "The couple moved from Liverpool to a charming cottage in Hornby, along with their loyal dog, Mix." I tickled myself with the skill I had in creating fiction, using details from my own life. The lager and the crackling fire made me warm.

"Didn't you say *you're* a doctor?" Mr. Scott asked.

"Merely coincidence," I replied.

"What did she look like? The woman?" Edgar asked.

"Was she young or old?" Jack piped up.

"Well if she was beautiful, then she was young of course!" Mr. Scott exclaimed.

I chuckled, "Of course." Now it just so happens that my wife has a rare beauty, and since she was on my mind, I described her to my companions. "She was slight—what the French call 'petite'—with shining auburn hair. She had eyes of chestnut-brown with flecks of amber streaked through." I closed my eyes and brought her to mind. "A dusting of freckles across her nose, and a smile that dimpled at the corners in the most alluring way."

"Was she Irish?" Edgar asked, interrupting my reverie.

"I don't—does it matter?" I asked with annoyance.

"Well, I like Irish girls," Edgar said. "I just wondered."

"Fine," I said. "She was Irish."

"What was her name?" Mr. Scott asked. "We must know that."

While I considered my answer, the innkeeper took up a great iron poker, stabbing the charred logs in the fireplace to revive the dwindling flames. The wood sparked, and with the addition of another log, the fire *whooshed* back to a full blaze. Odors of wood smoke and fat drippings wafted through the room, mingling with the scent of Mr. Scott's tobacco; I found it comforting.

"Bridget," I said. "Her name was Bridget O'Donnell. And her husband was James," I added, although my name is Henry. "James wanted to move to the countryside, but his wife wasn't so keen. In the city, they lived in a smart Georgian townhouse, with columns in the front and large windows that filled the rooms with light. She walked her dog in the shady park across the square and shopped at Harding and Howell's in the high street. Oh, and there was Cuthbert's of course, her favorite place to take tea with her friends. But her husband found himself fed up with the endless gray of the city, and the soot on every square inch of it. The bustling crowds, the constant traffic. The noise never stopped; he couldn't think in all that clamor, and grew rather miserable."

I ran my hand through my hair, remembering it all. "He convinced his wife that they would have a magnificent life in the country. 'There are fields dotted with sheep,' he told her, 'And leafy forests filled with chirruping birds. Skies of brilliant blue stretch out overhead, and the nights are so clear you can see the stars.' 'We'll live in a cozy, thatched cottage,' he said. 'I'll practice out of the house—we'll have more time to spend together.' And so Bridget agreed to move to make her new husband happy."

"She was a good wife to that doctor," Edgar said in his gruff voice.

"Yes, she is a good wife," I said, not noticing my mistake.

"Get to the good part," the innkeeper said, taking up a stool close behind me.

My cheeks were flushed, and it was hard to think as clearly as I had when I began. Watching the flames devour the logs in the grate I said, "Her husband went out one day to a local farm, where he delivered a healthy baby boy."

"I thought this was a story about a pretty Irish lady," Jack complained.

"I'll get back to her in a moment," I snapped. "James is important too."

"It's a ghost story," Edgar reminded Jack, "so you know it isn't going to end well."

My skin prickled with gooseflesh. It was true, ghost stories didn't end well. Why had I used a description of my wife? *Don't be daft*, I told myself, *it's only made up*. My pulse quickened, and with my head swimming slightly, I placed my fingertips against my temples to recover myself. After a few moments, I looked up at the innkeeper and held out my empty glass.

"Another, please."

"The bottles 'ill be out soon," he replied.

"Haven't you got any more?" My throat was dry again already.

"Not 'til the delivery day after tomorrow."

I tried to focus. "A terrible fog sunk over the countryside, and after the doctor delivered the baby, he had to walk out in it, carrying his heavy medical bag; water leaked into his boots, and his bones ached with the cold."

I glanced across the room, to where I had draped my own coat over the back of a chair near the fireplace, with my boots and black bag set down next to it to dry out. "He had sworn to his wife that he would be home by nightfall, but he wouldn't make it. Lost and frozen, he came upon a coaching inn, and drawn in by the light shining through the windows and the promise of some warmth and companionship, he decided to stop for a rest, planning to wait until the fog dispersed, but it only got worse."

"I don't know if I like where this story's goin'," Mr. Scott said.

I didn't much like it either, but something compelled me to continue. "James told his wife, 'I promise I will be home before the sun sets.'" The men all stared at me as I struggled to speak the next line, "'The only thing that could keep me from you is Death itself.'" That part was true. I had said that. My palms were slick against the empty lager glass. A chill ran down my spine, and I shivered. "Have you got a window open?" I asked the innkeeper.

"Course not," he said. "Though the place is in need of repair; there's plenty of cracks for the wind to get in."

"He shouldn't have said sumthin' like that to his wife," Jack said. "He'd have had her all upset for nothin' if he was stuck and couldn't get to her. Why would he tell her that he'd be dead if he didn't come home?"

"It was a reckless promise," I conceded. "But he hadn't imagined a fog too thick to navigate, or that he'd be confined by it. It seemed a romantic thing to say at the time." Looking forlornly into the bottom of my glass I added, "I'm sure he didn't mean to make his wife anxious. Undoubtedly he felt awful about it."

It had been a while since I'd checked the time, so I looked again at my pocket watch. Twenty minutes had slipped past. "I'm sure you can guess how the story ends," I said, with finality in my voice. This superstitious nonsense was straining my nerves.

I went to the window to have another look outside. The weather was even bleaker than before. Snow blowing against the side of the inn had collected on the windowsill and up against the door. Audrey had gotten the white Christmas she had hoped for, I thought ruefully.

"I can't guess how the story ends," Jack said. He chewed the edges of his fingernails. I didn't know if the talk of ghosts made him nervous, or if it was his usual habit.

"Neither can I," Mr. Scott added.

"You've got to give us the rest of it," Edgar said. "We've not heard this one before, and it's just getting interesting."

It was as though I was marooned on a desert island, like in that adventure novel filled with pirates and cannibals, but instead of an endless, unsurpassable ocean, it was a shroud of gloom that had me trapped. Foolishly, I had used my own life's details for my ghastly tale, with a description of my wife and myself as the central players. What had I done?

"Finish your story, Doctor," the innkeeper said.

I swallowed the lump in my throat. "The doctor's wife waited for him until the wick in the lantern burned down to a black stub, but that damnable fog didn't relent. James had sworn that nothing but death would keep him from her, so Bridget bundled herself up in a shawl of tartan wool and went out searching for him. She took a carriage lamp and the faithful dog Mix with her, planning to make enquiries in the village."

"How did she walk through that fog?" Jack asked. "When it had everyone else stranded?"

"Good question," I said. I mulled that over. "You're right." I looked at Jack, hopeful. "It is unlikely she left the house. It would have been unwise." I seized at the suggestion. Of course, Audrey would never leave the safety of the house. Not alone. Not in such murky weather.

"But it's a ghost story," Edgar said again. "Maybe she did go out in the fog and got lost in it. Was it her that died? Is she the ghost?"

"No!" I leapt out of my chair— my legs weak, my hands trembling.

"No, she does not die. She is not the ghost!"

Mr. Scott cringed when I cried out, his teeth clattering against his pipe stem.

I caught sight of my own flustered countenance in the mirror behind the bar. With my wide eyes, pale cheeks, and hair standing every which way, I almost didn't recognize myself.

The men looked at each other. I couldn't tell what they were thinking. There was only the snapping of the fire and the wind blustering around the inn.

"Tell us the rest," the innkeeper said.

I managed to regain my composure, though my stomach was queasy. "All right. You shall get your ghost." As I returned to my seat, the innkeeper poured the last of the lager into my glass, shaking every drop out of the bottle.

My voice faltered as I continued, "Bridget urgently needed to find her husband."

"P'raps a neighbor with a gig took her out," Jack suggested.

"That makes sense," Edgar said. "She was a pretty Irish lady; any man would 'ave taken her."

"Besides, it was Christmas Eve," Jack said.

"I didn't say it was Christmas Eve," I retorted, my jaw tight.

Jack knitted his eyebrows. "Of course it was Christmas Eve; it's a Christmas story."

My mind raced; I realized that I hadn't given the ending yet. All was not lost. "All right. Let's say that despite the fog, the neighbor took her in his gig, and they travelled without seeing another soul until they reached the Loyn Bridge." I felt more confident already. "But as the carriage crossed over the river, Bridget saw that a section of the bridge barrier had broken away, and a cluster of men were peering over the side of it. 'A carriage went over', she heard someone say. 'I reckon the driver couldn't see much in the fog.'

Somewhere out in the haze, the tragedy replayed itself. Bridget heard the pounding drum of horse hooves striking packed earth, the clattering of carriage wheels, the crash and rumble of the bridge barrier giving way. She put her hands over her ears to try and block out the screaming of the horse, and the deafening cacophony of the entire conveyance smashing against the rocks below before splashing into the freezing river."

My cheeks were flushed, and I found myself pacing up and down in front of my audience. It was as if the words spilled out of my mouth before I could think them through. I set my glass down hard so that the beer sloshed over the side of it. "It was one of the travelers on that carriage who died and became a ghost. *That* is the phantom that haunts the bridge to this day."

Again, I considered my ghoulish story had come to its end. Now I would take my leave.

"It *was* the doctor," Jack said.

"Sorry?"

"It was the doctor what fell off the bridge. It was him who was dead. It was him who became the ghost."

"I told you it wasn't," I said crossly. "It was some unfortunate traveler, that's all."

"I agree with Jack," Edgar said. "It must have been the doctor, the story can't end any other way."

It was only then I noticed how dim the place had become. Most of the candles had been snuffed out, leaving the light from the fireplace to cast queer, dancing shadows on the faces of the men seated around me.

"Unless it was the wife's carriage," the innkeeper said.

My stomach turned over.

"What a gruesome turn of events," Mr. Scott muttered.

Jack squinted his eyes and tapped his bottom lip with his finger. "But she was on the bridge *after* the accident, so how could it have been her what drowned in the river?"

"Well, if she haunts the bridge," Mr. Scott said. He removed his smoking pipe. "She mightn't know she was dead. Or how she got to be that way. She'd be doomed to relive that accident over and over." He took a draw of tobacco and blew a ring of smoke into the air. "For all eternity, I reckon."

Suddenly I was desperate to get to my wife, to stop her from leaving the house, to stop her from searching for me. I snatched my overcoat from the back of the chair, mashing my feet into my boots.

"Where are you going?" the innkeeper asked. "Not out there, are you?"

"I must get home to my wife."

The innkeeper looked at me as though I was mad, as though I was already lost. "Godspeed, then." He swung the door open.

The air outside was thick and heavy with snow, but I was prepared to plunge into it. As I attempted to determine where the road was, I heard the thudding of a horse's hooves and the rattle and squeak of springs and carriage wheels. Then a hazy light penetrated the gloom.

Steadily the light grew stronger, until it appeared as a blazing lantern fastened to the side of a carriage. The vehicle slowed as it drew up in front of the inn. The sleek, black horse pulling it had had a vigorous run; it blew hot vapor from its nose and nodded its head, making the tackle jangle. I could see the whites of its eyes.

The young driver kept the reins tight. He tipped his hat to us. "Is Dr. Reid here?"

"Yes!" I stepped forward.

"I've got your wife on board. We've been looking for you."

Without so much as a wave to my companions, I rushed out into the miserable night and clambered into the carriage. Audrey gazed out the opposite window— the curl of her auburn hair, the tartan shawl at once recognizable.

The carriage took off at a fast trot. "Darling, please forgive me," I said. "This unholy weather had me trapped! To set out in it alone would have been dangerous. I planned to leave the moment I had a chance to." I didn't want Audrey to think I chosen to stay at an inn, drinking, rather than spend Christmas Eve with her.

My wife remained silent.

I clasped her hand, cold and thin, in mine. "Let me make it up to you. Tell me how."

I thought she would punish me by not speaking, until at last she said, "I love you more than you love me." Her voice was so low I strained to hear it. "You said that nothing but Death itself would keep you from me."

My own vow had come back to haunt me.

"I shouldn't have disturbed you like that—"

As I spoke, the words died in my throat, for my sweetheart turned to look at me at last, with eyes that were blank and sunken into their sockets. Her pallid flesh had withered, and was stretched over the contours of her skull. A flap of skin hung from a large wound bisecting her cheek. Seizing me with her bony fingers, she drew me in for a kiss.

"I love you more than you love me," she crooned, "for *not even* Death will keep me from you."

The carriage thundered down the road, swaying wildly. I screamed, but the fog swallowed the sound.

My wife and I were together again. Forever.

CAROLERS
Kenneth E. Olson

Haley loved Great Grandma Vi. Absolutely and without a doubt. That didn't mean she wanted to spend Christmas out here in the middle of nowhere. She *certainly* didn't want to spend Christmas Eve alone with Great Grandma, but everybody else wanted to go to the Christmas Eve buffet at Ricky's Tavern in town. Because Haley was the eldest, that left her Great Granny-sitting a woman who probably had worn nothing but nightgowns and slippers since July.

Merry Christmas.

"Let her go," said G-Gran. Great Grandma loved when Haley called her that, "Gee Gran". She said it made her feel "hip" and any hip she could feel at her age was a good thing. "I'll be fine." Haley awarded the elder with a warm smile.

"You know someone needs to stay with you, Mom," Grandma said, slipping her jacket over her shoulders and snugging it into place.

"Rubbish. What do you suppose I'm going to do? Throw a party?"

"*I* might," Haley suggested.

"See? You should take her. Otherwise she'll get me drunk."

"Stop it you two," Haley's mother said. "Gran, you can't just sit there all night. What if you've got to go to the bathroom?"

"Depends," she said. Haley giggled.

"Well there you go. You two are perfect for each other. You'll keep each other entertained for hours."

"Hours?" Haley was mortified. "You're not going to be gone for hours! Mom?"

"Of course not."

"I wouldn't make promises," G-Gran said. "I hear Ricky's can get pretty full on Christmas Eve. They're the only thing open. The last fading beacon of full stomachs for those that can't make themselves a damned sandwich."

"Don't be so sour, Mom." Grandma opened the door, where a series of three concrete steps flanked by iron railings led to the ground. To the right, the car was running with its headlights on, warming up, with Dad and Haley's two younger brothers already inside. Snow flitted through the headlight beams, dancing on the wind as if happy to be in the spotlight.

10

"Mom," Haley pleaded. She lowered her voice to a whisper. "What if she has a stroke or something?"

"Oh for the love of…she's not going to have a stroke." But a look passed between her mother and grandmother because, well, who knew really?

"In or out," G-Gran said. "You're letting in all the cold air. And take her with you. I don't want her here. I've got company coming."

"You do not have company coming, Mom." Grandma sighed. She gave Haley a quick kiss on the forehead. "You watch her. Call Ricky's if anything happens, but only after you call nine-one-one."

"That's reassuring, Grandma."

"You'll be fine," she said. She waved at the car, a symbol of *we're on our way*, and walked toward it, her head bent against the cold.

"Mom?"

"We'll bring you a Juicy Lucy," her mother said. "Gotta go."

The door closed, and Haley was left alone with G-Gran.

She watched through the window as the vehicle pulled onto the main road (still a gravel nightmare of mud in the spring), taking its warmth and light with it. The area around the house plunged into that weird, oddly soothing color Haley thought of as "Winter Blue". Snow drifts in the yard shifted and rippled in the wind. Beyond that, dark trees rose into the night, blacker than anything else on the landscape. They looked like construction paper cut-outs pasted at the edge of reality.

"You going to pout about this all night?" G-Gran croaked from the living room.

Haley shuddered. She hated when G-Gran got ornery.

"I'm not pouting," Haley said. She turned, awarding G-Gran her best *happy to be here* smile. "I was just looking. It's beautiful out there."

"Yes," her great-grandmother agreed. She closed her eyes, leaned back in her chair, and smiled. "Yes it is."

Had G-Gran had a television, or a radio, or even a Commodore 64 computer—*anything*—it might not have been so bad. Haley supposed she should be lucky there was electricity. Everything else seemed to have locked down in 1940-something and hadn't moved a centimeter since. Even Haley's iPhone had begun to bore her, and that was saying something. Of course out here in the boonies there was no Wi-Fi and no signal strength to speak of, so the most she could do was play the games she'd already downloaded, until her battery gave out.

G-Gran had a landline. *A landline*, if you could believe that! With a handset that must have weighed at least twenty pounds, connected by wire to a base that had a disc you had to turn to dial the numbers. There was a list of phone numbers taped to the desk beside it, but most of them were doctors and businesses and stuff. Ricky's Tavern was listed there. No personal numbers at all.

The phone wasn't the only ancient item in the house. G-Gran must have kept everything she'd ever been given in her life. The walls were littered with photos, and shelves showcased knickknacks from all decades of the human race. Small porcelain angels, haloed with dust, glared at her from their spots above the windows. A small, plastic, dog-faced Wonder Woman figurine from the '70s brandished her magic lasso from the top of a bookshelf. Next to her, a bird with a bulbous bottom and a top hat dipped and drank from red water, dipped and drank and dipped and drank, again and again without end, Amen.

Fixed to the wall just to the left of G-Gran's lounge chair was a clock shaped like a cat. G-Gran called it Felix, after some old cartoon cat nobody remembered. The tail would swing one way while the eyes of the cat looked the other, a big stupid grin on its big stupid face. Tick-tock, tick-tock. The thing was creepy. Haley was staring at it and thinking, *Twenty minutes! It's only been twenty minutes!* when G-Gran, who Haley had assumed had fallen asleep, spoke.

"Can you hear them, Haley?"

"Hear who, G-Gran?"

The old woman chuckled at the name. "The carolers. I said I had company coming."

Perhaps she *was* asleep. Maybe dreaming.

"There's no carolers out here," Haley said. "We're too far out." It was only four miles, but houses were sparse in between. What chance was there of people caroling out here?

And yet, didn't she hear something? An echo, maybe? Sounds carried on the wind? She shook her head clear. This place was too quiet. It played tricks on the ears.

"Oh they're out there," G-Gran opened one eye at Haley. "Be a dear and get a saucepan of water boiling, would you? I want to have some hot chocolate ready for them. And I could do with a cup of tea."

There was a teapot on the stove with old water in it. Haley dumped it, then filled the pot about half-full before putting it on the gas burner to heat up. That was enough for tea for G-Gran and some hot chocolate for herself.

"We used to go caroling every Christmas Eve," G-Gran said from the living room. Her voice creaked in the way old people's voices tended to do, yet it filled the house. Not that there was much to fill. From any given room you could see two others and there were only five in the whole place.

Leaving the water to boil, Haley went back to the living room. "Be a sweetheart and hand me that photo album, third one from the top. There's a good girl."

There was a stack of perhaps thirty to forty photo albums just by the

12

arm of the couch. Haley removed the third down, steeling herself for the puff of dust she was sure to encounter, but didn't come, and then waited for the whole swaying stack to topple over. That didn't happen either.

She handed the book, a brown leather monstrosity with a cracked and peeling binding, to G-Gran. G-Gran grunted as she took it and set it heavily into her lap.

"Old memories are heavy memories, Haley," she said. "Don't forget that."

"I won't," Haley said, but thought the book was just damned heavy because it was old and had nothing to do with the memories inside. She couldn't have been more wrong.

G-Gran flipped to a point about a third of the way though the book, then flipped a couple of more pages for good measure. When she found what she was looking for, she leaned back and smiled. It was a sad smile. One Haley didn't like.

"Come look at this with me."

Haley knew what she was going to see. G-Gran showed the same photo to everybody every year, and it was this photo she pointed to with a gnarled finger.

"That's my little sister, Pearl. She was killed that year. Christmas Eve of 1936. She was six."

Not exactly, thought Haley, *Pearl went missing that night.* The assumption was that she was dead but there was no evidence to back that theory.

Pearl was the smallest of the group of seven carolers represented in the yellowed and cracked photo, and as such she was front and center in the picture. G-Gran, two years Pearl's elder, was just behind her, one mittened hand on her sister's shoulder.

Pearl wore a winter jacket with the fur-lined hood pulled up. Her head was bowed a little, a bright smile across her face, her eyes peering out from under the jacket's hood in an almost daring manner. Haley had always associated the color red with Pearl's jacket and blue with her eyes. Just like G-Gran's.

"She was a beauty, wasn't she?" G-Gran smiled and traced the outline of Pearl's face with one finger. "Could have been a star. *Would* have been a star I have no doubt. Maybe right up there with Patsy Cline and Loretta Lynn. Oh, she could sing. We both could. But her voice, her voice was something special. Like God Himself had touched her throat and said, 'With this you will bring joy.'"

Was there an edge to G-Gran's tone? Maybe, but maybe not. In the next moment G-Gran turned wet eyes toward Haley and smiled.

"I can still hear her voice."

Haley put a hand on G-Gran's shoulder. Part of the reason she hated this story was because it always made her sad. Imagine losing someone that long ago and still missing her. She couldn't wrap her mind around it.

"Can't you hear it? Pearl's voice?"

Haley stopped. Despite the warmth in the house, she felt a shiver run through her body. Part of it was the surety of G-Gran's voice. The other was worse. She thought maybe she *had* heard something.

"Gran, there's…there's no voice."

"Oh sure there is, dear. A lot of them. You're not listening the right way."

Haley opened her mouth to ask how to listen the "right way" when she heard them. Somewhere off in the distance there was singing, a chorus. She could even slightly make out the words.

O Holy Night! The stars are brightly shining,
It is the night of our dear Savior's birth

The idea occurred to her that she hadn't heard it before because she'd been actively listening for it. As absurd as it sounded, it felt right. It was the auditory equivalent of seeing something out of the corner of your eye, the thing that wasn't there when you tried to look directly at it.

Maybe it was coming from town. Was that possible? She'd heard sound traveled farther in cold weather, something about sound waves bouncing off cold air near the ground and warmer air above; science wasn't her thing. But four miles?

It was the wind whistling through the trees, that's all. G-Gran had placed the idea in her head that it was singing, so that's what she heard. The problem now was that she couldn't unhear it.

It was beautiful. Hypnotic. The voices blended seamlessly, as if the harmonies were being produced by one set of vocal chords. She could almost see it, each voice represented by a color, rising and falling in waves. Blue bled to purple to red to orange to green. It was like listening to very colorful and active northern lights.

And then it was done. Just like that. Just…gone. Haley felt a little ill, like her stomach wasn't quite in the right place. A little to the left of normal, perhaps.

"They'll be here soon," G-Gran said.

"That was the wind, Gran."

G-Gran gave her a look that suggested Haley might be the one out of her mind. "There's no wind that sounds like that, Haley, and you know it."

That was precisely the problem. Haley did know it.

In the kitchen, the teapot whistled with that sudden burst of anger all teapots have. Haley jumped at the sound, but G-Gran just looked up with disapproving eyes.

"That won't be enough for everybody," G-Gran said. "You should have used the saucepan like I told you."

"I'll put more on when they get here, G-Gran. I didn't want it to be cold for them." Lies. All lies.

"Pshaw. They'll be here in a couple of minutes. Go ahead and put a little more on." G-Gran turned back to her photo album, flipping through the pages and humming *O Holy Night*. Goosebumps stippled Haley's skin.

Haley pulled the screaming teapot off the stove, and the whistling died down like a man breathing his last. Setting it aside, she managed to retrieve a mid-sized saucepan from the jumble beneath the cupboard with only a few errant clangs. As bad as her hands were shaking, she was lucky the whole mess didn't come spilling out onto the floor.

She stood up. A face stared at her through the kitchen window.

It was a guy, probably not much younger than herself. He wore a dirty baby blue knit cap that had seen better days, its yarn frayed in a dozen places and the ball on top only a quarter of what it once was. His face was a pale mask, a finely detailed snow sculpture with coal-black eyes.

Haley gaped until the figure blinked. She dropped the saucepan, and it clanged off the floor. She didn't hear it. Her ears were too busy registering the sound of her own scream.

"Gran, there's someone out there! There's—"

"Of course there is. I said I had company coming. Nobody listens."

G-Gran was at the open front door, which blocked a good third of the living room and the chair in which G-Gran had been sitting. How could she have moved so quickly? And quietly? She always grunted, making a show of getting to her feet for the benefit of those around her.

The ancient face widened into a grin just as the carolers began singing again.

Long lay the world in sin and error pining,
'Til he appeared and the soul felt its worth.

Just as beautiful as before. Just as rich and entrancing. G-Gran stood with the snow flitting in and the cold wind disturbing her nightgown, lifting and flapping it against liver-spotted, too thin calves. A snowflake caught in G-Gran's eyelash, and she blinked it away.

"Pearl," she said. "Pearl you look so beautiful. Just like the last time I saw you. Come in. All of you, come in."

The uneasiness in Haley's stomach flooded through her body, firing her nerves. Despite what G-Gran was seeing, Haley knew—was absolutely certain—that whatever was outside the door was the same thing that had been at the window. And letting it in would be a mistake.

"No! You can't! You can't come in!"

G-Gran turned when Haley yelled, the wind blowing strands of silver hair across her face. She looked for a moment as if she'd been attacked by a handful of tinsel.

"Haley! What? How rude!"

"You can't let them in."

"This is my house, and I'll do as I damned well please. If I want my sister and her friends to come in, they can come in."

"Grandma Vi, I don't know what those things are, but it's not Pearl. She's dead!" Haley was on the verge of tears, and her voice shook as she spoke. The words coming out of her mouth, the thoughts she was having...they didn't belong in this world. Not the real world.

"Well of course she is. I killed her."

There had been times, mostly just before sleep stole over her, that Haley had been astounded by the amount of noise in her head, all the chatter and thoughts that filled it, echoing through her skull. She never realized it was happening until some errant noise or particularly strong thought interrupted it. At those moments, all would go eerily quiet.

The same thing happened here, all thought suddenly drained from her mind. The only noise was the ticking of Felix. It seemed amplified, thudding through the walls, and Haley could imagine its wide creepy cat eyes swinging left and right and left and right and left and right. Haley stepped toward Gran in time with the clock, unaware she was doing so.

"It...it doesn't matter," Haley said and swallowed. Hard. "It wasn't your fault. Whatever the accident was, it—"

"There was no accident, Haley," G-Gran said. Her lips fluttered. Her eyes sank to the floor.

On the steps just beyond the door, figures emerged. Twelve of them. *One day for each day of Christmas,* Haley thought wildly. They were different ages and dress styles, as if each of them had stepped out from a different era in time which, Haley supposed, was horribly accurate. The boy she'd seen in the window was with them, one of the taller ones standing near the back. In the front was the little girl Haley had seen in the picture so many times. Pearl. Only her coat wasn't red but lime green. And her eyes certainly weren't blue. They were black. All their eyes were black.

"Who are you?" She'd meant it as a demand, but her voice only managed a whisper.

"Those wronged," the girl who had been Pearl said, "and those who have wronged." Her voice sounded airy, distant, like it was originating somewhere miles away from where the figure actually stood.

"They're Collectors," G-Gran said, and her voice, too, sounded far away. As if she was in a trance, reciting by rote. "Their souls are darkened by their guilt, their forms caught forever at the age their pain first took hold. They come for those of us who have heavy souls, but they can't do anything if they're not invited inside."

She turned to Haley, her voice normal again. "They've been after me for over twenty years, but I never let them in. And I'm glad, no matter how my old bones ached for it. It gave me time with you and your brothers."

G-Gran knelt in front of her baby sister and took the emotionless face in her hands.

"Oh, Pearl, I'm so sorry. I was just so jealous."

"I am not the girl you once knew," the Pearl-thing said. Haley gritted her teeth, silently begging it to stop talking.

G-Gran waved the statement away as if it were an annoying fly. "It doesn't matter. You have her face. I need to apologize to this face." A tear tracked down G-Gran's cheek. She didn't bother wiping it away, if she was aware of it at all. "Once you started singing, once Mom and Dad knew you were better than I would ever be, all their attention shifted to you. Maybe that's not how it was, but that's how it felt."

The Pearl-thing remained stoic, blank. It didn't even blink. G-Gran stared at that face for a moment, her lips trembling. She looked like a child that had been caught with a hand in the cookie jar and knew she was one second away from punishment. Maybe she expected some sign, some token forgiveness. She didn't get it.

G-Gran sighed and stood. "Can we at least sing? On the way out? Can we sing one more time?"

The Pearl-thing nodded. It reached out one mittened hand (the mitten, too, was lime-green, Haley noted). G-Gran took it.

"No," Haley said. Her voice trembled. She could barely see through the tears in her eyes. "You can't go. You can't take her! I won't let you!"

Haley grabbed the forearm of the Pearl-thing in an attempt to wrench it away from G-Gran's hand. In an instant, her arm grew cold and numb to her shoulder and her body went rigid. Her mouth dropped open in a gasp that didn't quite emerge right away. To anybody watching it would have looked as if the video of life had frozen momentarily before catching up with itself again. A split moment, a skip, and that was all. To Haley it was an eternity.

Visions filled her head. Truths.

Two children she would have recognized as G-Gran and Pearl, even if she hadn't seen those old pictures. They were with a group of others, caroling, going from house to house and occasionally enjoying some hot chocolate. Snow fell lightly but was piling up. There would be a fresh two or more inches on the ground come morning. They posed for a picture, the same one in G-Gran's album. Gran slipped away from the group. Pearl noticed and went looking for her. Gran hid behind a tree. She pulled a knife, the kind fisherman use to clean their catch, from beneath the cuff of her jacket. Pearl walked past the tree, and G-Gran stepped behind her. The knife flashed.

And then Gran was on her knees near the old creek. Haley knew where that creek was. She recognized the large oak that teetered right on the edge of it, some of its bare roots, layered with snow and unnaturally pale, diving directly into the water. She didn't recognize the hole some of those tangled roots had created in the embankment. Maybe that hole was no longer there. But it was then. It was when Gran shoved the lifeless body of her little sister into that hole. She shoved and cried at the same time. Shoved and cried and cried and cried.

Haley snapped back to the present, stepping away from the sisters. Her arm was still cold and numb, and it fell heavily to her side. Her mouth moved but nothing came out. Her breath seemed locked in her chest. G-Gran, her eyes streaming, smiled wearily at Haley.

"I hadn't meant to kill her," she said, "so I suppose in some sense it was an accident. I didn't want her dead. I just wanted her silenced. But accident or not, I did it, and I have to pay for it. Jealousy is an ugly thing, and more so when it's between siblings. Sometimes the hate you breed is greater than the love you share."

She reached out, placed one hand on Haley's cheek. Haley stepped back involuntarily, afraid of more visions, but none came. Just G-Gran's cold hand on her cheek. A hand she could barely feel. Her chest unlocked and she gasped, able to breathe again.

"You weren't supposed to be here for this. You were supposed to be in town with the rest of the folks. This was to be my moment, and mine alone." She sighed, a great lonely sound filled with the secrets of years. "But I suppose things rarely work out the way you'd hope. Life is a messy thing, after all."

She rose and faced the black-eyed carolers.

"I'm ready."

The Pearl-thing once again reached out for G-Gran's hand. Gran took it.

"Please find her," G-Gran said to Haley, "Give her a proper burial. That's all I want this Christmas." The elderly woman, whom Haley had thought she'd known, bent and kissed her on the cheek.

Then G-Gran walked through the front door, bare feet leaving no prints on the new snow that whipped her hair and nightgown around. She raised her voice with the others, hesitant at first, and sounding vaguely crow-like. Soon it was as strong as the others, although it didn't mesh quite as well, a black bar in the chorus of color, the one voice distinguishable from the rest.

Fall on your knees! O hear the angel voices!

O night divine.

O night,

O night divine.

Nearly two dozen more of the black-eyed creatures emerged from the shadows of the trees at the edge of the lawn. The entourage reached them, and G-Gran turned, one more time, and raised a hand to Haley. Haley found herself returning the wave as the front door swung slowly shut of its own volition.

Then she was alone in the house. G-Gran's body slumped in her chair, the large photo album dangling precariously from her lap. The only sound was the ticking of that awful cat clock. G-Gran was gone. Felix still lived.

Slowly, dreamily, Haley picked up the phone (the handset was *heavy*) and dialed the number to Ricky's Tavern. No need for nine-one-one now. The other end rang, and Haley thought about a spot above her bed where Felix the Creepy Cat Clock would fit perfectly.

THERE MUST HAVE BEEN SOME MAGIC
Casey E. Hamilton

A pea green fog rolled in across the Thames, mixing with the smoke of the coal soot that poured from the chimneys to hold at bay the bitter cold. It smelled noxious, of rotting garbage and decomposing bones, and it filled the alleys and byways of Whitechapel and Piccadilly alike, making it impossible to see even the flickering flames of the gas lamps overhead in the thick, eerie green.

The fog swirled, and a top hat tumbled down the cobblestones, brim over crown, brim over crown. It seemed to go faster than the small breeze warranted, but it was full of holes with the silk shredded in places, so perhaps it was lighter than an average top hat. It tumbled. and the wind howled as if it were blowing through pan pipes, the melody jaunty and eerie in the green, the sound beneath the bluster a death rattle in the throat. The music was felt as much as heard, a part of the fog and the decomposing air. The hat blew sideways, tumbling along the low wall, and then the wall broke where a set of stairs led down to the river bank, and the top hat fell, brim over crown, brim over crown, onto the frozen embankment.

The wind was less here, and it rested in the filthy air on the cold snow.

It whistled.

It waited.

* * *

Sam knew cold, and he knew that the thick green wind coming off the Thames meant that he couldn't enjoy his usual sewer pipe that night. It was out of the way, and he had never been robbed there. But when the wind blew, it whipped through the holes in his wool sweater and made his teeth chatter. This wasn't even teeth chattering weather. This was the sort of weather where a chap falls asleep and never wakes up again. He would just have to face his father and hope the noxious green air cleared in a few days. Black eyes were better than being dead, anyway.

He trudged down the snowy street with his hands in his pockets, his cap pulled low, and his thin scarf wrapped too many times across his nose. The sole of his boot flapped as he walked. The scarf did nothing to help with the smell, but it made him feel better to breathe in the oily scent of wool along with the other, for at least the whole world didn't seem like it was rotting then. He could tell that others were in the fog with him, scurrying to their own homes, but all he saw was the patterned plaid of a skirt as it swooshed past him, the outline of a man in the fog, the sound of footsteps in the distance, the click of a cane.

The green swirled. A little girl stood in front of him. She had a white fur hood and fur muff on her hands, resting atop her red wool coat. Her black buttoned boots shone, though her curls had gone limp in the damp air. She looked warm. She also looked frightened.

The fur hood came right over the little girl's ears, and the muff was infinitely more protection for the hands than Sam's threadbare pant pockets.

"Hey— " Sam started to say.

A set of hands reached up and plucked her from the mist. Brown wool pants and shiny shoes stood in front of him. "You!" the man yelled. "Be off with you, urchin. If you so much as touch my daughter...."

"Now, Guvnor, I didn't mean—"

"Scat!"

Sam turned, and he heard the man's voice change. "Gwen, darling. It's alright. I'm here..."

She was likely going home to plenty of warm tea and a grate full of coal. Sam didn't know what he was going home to. It all depended on a small amber bottle on his father's shelf, but likely the bottle would be empty and the coal box too.

Would his lot be easier to bear if others didn't have so much more than he?

Sam started to whistle, but the way the fog took the sound made the hollow at the base of his spine tingle, so he stopped. Instead, he hurried over the cobblestones. The cold settled into his bones, making them feel as though he would shatter from the inside, like an icicle falling from a roof.

* * *

Three days. The fog lifted and the cold settled into something half bearable. And in a cold like the one that had passed, of course the Thames would be frozen right through the middle now, and maybe thick enough to stand on.

Sam waited until his father drank himself into an insensible heap in the corner of the rented hovel, then left for the river embankment. In the cold, which made everything hurt, it was easy to ignore the unique pain of his bruised shoulder and thigh.

The flags and booths, dark brown and dingy on the white snow, were already going up on the hilly ice of the river. White flags and Union Jacks waved from the top of the triangle-shaped tents. Along the banks were the heaving, tilted masts of frozen schooners. Wisps of cloud unfurled across the sky.

Sam thanked his stars that he was early enough. There wasn't a man at the steps yet, to insist anyone pay a penny to get to the fair or get his ears boxed. Sam ran down the icy stairs, skittering and gripping the hand rail with his holey gloves for purchase.

He saw the hat when he got to the bottom, pressed up against a drift with the crown toward the sky. It looked like the top hat had been expensive silk once, though now it wasn't any good to anyone.

Sam picked it up.

The wind whistled through the holes, and the blue sky shone through.

Sam smiled. He might make a few pennies himself this afternoon. The hat was begging for a snowy occupant. He tucked the hat under his arm and ran towards the assembling fair.

* * *

Sam chose his spot with care. Not near the booth with small cards that said "Printed on the River Thames in the Great Frost, 1814," nor near the lady selling gingerbread and sausages, or the potters selling expensive wares with the date on them. He made sure to avoid the edges of the river, where coaches and horses would wheel along the ice between the tipsy ships frozen to their moorings. He would set down by the large drift of snow next to the carnival rides. That would do perfectly.

The snow was easy to mold under his fingers. He made the snowman a lavish costume of swirls and patterned stones, carving his face in a jaunty, rakish grin. He placed the top hat on the snowman's head.

A gust of wind picked up, whipping the white flags of the tents into a billowing frenzy when Sam laid the hat on. The hat stayed put, never tipping with the bluster.

The wind was bitter, whipping through Sam's sweater. He rewrapped the scarf around his neck, using his unbruised arm.

Sam took his own hat off his head, and held it out to a group of men walking by. "Penny for the Guy?"

Two of the men dropped a penny in Sam's hat without making eye contact, striding without break after the others. Their top hats were the soft velvet of beaver. Their ties were silk, their overcoats thick wool. The wind died down.

* * *

The night was cold and clear. Sam sighed. "Wish for a sausage," he muttered under his breath. He sat on the snowbank next to the snowman and listened to someone playing an eerie melody on the pan pipes. And then he remembered the hat full of pennies. He splurged and bought a sausage from the woman near the bridge, and then went back to the Guy. He hadn't had meat in ages.

He would have to find a place on the ice to sleep tonight, before someone else claimed his handiwork. The frost fair was likely to last several days, and already his pocket was full of change, maybe enough to keep him from his father's house for a few months, even if it did get cold again.

But when Sam went back, the Guy was not where he had left him. Instead, he was sitting on the snowbank. The hollow where his eyes weren't followed Sam as he approached.

"Hullo!" said Sam. "Did someone knock you...no, you look fine. What the devil?"

I am quite intact. Thank you for your concern.

The snowman hadn't spoken. The words found Sam's brain and resonated inside it. He dropped his sausage and backed away.

Please stay, said the Snowman.

"I don't need no trouble," said Sam. "I ain't...I ain't had nothin' to drink. Not a thing. Nossir. Begone ye devil—"

I am not a devil. If you would only stay a moment. I am not a figment. You must know. You made me, Samuel. I wish to thank you. Only to thank you for my life.

Sam stopped moving.

"I ain't had nothin' to drink," he muttered.

Finish your dinner. We will converse.

Sam stood for a moment. The snowman didn't move. He picked his sausage back up off the ice. It was cold, but at least it wasn't half rotten like most of his meals. He took a bite. He edged back toward the Guy.

"What do you want?" Sam said. It still hadn't moved, and then it did. Sam jumped.

The snowman jerked his hand up, thrust it mechanically into a fold of the costume Sam had sculpted for him, and pulled out a set of wooden pan flutes. They had come from nowhere, and yet they looked solid enough.

Want has nothing to do with me. I am a man of snow. I cannot want, but you can. I have heard your own wanting, and I have come. Tell me what you wish for and I will grant it with my music. Tell me.

"I don't want anything," Sam lied.

Every human wants something, said the snowman. *Like you wanted that sausage a moment ago. Let me give you a big wish. I will wait until you know what you want. I will be here. Take the time you need to consider.*

Sam stared at the snowman for a long time. He stared until his hands turned numb, and his feet tingled from standing too long. Around him, the gold pinpoints of can fires among the dark tents winked out as merchants went to sleep. The Guy still stared forward, hand upright holding the pan flutes as if Sam had sculpted him like this instead of upright. Not a stone was disarranged on his patterned body.

Did he want anything? Or, more to the point, how would he choose from the thousands of things he longed for? If this wasn't a figment of his imagination, of course.

"Just one wish?" Sam asked.

Three, said the snowman. *Though you have already used one when you wished for dinner. It was your longing, your hunger, which brought me into being. You honor me by letting me serve you.*

It wasn't even really a wish at all. And it had been granted by the pennies in his pocket, not by the snowman. Not like magic in the stories.

Sam frowned at it. "A heap of blankets and a fire to sleep around," he said.

"Hey you!" a voice called from over in the tent city.

Sam tensed his muscles to run, but it was a woman who was walking toward him, shawl pulled over her head and tucked under her chin. She waved her hand, beckoning.

"You! Boy!" she said again.

"Hullo?" said Sam. "Me?"

"'Tis no night to be sleepin' in the cold. Come on. I've a heap of blankets and a warm fire. Your Guy will still be there in the mornin'."

The wind blew, heavy with the lilt of pan pipes. He shrugged at the snowman and walked toward the woman, toward warmth.

* * *

In the morning, the snowman was standing again. He was just where Sam had sculpted him, only his hand still stood upright holding the pan flutes, the only thing to show that he had not dreamt the night before. He did not know whether to be glad or afraid.

Perhaps he had dreamed it all. Perhaps he had imagined the thing sitting there, the lilt of pan pipes in the air, the wishes granted.

Still, he had woken up warmer and safer than he had been before in his life. That was no dream.

And he only had one wish left, if the wishes were a true thing.

It was barely dawn, and the ice was cast in the red light of sunrise. The bright swinging boats on tripods where so many children had squealed, flying back and forth into the air, were still.

The sun rose higher, and people began to fill the spaces between the tents again. A group of laughing girls strode past in bright coats and silk dresses, their bonnets cakes of lace framing their ruddy faces.

"Penny for the Guy?" Sam said, taking his hat off his head and holding it out to them. The sole of his boot flapped when he moved. The bruise on his shoulder had turned yellowish overnight. His sweater had sprung another hole under mysterious circumstances.

What would he wish for? It had to be something grand. Something that would keep him in comfort. Maybe something that would keep everyone in comfort, so no one had to brave the streets or sleep in the sewers. It would be noble to wish for everyone, wouldn't it?

"Penny for the Guy?" Sam said, standing in the middle of the makeshift pathway on the ice and brandishing his upturned hat. A passing woman slammed into his good shoulder. Two children gripping ice cones ran past. An old lady dropped a penny onto his brim.

But everyone couldn't be rich. If everyone was rich, then some people had to be poor. That was the way it worked. What could he wish for, that would make everyone happy?

The sun was high overhead now. Sam's stomach rumbled and he thought about his pennies, of the tragedy of wasting them on food. The snowman still hadn't moved. He turned to it.

"You still there?" he whispered.

I am waiting for your wish.

"I wish for…," said Sam. "Uh…I guess for same. For everyone to be the same."

The snowman raised the panpipes to its lips in a single jerk. Sam hadn't noticed, but the snow on the man seemed to have melted during the morning. The lips of his grin were ridged with rivulets of water, making a grid of teeth on its face. The divots of its eyeholes had widened and its body had slimmed. It looked like a snowy decorated corpse in a top hat.

There is only one way to grant equality. I shall play you the Danse Macabre, it said.

"No," said Sam. He didn't know what the song was, but he knew that anything the snowman sang would be terrible, knew it in a flash as he watched the sun glint off the snow of the thing's face. The wind picked up around the tents, snapping the flags in the breeze. Sam's protest got lost in the din.

"No!" said Sam, louder.

The music began. The snowman sang. Its voice was deep, raspy, and hollow.

"Thumpety Thump, Thump
Death is dancing
Striking the ice with a heel
Ziggity Zig, Zig
Death plays a dance tune

The pan pipes start to squeal"

It sang and blew the pipes, despite the lack of breath a human would have had for both, and it lifted its snowy leg to thump the ice, as the song said it would.

When Sam heard the squeal of the pipes now, he felt an easing in his stomach. He felt something lumpy and earnest well up inside his throat that might have been laughter, or hysteria. His bones felt gleeful. He took two steps toward the snowman, and two steps back, and then he found that he was wheeling around the Guy, kicking up his heels and toes. Next to him were three more children, placing their feet heel to toe, kicking high, grinning. A man in ripped trousers asked a befeathered woman to dance, and they also joined in. A priest slid on the ice, into the folly, and moved his feet in a vigorous jig.

"The winter wind blows, the night is dark;
The pan pipes start to moan
Over snow drifts, white and twirling
Dancing you to home

Thumpety Thump, Thump
Out on the ice
The veil betwixt is thin
Ziggity Zig, Zig
King and Peasant
All hold hands and spin"

The dance was huge now, spinning out of control over the ice. The more people danced, the louder the song became. It felt to Sam like the whole frost fair was dancing now, grasping hands, kicking legs, twirling to a new partner and dancing again. Dock workers danced with fine ladies. Washerwomen danced with bank executives. A man in a velvet cloak wheeled past, a paper crown cocked over one ear.

Somewhere in his depths, Sam knew that this wasn't right. But he didn't want to stop feeling joyful. He didn't want to take the aching smile off his face. It was beautiful, the spinning masses, the people coming together. In this place, neither fur muffs nor torn shoes made any difference.

"How long will…?" Sam said to the Guy as he twirled past.

Many days. You have started the macabre. It does not stop until it is over. It does not stop until it has claimed its due, until everyone has achieved your wish. Until everyone has reached the end.

The song never broke, nor did the music. Nor did Sam's dancing feet pause.

"The dance continues for a time
The dancers never stop
And when the river thaws they drown
Still turning like a top

Thumpety Thump, Thump
Hear the song
Compelled to take the chance
Ziggity Zig, Zig
Follow now
And join me in the dance"

Sam heard it in the back of his mind somewhere, the lyrics to the song. They echoed and they took root: "The dancers never stop. And when the river thaws they drown."

The words weren't right. They weren't what he had asked for. A laugh bubbled on his lips and spilled at the thought that it had all gone so awry. He did not want to drown. He didn't want the people whirling around him to drown either. It was a glorious joke on him.

He doubled over, chuckling, still dancing.

Underneath the glee, the truth pierced his heart like an arrow: He had made the wish, unpondered though it was, and it belonged to him. They belonged to him, these dancers. He must stop the music somehow; it was his only chance to make this right.

But to stop the music meant trading away this glorious euphoria. He smiled, and he twirled again. He danced now with an old lady who carried a lace parasol on her wrist.

No. No, he had to stop it.

He grasped the parasol and wrenched it from the lady. She cried out and rubbed her wrist, twirling away with a scowl. Sam took the hand of a small girl who was spinning in the direction of the guy, and together they danced past him.

"Over snow drifts, white and twirling
Dancing you to home."

Sam raised the parasol and spun it over his head like a baton, a majorette in the glee happening around him. Sam raised the parasol, and this time when he spun it around, he whacked the snowman on the neck.

Except that he hadn't. It stood there still, just as before, untouched and whole.

Sam could concentrate long enough to dance close to the guy. He could lift his arm, he could thrust the umbrella forward, or swing it violently. But it never hit the snowman. It never touched a flake on the thing's beastly head. The music went on, unchanged, and Sam danced on with it, his feet carrying him as his heart would not.

And why do you even care? something else whispered beneath the music to him. *Life has not been good to you, and so why would death be any crueler? It comes to us all in the end, and who is to say when is the end?*

It seemed obvious now, too, that there was no equality in life. Of course there wasn't, for there never had been. There was equality only in death and in birth, in the way humans enter the world and the way humans leave it; in the single breath they take, first or last.

But Sam did care. His heart thudded in his chest, and he remembered. Warm sun soaking through to his bones as he sat on a park bench, trees white with spring above him; buttery crust melting in his mouth, sharp apple on his tongue. An old woman handing him the sweater he wore, the soft warm pressure of her lips on his forehead before he left; the heat of rum burning down his throat and settling like fire in his stomach. Cold rain on his upturned face; the colorful flags on the white ice that flew from the tents around him; breathing in fresh, cold air.

He knew it then. The answer was in the wind somehow, in the breath of the earth that passed over them as they danced, the wind that swirled whenever the hat was near. He had to use it, to get inside of it somehow.

He dropped the umbrella onto the ice, and concentrated. He spread his arms wide, still twirling, and tried to feel the wind as it rushed over him, through the holes in his sweater, over his fingers, over his eyes.

It wasn't enough. He knew that he needed more to be able to get inside it, to know what it was made of and to find its origin. Sam pulled off his own hat and sent it wheeling into the sky. He pulled his sweater over his head and waved it like a flag.

Better. It was better now. The music drifted over the top of him. He could feel it in his hair, whipping the tips across his ears. He could feel it on his bare arms.

But he still couldn't see how to get into it.

Sam dropped the sweater onto a group of three girls in white dresses, spinning in their own circle. He pulled his shirt over his head and dropped that, too. He thrust his heels from his shoes and kicked them onto the snow, and he tore his socks from his feet.

And there it was. Like a gift, he felt it whisper around him as the music died away and the ice spread through his chest. It hurt as it expanded through him, too much to cry out; hoarfrost in his heart, icicles in his lungs. He stopped dancing and breathed in the stillness, breathed deeper. The cold turned to something else, something that even felt warm. Sam looked at the scene and found he could see the currents in the air around them all, blue for the wind, a ghostly green for the music.

The music was like a tether coming from the pan pipes, a thousand thick green ropes that spewed from the top of the instrument and took root in the hearts of the people there. The rope went into their mouths, and in their chests a green orb pulsed through their skin in time to their heartbeat. The hat pulsed green with them, growing ever brighter as the music continued. The harmless ribbons of blue wind swirled around them, unconnected.

The knife in Sam's boot was long gone, and even if he had it he didn't know if ordinary steel would cut ropes of whatever that was.

He strode forward towards the thing. It wasn't even human shaped anymore, just a blob of snow with two long ovals holding the pan pipes, a smaller round blob at the top with no features, but a dark divot where the mouth used to be. It turned to look at Sam though it was eyeless, and swatted at him with its semblance of an arm.

Sam didn't pause. He watched the top hat pulse and knew that he was outside of time now. He knew it couldn't touch him; not to harm him. He raised his own arms and placed them on the brim of the top hat.

He pulled.

There was a snapping sound, a light cracking where Sam pulled one side of the hat. It felt like pulling weeds, like the moment a root dislodges, though the rest are still attached deep in the dark earth. Sam wrenched again, and one whole side of the hat came free.

The light stopped pulsing, though it didn't wane. The snowman wrapped his arms around Sam's chest in a hug. He could feel the cold burning his stomach, and the water dripping down his sides where the arms of the thing melted in the heat of his body.

Sam pulled a few more times, cracking more roots. He felt them give, straining, but he still couldn't pull the hat fully loose.

The snowman squeezed, and Sam found it even harder to breathe. He worked his hands underneath the hat and gave it another sharp tug, as hard as he could.

The hat came free in a single jolt, throwing Sam backwards with the force of it, out of the snowman's arms and onto the ragged ice.

The head of the Guy broke into a thousand pieces, crumpling downward in kind until the whole snowman dissolved into powder. The music stopped, and the dancing halted. The people looked around, dazed. The body crumbled back into a messy snowbank.

* * *

Two policemen stood in front of a small snowdrift, just near the carnival rides. Their uniforms were dark on the white ice. Both stared down at a small, shirtless and shoeless boy who was crumpled in the snow. His flesh was blue, and he wore a ragged top hat.

The first policeman shook his head. "Cold night, Mac. Don't know what he was thinking."

"Maybe he warn't thinking, Niles," said Mac.

"Maybe he warn't," said Niles. "Well, it don't matter now. He's for the coroner, and that's that. Mark it in your book."

They both shook their heads as they walked back to the main festival. They would catch a pick-pocket maybe, or someone nicking goods from a booth. It was too late for that chap, and no use thinking any deeper on it. He'd obviously lived hard.

The brilliant cobalt of the sky arced above; the red and green flags whipped from the tops of the tents; the painted colors of the booths stood bright. Children shrieked, throwing dull darts at blown-up pig bladders on a wall at a carnival booth. Small blue boats on tripods swung high, the boys inside squealing.

The wind blew.

SOL INVICTUS
Kevin Wetmore

Snow on Christmas always reminds me of my Uncle Mike and scares the hell out of me. Mike's the one who got me to notice the sound of snow, the noise it makes when it comes down. It's not silent. The sound has this soft, heavy quality.

My uncle was eighteen years older than my mother. My grandparents had spread their three children nine years apart each, so my mother, the baby, was not yet born when he, at the age of seventeen, used a borrowed birth certificate to join the army during the Second World War. So she never knew him as she grew up.

My mother had me in her early thirties, so by the time I was seventeen, her brother was in his late sixties. He and I were not close by any stretch of the imagination. In fact, I only saw him maybe once in my life (at my grandfather's funeral in 1976), until the mid-eighties. Further complicating things was the fact that our family lived in Connecticut, but after the war he moved to Southern California and lived in the desert outside of Los Angeles in the Antelope Valley. The distances of age and geography meant that he and my mother were virtual strangers connected by biology alone, and I was even further distant from him. But when my grandmother passed away in 1982, my uncle decided he should know his family a little better, and we began to visit back and forth on holidays.

It was one Christmas in the late eighties that, in my seventeenth year, I learned much of why my uncle was the way he was. My uncle had divorced several years before (probably another factor in his decision to reach out to my mother and her older sister, my Aunt Kat, who lived near us with her husband and my three cousins), so Uncle Mike came and stayed in our guest room for a few days every year at Christmas time.

A "White Christmas" is an idea more honored in the breach than in the observance—in central Connecticut, as often as not, it is a dull brown and gray Christmas that awaits as one awakens to open presents. That year, however, there was already snow on the ground by mid-December and a huge blizzard forecast for Christmas Eve.

There was a fire in the fireplace, the tree had been decorated the week before, and Christmas carols were playing on the stereo, while my sister flipped back and forth between *It's a Wonderful Life* and *A Christmas Story*. When she went to bed, I stayed up reading by the firelight. It felt good, comfortable.

I heard movement before I saw it, and realized Uncle Mike had come into the room. He was opening up the curtains on the picture window looking out on the woods behind our house. He sat down in my father's easy chair and placed a bottle to his lips. He'd been drinking all day, much to the consternation of my mother. I tried to ignore him as he took a long pull and stared out the window, but the silence was becoming unbearable. I heard every crackle from the logs in the fire, each inhale and exhale of his beery breath, and both of us shifting in our chairs.

"Everything okay, Uncle Mike?" I ventured.

I almost thought he hadn't heard me or was too drunk to notice I was there. Instead, he turned from the window and said to me, "You're seventeen now, right Geoff?"

"Yes, sir."

"When I was your age I joined the army to fight in the big one." He took another pull from the beer and wiped his mouth and moustache with the other hand. In this light, sitting in the chair between the fire and the window, he reminded me of old photos of Orson Welles, whose films I had discovered on VHS the year before. Maybe it was the firelight on his face, maybe it was the big thick beard, but the resemblance was uncanny.

He broke the silence. "You want a beer?"

"No, sir. I'm seventeen."

"When I was your age I drank a lot of beer. World's changed since then, but don't make an old man drink alone. You telling me you never had a beer?"

I realized no matter how I answered, I was in trouble. So I said, "Sure, I'll have one. But don't tell my parents."

"Good man," he responded, and pulled a beer out of his sweater side pocket. "We'll tell your mom I drank it. Now put your damn book down and talk to your Uncle Mike."

"What shall we talk about?" I asked as I took the bottle from him.

Again, silence for a while as we drank. "How's school?" he finally asked.

"Fine. I'm thinking about going out for track in the spring."

"Oh yeah?" More silence except for the crackling of the fire. Without warning he stood up. "Come with me." He moved from the living room to the kitchen to the back door, pulled on his boots, and then opened the door without hesitating and walked right out into the blizzard.

I followed, more out of concern for him than in any interest in being out in the cold, pulling on my boots without tying them and racing after.

"Uncle Mike, what…"

"Shut up and listen." He stood with his face pointed up but his eyes closed.

After a few seconds of not hearing anything, I said, "What are we listening for?"

"The snow."

I began listening. I could hear a light wind blowing, the branches of the trees creaking under the weight of the snow, and leaves skittering across the surface of the snow.

Then under all that, I heard it: The sound of the snow hitting the accumulation already on the ground and even the sound of the snow coming down. It is quiet, soft, and heavy.

Uncle Mike lowered his head. "This is why I've been drinking today. Don't like to think about the snow or what's in it. Hell, it's why I moved to Antelope Valley. Hasn't been any snow there since before California was a state." He placed the bottle to his lips and took another pull, staring out at the black night interrupted by falling white in the porchlight. "Colder than a witch's tit out here," he spat. "Let's get back in."

We walked back in the house, took off our boots, shook off the snow, and returned to the fireside. Uncle Mike pulled the drapes on the picture window closed and drank the rest of his beer. He immediately opened another from his sweater pocket as I sipped mine. He set the new one down, untouched, and began to speak in a low voice. The fire had dropped lower and his face was mostly in shadows.

> "After the Nips bombed Pearl Harbor all my high school buddies were signing up to go give them, the Nazis and the Eye-ties, what for. They were mostly older than me, but you gotta understand, it's not like now. You kids are soft. You're worse than your mother's generation with their protests and free love. We wanted to defend our country. So I borrowed my cousin's birth certificate and at seventeen went down to the induction center in New Haven, passed the physical, and was in the army. Your grandparents were none too happy at the time, but they knew why I did it.

> Got sent to Fort Sam Houston. Went through basic training and was put into the infantry in the Fifth Army. The night before we shipped out, Sarge told us we were going to get on a transport and find ourselves soon

enough in Italy, making Il Duce see the errors of his ways.
We were full of piss and vinegar and hot air. Buncha kids,
really, talking tough so no one would know how scared we
were, not even ourselves.

Half the guys from Fort Sam got seasick on the first two
days out of port. Navy ran us over and dropped us off in
Naples, and we figured it would be a cakewalk up to
Rome. Boy, were we wrong. Krauts were waiting for us all
the way up. 'Operation Avalanche' they called it. More like
'Operation Slow March up the Old Roman Roads.' We
landed in September of '43, but had only gotten as far as
the Winter Line by December.

Right before Christmas, we were outside Monte Cassino,
this was a few days before the big battle there. Blizzard hit.
Like this one."

He gestured toward the closed curtain, and in my head I could hear the
snow falling.

"Drifting snow and zero visibility caused the advance to
grind to a halt. We hunkered down in the cold and the
snow to wait. Regular patrols were sent out, but you had to
be careful and be quiet, because we knew we were just a
few miles from a whole bunch of Kraut and Eye-tie units.
Didn't want to get killed or captured."

He finally picked up his new beer and took a drink, but it no longer
seemed like he was drinking to get and stay drunk.

"Arunci Mountains, Liri Valley, just below Monte Cassino,
a few days before one of the biggest battles in the Italian
campaign, and my buddies and I drew the short straw. We
were to go out on patrol in the mountains around camp on
Christmas Eve. Make sure nobody was out there, and let
top know if anyone was coming down the hills for us. We
picked up our weapons and headed out into the snow.
Merry Christmas, right?

We were moving real quiet-like. The snow was coming
down hard and fast. It felt like fingers hitting your
shoulders. It was a wet, heavy snow. You could hear the
sound of your boots and the boots of the guys in front of
and behind you. But we were not talking.

You have to understand, by this point we were four

months out of boot camp, and we had learned that nothing actually prepares you for battle. The sights, the sounds. It's horrific. Like I said, we thought it would be a cakewalk. Instead, we fought for every mile. Didn't expect the Nazis to be there, but they were. Johnny Breen, nice kid out of Cleveland. We were friends in Basic. Second day in Italy I saw a German shell land right next to him. My friend was there one minute, the next there was a hole in the ground, blood and…parts. There wasn't enough to send back to his parents. He loved Indians baseball. Big Cleveland fan. Was gonna marry his high school sweetheart when he got home. Was lousy at poker. Then he was blown to pieces."

Uncle Mike tilted back his beer and took a deep drink, then stared at the fire for a while.

"In a way, that's worse than the actual physical wounds. Seeing people you know just suddenly gone and realizing everything they were just ended. I mean when you're seventeen, eighteen, you think you'll live forever and that you're kind of invulnerable. Then you're confronted by death on an almost daily basis but you still never think it could happen to you.

So, me and the boys are out on patrol, keeping quiet in case there's an enemy patrol out in the same blizzard. You can't see more than five feet in any direction, and we're on these mountain paths over the Liri Valley. The snow is coming down, and I focus on the sound of the snow. After a few minutes, well, I say a few minutes, it could have been two, it could have been twenty, I was so focused on the snow. But after a few minutes, I realize I can't hear the other boots anymore. I pick up the pace and jog a little to see if I can catch up with the guy in front of me. After a minute of running, nobody. I then stop to see if the guy behind me comes up. He doesn't. So now I'm alone in the snow in the mountains near the front line, wondering if I took a wrong turn or went up a path when I was supposed to go down. I realize it doesn't matter, because I'm alone, in the snow and freezing cold with no idea where I am.

So I'm just standing in the falling snow. It's all I hear. That sound can drive you mad. Well I'm not going to die in the snow in Italy, dammit. I decide I'm going to find my way back to camp. So I start retracing my steps, and I find myself on this narrow path halfway up a cliff, and I come across the opening to a cave.

Now I know I'm lost because we never passed this cave. But at the same time, I figure this might just be a gift from the Almighty, since I can get out of the snow and cold for a while, maybe eat something and warm up, get my bearings and figure out how to get back to camp. So I point my weapon, drop down, and walk in.

I first make sure there is nothing in the cave. I realize that it goes back into the mountain, but there is no one in this front chamber. No Krauts, no Eye-ties. I didn't want to risk a fire, but I did want to get warm. So I lit a cigarette and did some jumping jacks to get the blood back in my feet, then pulled out the K-rations from my pack and got some food in me.

As I was eating, I faced the entrance of the cave with my weapon at the ready in case an enemy patrol passed by and decided to take the same shelter I did. I heard a noise behind me, grabbed my M1 and turned. I forgot that I had taken off my gloves to eat, so the metal parts of the M1 froze to my hands. I wasn't even sure if I could fire, but I wasn't gonna go down not fighting.

There was a man standing there, a young man. He looked to be just a few years older than me—in his mid-twenties. His skin was a grayish white, his hair black, and he stood about six feet, which made him taller than many of the Eye-talians I had met. He was wearing the strangest thing—a leather skirt-looking thing and a red tunic. Sandals on his feet. Middle of a blizzard and this guy doesn't look cold at all. I have my M1 trained on him, but I must have looked in pain, because he asked me if I was suffering."

"Wait," I interrupted, "he spoke English?
"That sumbitch was speaking Latin."
"Latin?"
"Mmmhmm. And we began to talk."
"You speak Latin?"
"You think your uncle's an idiot? Eleven years of Catholic school before Johnny Twenty-Three made everyone start speaking English for Mass. Damn fool decision if you ask me. Mass lost something. Don't matter to

me anymore, I suppose. Haven't gone in years."

"So who was this guy? What did he say?"

He gave me the look again, took a pull from his beer and continued. "He asked what year it was."

"What?"

> "He asked me what year it was. I didn't answer. I kept that gun on him and demanded to know who he was and what he was doing there. He didn't answer, instead he walked past me and looked out the cave entrance and smiled. I have to tell you, that smile was colder than the blizzard.
>
> He turns back to me and stares at me, and I realize he's checking me out. He is looking at my clothes and my weapon and then looks at my K-rations. Then he asks if my M1 is some kind of weapon.
>
> 'Damn right it is,' I tell him in Latin, and then ask again who he is. He says his name is Sandalius and asks again what year it is. I ask him what year he thinks it is. He tells me he lost track a few centuries ago. So now I know I'm dealing with some crazy guy. I figure he's some Eye-tie soldier who went stir crazy, ran off from his unit, and is now acting crazy in this cave until the war's over. I lower the rifle a little and ask why he isn't cold.
>
> He says temperature doesn't matter to him anymore, but the light does. He looks out again and says he wakens every year on this day to mark Sol Invictus, or more accurately, '*Dies Natalis Solis Invicti*,' the birthday of the Unconquered Sun."

"Son?" I asked. "Like Christmas? Birth of Jesus?"

"What do they teach you kids in schools these days? No, Sol Invictus, the birth of the unconquered sun, like the thing in the sky. Roman holiday celebrating the passing of the Winter Solstice and the days getting longer again. It's the Christians who came along later and said that it was Jesus's birthday, too. Another reason why I figured I didn't need to go to church anymore."

"Let me get this straight, Uncle Mike. This guy says he wakes up every year to celebrate this Roman sun holiday?"

> "Right? I figure he's a whack-a-doo. Don't want to shoot an unarmed man, but don't trust a crazy one. I kick myself for letting him get in between me and the cave opening. My fingers on the cold metal are burning beyond belief. So

I figure I'll play his game until I can get out of there. I tell
him it's 1943. He grows grim. He asks me why I am
carrying a weapon. I tell him we're at war. He asks with
who, and I tell him the Krauts, figuring since he's Eye-
talian he doesn't need to know I'm there to shoot his
buddies. He nods knowingly and says something like,
'Always war with Germania. They have always been a
difficult people to quell.'

'What's your story?' I ask him. 'Like you,' he says, 'I am a
soldier. Conceived in incest, sold by my father when I was
three as a slave. By the time I was a decade and half I was a
soldier in the legions. Fought in Germania, like you.'"

"So he was a whack-a-doo," I say to my Uncle Mike.
"That's what I thought. Guy thinks he's a Roman soldier."

"So I ask him: who is the emperor? He says there is no
emperor. The empire fell centuries ago. He tells me he is a
Strix. He had been sent to fight in Greece, his legion was
attacked by...something...I didn't recognize the words,
but he said that as a result he was a 'Strix.' I've learned
since then it was something like a vampire."

Now it was my turn to take a long drink from my beer while the
thoughts ran through my head.

"So...Uncle Mike...you met a vampire in Italy during the Second
World War? Is that what you're telling me?"

I could not see his face, but I could sense the change on it. "Watch your
tone, boy." He let the threat behind the words hang between us for a long
moment, then after a quick swig he said, "I know what it sounds like—why
do you think you're the first and only one I told this to? But he said he was
a Strix. And since I needed to gather up my stuff and get past him, I chose
not to fight with him in the moment about it."

"'So why are you fighting Germania in Roma?' he asked.
And before I could answer, he moved across the cave
faster than my eye could follow and grabbed the M1 out of
my hands. The skin that had been touching metal tore off
and blood dripped from my fingers and palms. It took a
second, maybe because it was quick or maybe because the
cold had numbed me, but once the actual sensation of my
skin being ripped off hit my brain, I'm not ashamed to
admit I screamed in pain.

He ignored me while staring at the M1. He made some

comment about it being a strange and silly weapon. He then licked the blood, my frozen blood, from it. His tongue did not stick to the metal, but I noticed it was forked. That was when I started to think he might not be a whack-a-doo. He looked out into the snow again.

'Tomorrow we celebrate Apollo and the Unconquered Sun. I like to be present when the sun rises and sets on that day to remind the sun I remain unconquered as well. This is even better.' He walked out into the snow. I waited for a minute. Then another. Finally, I got my gloves back on, threw my things back in my pack and shouldered it. I walked out into the snow, and he was standing there, looking up.

'It is up there, on the other side of the clouds,' he said, not looking at me. 'The Unconquered one. Yet right now, in the daytime, I walk and it cannot harm me. Tomorrow, perhaps, but today I have conquered the unconquered sun.'

He turned to me and threw the M1 in the snow at my feet. 'A gift,' he said, 'as is your life. I will not drain your blood today. Go, kill more men from Germania.' He laughed low. I realized in that moment that he had been at war for far longer than I."

"Against the Germans?" I asked my uncle.

"No," he sighed, as if I were a disappointing pupil. "Strix...vampires, don't just hate the sun because its rays kill them. It is the one true reminder that they are not immortal, that they can and will die someday." He looked at the clock at the mantle and then looked me right in the eye, taking my measure. "I knew how he felt. I was seventeen for Christ's sake. Like I said, when you're that age you feel immortal, even when your best friends are being blown to pieces by German mortars all around you, you figure it can't happen to you. You think you're gonna live forever." Another pull from his beer. He swallowed. "Until you don't. I think on some level, me at seventeen and him at two millennia, we understood each other in that moment."

"I dug into the snow, pulled out my M1, and slowly moved backwards away from him and then ran in the snow down the mountain, into the valley. I watched him for the twenty or so feet of visibility there was. He just kept looking at the sky, the snow falling, smiling that cold smile.

I got back to camp about three hours later. The other guys on patrol didn't realize I was missing until they returned. Sarge said it was snowing too hard to look for me. Doc treated me for frostbite and the torn flesh on my hands. Three days later all hell broke loose. But like all wars it ended and like most wars we won it, so the story turned out okay."

We sat, in silence, for a few minutes.

A loud crack from the log dying on the fire broke the silence, allowing me to speak. "So he's still there, huh?"

He took a final pull from the bottle and set it down. "Nope."

"No?"

"No. When I got back to camp I gave artillery the coordinates of the cave and told them it was a German sniper nest. I told them I stumbled across it while I was lost in the snow, but figured out where it was once I got my bearings. They rained mortar fire down on it at dawn's first light. Merry Christmas. When we passed it later I saw that the cave had been blown open to the sky."

"What? Why?"

"It was war. He was the enemy. Not just of the United States, but of humanity. Couldn't let him live. Some things just should not be. So we blew the cave to hell and a few days later we went up against the Nazis and Eyeties at Monte Cassino, and I figured he was good and dead. We opened up his tomb to the unconquered sun. I hope it burned him to a crisp. Anything that had seen as much war and death as that thing, but still wanted more was a threat to everything. But we never saw the body, nor was there any evidence that he was real, or that he was now dead. I might have dreamed or hallucinated the whole thing. So when it snows like this I remember that winter that I just want to forget. And on some level, maybe, just maybe, I worry he might be coming for me. It would take a long time to get from Italy to here, but when it snows…

I figure if he is afraid of the unconquered sun, Southern California is the perfect place to be. Sumbitch wouldn't try to get there, because let me tell you: nothing, but nothing conquers the sun in the Antelope Valley."

"And that, boy, is why today I needed to drink. To try to forget. Tomorrow while we celebrate Christmas, I will also, in my heart of hearts, be celebrating the feast of Sol Invictus—the unconquered sun that will rise tomorrow morning and shine on all this snow."

And without another word, or acknowledging me in any other way, he simply got up and walked steadily up the stairs to the guest room. I sat in the dark, watching the fire die down to embers, and the embers die down to ash, until a hand shook me awake in the morning and my mother said, "Merry Christmas. Did you sleep here all night? That must have been a good book." Then, looking at my feet, "Is that a beer?"

Uncle Mike was his old self Christmas Day, and nobody mentioned the day before to him or each other. He said nothing to me, other than general pleasantries, and we never spoke of his war experience again.

Two years later my uncle was gone. We were told he had had this massive heart attack, but the weird thing was that he walked out of his house and into the back yard while he was having it. I was off at college and didn't go to the funeral. My mother told me it was a closed casket funeral because he supposedly had a look of absolute terror on his face. We found out later that it had snowed in Antelope Valley that night for the first time in six decades. I don't know what happened to him. Could be nothing. But even now, decades later, every time it snows at night, I will stand outside my door for a few minutes, listening to it come down, and I am afraid.

'TWAS THE FIFTH OF DECEMBER
Brad P. Christy

The final bell rang and middle schoolers flooded into the hallway. Rumors had been swirling all day about a fight and nobody wanted to miss it.

Robby Murphy was big for a twelve-year-old; certainly bigger than Jason Fisher, whose head Robby slammed into a locker. Tennis shoes squeaked on the tile from melted snow as kids tried to get close to the action. The more Robby hit Jason, the more the hooting, laughing mob wanted to see.

Robby's face tightened into a flushed-red knot as he kicked Jason while he was down. All Robby wanted was to be left alone, but Jason just wouldn't let up with the teasing. He had warned Jason what would happen if he didn't shut up. There was nothing left to say to the crumpled boy shielding his face and head, huddled against the lockers, that Robby hadn't already said a hundred times before about leaving him alone.

"That's enough, Robby!" said Mr. Christiansen, the seventh grade history teacher, as he grabbed the back of Robby's flannel jacket and pulled him away from the fight.

"He's crazy!" Jason's voice cracked. He was shaking and his lip was split open. Tears steadily dripped from his chin.

Robby took one more kick at Jason before giving in.

"Alright, that's enough," said Mr. Christiansen. "The two of you are coming with me to the principal's office."

The fight was over.

Robby tried to catch his breath. The fight had only lasted minutes, but it felt like hours, and he hadn't taken a breath the entire time.

Mr. Christiansen looked at Jason's face. "On second thought, go to the nurse's office and have that lip looked at," he said before marching Robby down to the principal's office.

"He said-," Robby started.

"Not now, Robby," interjected Mr. Christiansen, pointing at the wood bench outside Principal Morse's office.

The bench reminded Robby of a church pew, only less comfortable.

The school secretary's cataract-laden eyes crested the top of her horn-rimmed glasses as she glanced up from her files. When she pursed her lips, the deep wrinkles around her mouth made the lower half of her face look shattered. She slightly shook her head and went back to work. She did this every time he sat outside the principal's office, which was becoming more and more frequent.

Robby could hear his teacher and principal in the office behind him. He heard Principal Morse say that Robby should be expelled, and Mr. Christiansen saying that Robby's been through a lot for a boy his age and that he wasn't the instigator. He heard Principal Morse say that Jason's parents had donated a lot of money to the school district, and he heard Mr. Christiansen say that Jason used his social standing to goad Robby into fighting.

Something scratched inside the wall near the bench. Robby wondered if the school had a mouse infestation and wanted to say something about it, but it didn't seem like the right time to criticize the school's sanitation.

Robby stared at his shoes. His head down, his long bangs hung in front of his face. His shoes were still wet from walking to school in the snow that morning, which made them smell like old cheese. The holes in them let his socks get wet too. He wiggled his toes and wished he was closer to the heating duct.

The office door opened so hard the window shade nearly fell off.

"Come in Mr. Murphy," said Principal Morse, frowning and brows furled. He had the same intense look whenever he collected troublemakers from the bench. It used to scare Robby, but now he was used to it.

Robby grudgingly got up from the bench, but turned around quickly when he heard somebody snicker. The secretary was focused on her files.

"Am I holding you up from something, Mr. Murphy?" said Principal Morse.

Robby looked back at the secretary a last time before walking in to the office. She didn't seem to notice.

Mr. Christiansen was standing by the chair in front of the principal's desk, arms folded and straight faced.

Principal Morse sat down and pulled a bottle of peppermint flavored chewable antacids from the top drawer. Chomping on a fistful, he didn't bother to look at Robby when he spoke. "How many visits are we going to have this year, Mr. Murphy?"

Robby noticed that Principal Morse had four pictures on his desk, all of them facing outward and all of them of himself. There were also twelve pens of different colors lined up on a coffee-stained desktop calendar, a mahogany nameplate with gold inlay lettering, and a half-eaten candy cane poking out of a steaming coffee mug bearing a 1950s era picture of Santa Claus reading a book to a group of children on it.

Robby didn't quite catch the question. He looked up at the principal to see if he expected an answer. The strong smells of pine from the fake wreath hanging behind the principal's chair, burnt coffee, and musk cologne made Robby's head hurt.

"In all fairness," said Mr. Christiansen, "it was Jason who apparently started it."

Robby looked up at his history teacher.

"Be that as it may," said Principal Morse, "Mr. Murphy here has made a name for himself by leading with his fists rather than his words. Wrong or not, I can't let it slide this time." He turned his attention to Robby, "I'm calling your mother to pick you up. In the meantime, I want you to go with Mr. Christiansen and wait."

On their way to Mr. Christiansen's classroom, they passed Jason's parents in their matching evening wear. Officially, Jason's parents put him in public school because they thought it would help develop his social skills and appreciation for finer things, but it was widely rumored that he got kicked out of the private school he used to go to. Mr. Fisher didn't acknowledge Robby or Mr. Christiansen, but Mrs. Fisher glared at the boy who had struck her son. Her beady eyes made Robby walk faster.

Shadows seemed to be following them, and Robby was glad to be out of the hallway when they got to the history room.

Reference books haphazardly lined the shelves of Mr. Christiansen's classroom. Posters of famous people like Edison, Lincoln, Washington, and Poe papered the walls. The next day's assignment was written on the dry erase board behind Mr. Christiansen's desk.

Mr. Christiansen plopped down in his chair, ran his hands through his hair and sighed. "Robby," he said, placing his elbows on the desk. "I know it's been tough since your dad passed away, especially now."

Robby picked at his fingernails, "He didn't pass away. He killed himself." Robby didn't like talking about how he woke up on Christmas morning to find his dad's body under the tree, but it seemed inescapable. A shadow next to the classroom door moved in his peripheral vision.

Mr. Christiansen sat way back in his chair and massaged his temples. He couldn't break eye contact with the boy. "Listen, Robby, we both know that your dad was not well for a very long time."

Robby noticed that the history teacher's desk had three resource books stacked on top of a copy of 'Time' magazine. There was a 'Star Wars Bounty Hunters' cup filled with pens and pencils, and a day planner highlighted in yellow, pink, and green. December 25th had a big star scribbled on it. Mr. Christiansen made a quick notation on today, December 5th.

"I'm sure he didn't mean for you to find him like that."

Robby looked up at the water-stained ceiling tiles. It sounded like the mouse that was gnawing on them might fall through at any second.

"What I mean is: you that can't let your dad's tragedy define who you are," said Mr. Christiansen.

Robby examined the snow globe on his desk with garland painted around the base and a palm tree baring a single red Christmas bulb inside. The shadow moved again, this time behind a bookshelf. Tiny white flakes fell from the palm tree and floated to the snow-covered desert island below. Robby gripped his knees.

"Don't be nervous about your mother being mad," said Mr. Christiansen.

Robby looked around the room for the shadow. "I'm not." Through the window, the winter sun was almost completely set. He was right, thought Robby. Todd, his mom's boyfriend, was the one to be scared of.

"Want to hear a scary Christmas Story?" said Mr. Christiansen to change the subject.

Robby stopped looking around, "Yeah."

"Ever hear of Krampus?"

"No," said Robby questionably.

"I'm not surprised. I hadn't either until I was doing some research on the old Germanic Saint Nicholas legends in college." He reached into his desk, pulled out a candy cane and handed it to Robby.

Robby took the candy cane and leaned in to listen.

Mr. Christiansen sat back and unwrapped a candy cane for himself. "Legend has it that Santa Claus is only one side of the Christmas coin." He sucked on the candy cane. "He's the bright, jolly side that hands out gifts to good boys and girls.

"Krampus, on the other hand, is the opposite. For hundreds of years people were terrified of Krampus, especially on Krampusnacht, which I believe is December 5th." Mr. Christiansen looked down at the calendar and tried to keep a straight face as Robby's went pale. The teacher leaned in, making his voice dramatic, "Imagine a demon disguised as a wild man all covered in hair, with horns and a long tongue, following Santa around. His sole purpose: to find naughty boys and girls to punish."

"Punish how?" said Robby, leaning in.

"Well, let's just say you were lucky to get coal." Mr. Christiansen bit off the curved end of the candy cane. "Krampus, you see, likes to shackle and whip naughty children. If they are exceptionally bad, he throws them in a sack and carries them off to his lair in the underworld to be drowned or eaten. And just like Santa, he is always watching; making his list, checking it twice."

Mr. Christiansen popped the rest of the candy cane in his mouth and munched on it loudly. "And, supposedly, Krampus would smell of rotting flesh if it weren't for his voracious appetite for peppermint," he said with a wink.

Robby dropped his candy cane on the desk and scooted away from it.

Mr. Christiansen laughed. "It's just an old story. Then again, you do have an impressive disciplinary record this year. So, next time you get the urge to smack around a kid smaller than you or cheat on a test or steal, yes, I know about that too, just remember that some old stories are true."

Robby's palms were sweating. The gnawing and scratching at the ceiling tiles was getting louder.

A loud knock on the classroom door made both of them jump. Robby's mom stood in the doorway, still wearing her yellow waitressing uniform from the diner she worked at. One hand on the doorknob and one on her hip, she looked like she was on the verge of tears.

"It looks like the history lesson is over for today," said Mr. Christiansen, who got up and shook Diane Murphy's hand.

"Get your bag and let's go," she said at Robby through her teeth.

She firmly shut the door behind them. "I can't believe that I had to lose my shift because of you." She knew better than to hit him on school property.

The rusted Buick Skylark's windows were frosted around the edges. Robby breathed on the cold glass, making it fog up.

"God! You had to beat up Jason Fisher, didn't you? You know his father owns the diner, don't you? Are you trying to get me fired for Christmas?"

Robby wiggled his soggy toes under the car's floor heater. Looking out the window at the school, there were few lights on as they pulled out of the parking lot. From inside one of the darkened classrooms, the black silhouette of a person with enormous horns was looking at them.

"And," yelled his mom, "you managed to get suspended…again!"

Robby didn't hear much of what was said on the ride home. The Skylark slid to a stop on the packed snow along the curb. The path to their front porch needed to be shoveled. Plastic covering the house windows flapped in the frozen wind. Snow pushed into Robby's shoes through the holes as he got out of the car.

Robby could hear the television before they got in the house. His mom once told him that Todd had to have the sound up because he'd lost part of his hearing when he was wounded in Iraq. The Army tried to fix him before they kicked him out, but the scars were still there. Todd liked to tell his friends that he refused to shave or cut his hair as a protest of the Army's treatment of wounded veterans.

The only light in the house came from the television and the Christmas tree. Todd was sitting in a recliner with his feet up, back to the front door, watching 'A Christmas Story.' A bowl of pink peppermint ice cream soup sat on the floor beside him next to a half-bottle of peppermint schnapps.

46

Todd sat perfectly still, except for swirling around a nearly empty glass of schnapps. The crossed pistols of the Military Police Corps and chain-linked handcuffs tattooed on his forearm flexed and danced in the Technicolor glow.

Robby kicked off his wet shoes and quietly hung up his jacket. His mom didn't have to say anything; he'd been in trouble enough times to know he should go upstairs to his room as fast as possible. As he passed the living room, he caught a glimpse of Todd taking a drink of peppermint schnapps, and an extremely long tongue licking the inside bottom of the glass.

Sprinting up the stairs, Robby slammed the door behind him and braced his back against it. His heartbeat pounded in his ears. He didn't turn the light on, not wanting to draw any more attention. There was a faint sound of breathing on the other side of the door, but nobody had followed him up the stairs. The street light outside the plastic covered window cast blurry shadows that swayed through the bare trees in the wind.

A muffled argument from downstairs peeled him from the door. He ran to the floor vent next to his unkempt bed and flipped it open. From his room, he could clearly hear every angry word between his mother and Todd, even over the television.

"Jesus, Dianne, what'd he do this time?" said Todd, his words slurring.

Dishes clinked. "He got into a fight with a boy who called him a name or something," said Dianne.

"What'd the kid call him," asked Todd.

"What does it matter? He's suspended until Winter Break is over."

The refrigerator opened and closed. Todd snickered.

"What?"

"Getting into a fight over name calling," said Todd. "That's just crazy."

There was an awkward silence.

"You're incredible," said Dianne sarcastically.

Todd snickered again.

"He's not crazy."

"Are you sure?"

A floor board squeaked inside Robby's closet. Branches outside his window creaked and scraped the plastic. A cobweb tickled the fine hairs on the back of Robby's hand, making him flinch.

"The fruit may not have fallen far from the tree, is all I'm saying."

"I can't believe you would bring that up," hissed Dianne.

Schnapps poured into a glass. "What? Last time I checked, schizophrenia's hereditary. Could be his problem, you know. Think about it, Dianne. The kid's grades are slipping, he's always getting into fights, and he keeps looking out the corner of his eyes like he's looking for something that's not there."

Robby's face flushed hot. His fists clenched. Something scratched on the window sill outside.

"My son is not crazy!"

"I'm just saying that he's either a schizo or a punk. So, which is it?"

There was more awkward silence. Robby could feel something watching him from the shadows around his closet.

"Cause if he's a punk, I can fix it right now," said Todd.

"Oh, leave him alone."

"Quit coddling the kid, Dianne."

"You're drunk."

"He's a punk then?" said Todd.

A scuffle broke out, along with his mom saying, "Todd, Don't." The scuffle moved through the house. His mom saying, "Keep your hands off my son."

Todd stomped up the stairs.

Robby's heart raced, and he couldn't control his breathing.

Suddenly, Robby's room seemed smaller than ever. Shadows were moving in from the corners, from under his bed and behind his dresser. There was nowhere he could hide.

"Todd, no!" yelled Dianne when they got to the top of the stairs.

Someone was thrown against the wall outside Robby's door. A picture fell and smashed on the floor. Robby's mom screamed.

Robby charged through his door, yelling for Todd to get away from his mother.

Drunk and off balance, Todd couldn't keep his footing as the door smacked into him. He tumbled down the stairs, taking a couple of family photos with him.

Dianne crawled through the broken glass to check on Todd.

Robby stood still, hand on the door handle. He looked down the stairs at Todd, who was almost upside-down and not moving. Robby couldn't move. Todd deserved to be pushed down the stairs, but his mother was upset. He couldn't tell if he'd done the right thing or not.

A voice whispered behind him, "Naughty."

Robby only paused for a moment before deciding to squeeze past Todd and his mom on the stairs. He tried to be as quiet and careful as possible. Dianne, who was bleeding from her lip, patted Todd on the cheek. The skin above each of Todd's eyebrows was swollen, raised up like horns were trying to break through.

The narrator from 'A Christmas Story' spoke loudly in the background about being tormented by the neighborhood bully.

Todd's eyes blinked open.

Robby tried to run by, but Todd caught his pant leg, making his trip and fall. Robby chipped a tooth on one of the last stairs. His vision was fuzzy, but he could see the front door just ahead of him.

Todd lifted Robby up by his collar and dragged him into the living room. Dianne pulled on Todd's shirt and slapped the back of his head. Todd backhanded her, knocking the woman into the kitchen.

Todd pinned Robby over the arm of the recliner with his knee and ripped the table lamp's electrical cord out of the wall. The lamp fell and broke as Todd used the wire to bind Robby's wrists. Todd stepped in the bowl of ice cream soup and violently pushed down with his knee in the middle of Robby's back, knocking the wind out of him.

With one hand in Robby's red hair, holding it in a tight fist, Todd pulled off his leather belt.

Looking up, Robby could see Todd standing over him in the mirror, only Todd's eyes glowed yellow and fangs sprouted from between his beard and mustache. The tips of black horns broke through the skin on his forehead. The smell of peppermint was everywhere. The beast in the mirror smiled in the blinking lights of the Christmas tree.

As Todd raised the belt, Robby saw his mom smash the bottle of peppermint schnapps over the side of Todd's head. Todd stumbled and fell against the television, knocking it from its stand and breaking it. There was no longer a narrator talking about anyone shooting their eye out, no more white light filling the room. There were only moans and the blinking lights of the Christmas tree.

Dianne stood in shock, holding the broken neck of the schnapps bottle in her trembling hand. Blood stood out on her yellow waitress uniform.

Robby slipped his hands free from the wire and hid behind the Christmas tree as Todd rose slowly to his feet.

Todd's bushy hair was matted with blood. He wiped his face. A long tongue flicked out his mouth as he wobbled and went slack.

Robby grabbed a glass icicle off the tree and thrust it into Todd's stomach.

Todd let go of the belt and dropped to his knees. Blood soaked the front of his shirt. His breath became heavy and erratic.

Robby shook. There was blood on his hands and clothes. The beast that Todd was a minute ago was no longer there, just the bearded face of a man in the blinking lights of a Christmas tree.

Todd looked over Robby's shoulder. His eyes opened wide and he scooted backward.

"Very naughty," whispered a voice from behind Robby.

Before he could turn around, a burlap sack went over his head.

All went dark.

A PERILOUS GIFT
Amber Newberry

Lady Cassandra Beaufort slammed against the wall of her carriage as it sunk into a deep puddle along the path through the woods. She cried out in pain.

"So sorry, madam, I couldna avoid the puddle an' she were deeper than I 'spected 'er to be," the driver called back to her. She rubbed a hand over the place on her shoulder which had crashed against the wall of the carriage. It hurt more than it should have on account of the large, purple bruise in the shape of Lord Beaufort's hand. She'd dressed carefully that morning, choosing a high collar to cover the part of the bruise that extended across her collar bone. She was grateful for the thick, long sleeves which covered the fading wounds down her arms from the many terrible interactions with her husband in the previous few weeks. Lady Cassandra hoped the browned bruise on her hand would not be too visible to her grandmother when she took off her travel gloves for tea.

What had set him off this time? She tried to remember as she stared out the window, watching the trees race by as the carriage rambled along. Of course, it was usually the third glass after dinner which uncorked his rage, but there was always a reason. There was the evening Lady Cassandra had spilled her wine during dinner with a very distinguished guest. The laughter and judgment of the Countess had not been punishment enough, and that was the first time Lord Beaufort had laid his hands on her. They were newlyweds at the time, in an arranged marriage. Lord Beaufort had tried to make amends the following day with a gift of fine lace and a new comb for her hair. He had succeeded in convincing her that this was an isolated incident, until she made the mistake of confronting him about his mistress. That time, he hadn't held back, and that was the night of her first miscarriage. Then he blamed her again and again for her failure to conceive. The second miscarriage had also been at his hands, having forced himself upon her relentlessly; he blamed her for the loss of the second pregnancy, as well.

As her childhood home came into view, Lady Cassandra's mind went to Grandmother Granger, who'd requested her presence for tea that afternoon. Being too fragile to travel, she'd asked her granddaughter to come for an early gift exchange, a few days before Christmas. Lady Cassandra's heart warmed as she watched the sun glisten over the snow that rolled out in waves before the sprawling old manor house. For a moment, she reveled in the joy of snow for the annual Yuletide celebrations.

On her arrival, Mrs. Rosemond, the housekeeper, immediately took Lady Cassandra to the solarium, where Grandmother was already waiting. The old woman, seemingly ancient, did not rise as her granddaughter entered, but reached out for the young woman to take her hand. Lady Cassandra took it gingerly, and kissed her grandmother's cheek.

"Merry Christmas, Grandmother," Lady Cassandra said as she took a seat on the divan across from the old woman.

"A Happy Christmas, my dear," Grandmother said, "I do hope you had no trouble getting here because of the snow."

"None at all, it was just enough to cover the ground, but not enough to make our short journey difficult. Of course, you know nothing could prevent me from visiting my dear Granny for Christmas." This made her grandmother smile. Cassie was her favorite of eight grandchildren.

A young maid entered with a tray of tea and small sandwiches, and a second maid followed carrying a tray of scones and an array of sweets.

"My goodness, Granny, it is just the two of us, is it not?" Lady Cassandra queried after seeing the many treats placed neatly on the table between them.

"Oh yes, but I do so love to spoil my darlings," Grandmother said indulgently, and her granddaughter returned the smile.

"Then I shall spoil you, too!" Lady Cassandra said as she stood and rang for the butler. Expecting the summons, Wilson entered with a sizeable parcel wrapped in a bow of gold ribbon.

"Thank you, Wilson," Lady Cassandra said as she took it from him, and he was dismissed as quickly as he'd arrived. Immediately, there was a whimpering sound coming from the parcel, along with faint scratching, which caused the parcel to sway in Lady Cassandra's arms. She quickly set the package on her grandmother's blanket-covered lap.

"You've brought me a hound?" Grandmother asked, incredulously.

"I knew the little fellow would give himself away before you could pull the ribbon."

"Oh my, let us see him, then!" Grandmother said as she pulled the ends of the golden bow. The lid of the box was lifted off by the black nose of a Cavalier King Charles Spaniel, who promptly began to kiss the face and hands of the old woman.

"Isn't he sweet?" Lady Cassandra doted on the puppy.

"Dear little thing. I suppose I do need a companion. It has been rather lonely in this big old house since…well, there's no use in saying it. We needn't bring ourselves down at a joyous moment," Grandmother said, not wanting to speak of her late husband.

The ladies cooed over the puppy, petting him until he curled up in a tiny ball at the skirt of his new madam. It was then that Lady Cassandra poured out the tea, and plated a scone at the request of her grandmother. They talked over names for the old woman's new companion and settled on Pippin. Then the subjects flowed through the usual discussions of health, weather, and family news. When the two had finished their tea, they rang for the maids to clear it away. Lady Cassandra scooped up Pippin and held him like a baby.

"Little cherub," she said, as he immediately returned to a deep slumber within her arms. It pained her grandmother to see her treating the puppy as she should've been treating her own babies. Had Lady Cassandra not miscarried, Madame Granger would have been blessed with a toddler and a brand new baby by that Christmas. As Lady Cassandra gently patted Pippin's head, Grandmother noted the diminishing bruise on her granddaughter's hand. It was no secret that Lord Beaufort was a violent man, and of course the servants talked. In these country houses, the maids and butlers often had relatives working in the nearby manors. Things made it back to Madame Granger, and she knew that this marriage had proved to be a poor match for her favorite grandchild.

"Cassie, dear, will you go to the mantle and fetch the brown case? I had Margaret leave it there for me," Grandmother said. Her granddaughter did as she was told, after placing the tired puppy on the rug near the warmth of the hearth. She brought it back and was instructed to have her seat back on the divan and open the leather jewelry case, which she did. The old woman watched silently as her granddaughter examined the case, and then the contents of the box. Lady Cassandra sat quietly, looking down at the strange gift her grandmother had seen fit to bestow on her that Christmas.

"What do you think of it, child?" Grandmother asked of her granddaughter, who stared down at the present, almost entranced with it. The case housed an exquisite, white beaded necklace. It alternated strange, jagged pieces, with beads carved with tiny delicate floral detail. At the center of the necklace, a larger piece was gracefully formed into a large and intricate flower.

"Is it ivory?" Lady Cassandra wanted to know, but her grandmother ignored the question.

"It has been almost sixty years since the Christmas this necklace was given to me," Grandmother said, watching her granddaughter's fingers move gently over the carved beads, "and now, I am giving it to you."

"It is marvelous, Grandmother, simply marvelous," Lady Cassandra said, finally lifting the piece from the case to more closely examine the fine details.

"As you know, my father was a man of science, an explorer. He travelled the world learning, studying, and writing of the places and people he encountered. When he was away at Christmas, he made it a tradition to send me something special, to arrive on Christmas Eve. He never failed with this practice. The first Christmas he was away, he sent the most splendid Arabian horse."

"How wonderful!" Lady Cassandra said.

"On his next excursion, he sent home fine linens and spices from India. That was also the year he sent me the lovely porcelain vase that now sits in the grand foyer. And, in 1880, the year I married your grandfather, he sent me this necklace, from his expedition to the Himalayas. He would never return from that journey." Grandmother was silent for a moment's reflection on her father before she continued, "Come and sit by me, I should like to see it again."

Lady Cassandra placed the necklace back in the case and took a seat beside her grandmother on a divan identical to the one she'd moved from. The old woman looked down at the remarkable piece and thought of the last time she saw it. This artifact had caused her such pain, such sorrow; and it was why she would bestow the dangerous gift on Cassie, her dearest grandchild.

"Dear girl, I must tell you about this necklace. It is for you, and for no one else, and you must always remember this." Grandmother spoke in a tone her granddaughter had rarely heard from the sweet, elderly lady, "Do you understand?"

"I do," Lady Cassandra said, not fully comprehending the magnitude of this statement.

"When my father wrote to me from the Himalayas, he talked of a woman he had heard spoken of in the villages along his excursion. Some referred to her as a healer; others claimed her to be a witch. My father said she was called Mamo Rikye. He followed the stories, putting together a trail, which he followed until he finally met her face to face, high in the mountains. He wanted to know of her healing powers, what herbs she used and how. His last letter arrived with this necklace, which you will find folded beneath the velvet." Just as her grandmother said, Lady Cassandra found the letter below the velvet which cradled the necklace. It was frail and browned with age.

Lady Cassandra gently unfolded the page and read it aloud:

"Happy Christmas, my child,

I have found the red witch of the Himalayas. Two years, I have searched, and I have been welcomed into a small village called Shailas. Their ways are strange, but I daresay this simple people got it right in letting the women rule. The men are workers and servants, and the women are revered as deities. Mamo Rikye is their witch goddess. There is so much to learn from her. She teaches me of the flora and of their healing abilities, and how to combine them for greater uses. I have learned of deadly plant life that, when used properly, can heal cholera. She has even shown me a flower which numbs your skin temporarily, so that even a pin prick cannot be felt.

I do so miss you, dear Elizabeth, and long to tell you of my adventures in person. I hope to be home by Christmas next. I know it is a great while to wait for your father, but I feel that I am on the verge of discovering something exceptional here in these mountains. I had hoped to be sending you something splendid this year, since it will be many months before I see you again. The witch goddess makes adornments of bone and teeth; odd, but so beautiful to behold, with intricate hand carved designs. Mamo Rikya is selective, and refused to allow me to make purchase or trade for her exquisite jewels. She makes gifts of them to the women, but never to the men. I do have my ways, where my Elizabeth is concerned, and this necklace was given to me in trade for the last of my cask. You know what a price that was, as your father is critical of flavor.

When I was told that this necklace was for protection, and that the flower was the witch goddess's symbol for the guardianship of young women, I knew that I must have it for my daughter. As you know, I am not a superstitious man, but I hope you appreciate the sentiment. I also recall your love for the anatomy charts in my books, so you will recognize these odd beads as the vertebrae of a snake. I am told they are the bones of the Gloydius Himalayanus, or what has been called the Himalayan Pit Viper, a reptile known for deadly venom, which the people here harvest regularly. The woman who traded this necklace to me also said the flower was carved from the breastbone of Mamo Rikya's very own mother. She claimed that this is what gives it protective powers of a feminine nature, though, I'm not sure I believe that it is truly of human bone. Who can say?

Please cherish this gift, and think of me when you wear it. Merry Christmas, my Elizabeth.

All my love,

Father"

"That was the last you heard of him?" Lady Cassandra asked.

"It was. When the correspondence ceased, we sent word to a man who could track Father down. The following Christmas, we received the news that Father had fallen a great distance, and met his demise before he ever made it back down the mountains."

"How awful that must have been for you, and I don't wonder at why you never told me that story before. What a dreadful way for a man to die," Lady Cassandra said, and she squeezed her grandmother's hand. "Is this why you say this gift is for me, and me alone? Because of the connection to your father?"

"It is a part of the reason, yes, but the story goes far beyond my father's part in all of it," Grandmother said as she stared down at the necklace.

"There's more?" Lady Cassandra asked.

"So much more, child," Grandmother said, and then paused, "And I should make clear at this moment that this necklace is cursed."

"Cursed?" Lady Cassandra asked, and laughed, "We are not a superstitious people, Grandmother, your father even said so in his letter! I've never heard you talk this way."

"It *is* cursed, dear. I shall tell you how I know this, but I must give you the entire story for you to understand." Grandmother frowned, knowing that what she had to say would be unpleasant for both of them.

"Why would you give me something that is cursed?" Lady Cassandra asked with amusement in her voice, skeptical that her grandmother could actually believe in such nonsense.

"Father was a meticulous planner," Grandmother continued her story, "When he wanted something to arrive somewhere on a specific date, it arrived on that day, without fail. Each of the gifts Father sent while he was away at Christmas arrived precisely after nightfall on Christmas Eve. It is a guess, but I believe he planned for his gifts to arrive in London well before Christmas, and hired someone to make their delivery at nightfall, to avoid allowing it to be late. My father was nothing, if not dependable. So, on the

Christmas Eve this necklace came to me, I was already waiting in the drawing room, expecting a parcel of some sort.

When it grew dark, there was the immediate notice that a young courier had called with a package that had come from a great distance. It was brought to me right away, and I noticed that it seemed to have been opened. I knew I should have to question the courier about tampering, but I wanted to read the letter and see the gift, so my questions would wait until morning. I read and re-read my father's letter, and admired the beautiful necklace. I was enamored. It was the most unique gift, and I missed my father deeply that year, it having been the longest he'd been away on such an excursion. I refused to let anyone touch my new adornment, I was selfish about it. Perhaps it was the protection my father spoke of, that made me want no one else to touch the piece."

"How do you mean?" Lady Cassandra asked.

"You will know when we get to that point. There is more to tell, my dear," Grandmother told her, and she caressed the necklace as she spoke. "It snowed heavily that night, and due to the late arrival, the courier stayed over in the servants' quarters. The following morning, I sent for the young man so that I could enquire about why the parcel had appeared to be previously opened or tampered with. I waited a long time for one of the maids to bring the boy up, but to my horror, the housekeeper came to inform me that the young man had taken ill overnight and died before daybreak on Christmas morning."

"How grim! And on Christmas, too!" Lady Cassandra fretted. She noticed that her grandmother still seemed to be caressing the intricate beadwork of the necklace, telling a ghastly story with serenity on her face.

"Yes, how grim," Grandmother said, "But, I must tell you, when we sent for the boy's family to give them the news of his death and to have them come and retrieve his body, we were informed that we had harbored a thief that night. The young man was a known criminal, and had he not been taken ill and died in the night, he would have, most assuredly, robbed us that night."

"Surely you can't know if he would have done such a thing—"

"He would have," Grandmother said sternly. Lady Cassandra hushed her protest and waited for the old woman to continue.

"He would have, because he had succeeded in doing so on many occasions before, and it would've been his final robbery, because a constable arrived that afternoon in search of the courier. He explained that he had tracked the young man all the way from London. Had he not been ill…" She paused and looked her granddaughter in the eye, "Had the necklace not made him ill after he tampered with the parcel, he would've robbed us overnight."

Lady Cassandra was taken aback. Her grandmother was a well-educated woman, her father had believed in the enlightenment of his daughter. She was taught by tutors, as all young women of great families were, but her father had insisted she learn the sciences. When other young women were learning dance steps and the finer points of polite dinner conversation, Elizabeth was learning about equations, and anthropology, and studying the anatomy of birds' wings. This was a woman who did not believe in ghosts, and instilled these same ideals in all of her children and grandchildren. Lady Cassandra began to doubt her grandmother's mental clarity, and started to wonder if this was what senility looked like.

"Granny, you seem tired. Perhaps you should rest awhile," Lady Cassandra urged, hoping that a rest might bring her dear, logical grandmother back.

"No, I must finish this story, and there is so much more you must know," Grandmother barked. A rare occurrence, which took Lady Cassandra by surprise, as this harsh tone had sometimes been taken with the servants, but never with her, personally. She silently waited for her grandmother to begin talking again.

"After I received the news of Father's death, I could hardly stand to look at this dreadful thing," Grandmother said, stroking the bone flower at the center of the beads. "I put it away in my oak chest, and tried to put it from my mind, and I did for a long time. It was twenty years before I saw it again, when we were asked to make a contribution to the Museum of London. It was the fashionable thing to do, to provide unique pieces, and, because of Father's expeditions, we had quite the collection of rare items.

I chose a few pieces to be displayed temporarily, and I remembered the necklace Father had sent to me the year he died, and the story about the witch goddess. I sent Carter, the head butler in the house at that time, to find the chest, which had been moved to the unused part of the house. I described the piece and asked him to go and retrieve it for me. Oh, it took some time to find, but he brought it back to me that afternoon. I had forgotten how lovely it was, so strange and interesting to look at. It made me think of Father, and I knew that now it was back in my hands, I could not part with it, even temporarily. I took it to my room and placed it in a drawer beneath my gloves, so that I could look at it whenever I wanted."

"You kept it there all these years?" Lady Cassandra asked.

"Very nearly all these years, but I'll explain that when the time comes, dear," Grandmother said, and she seemed to be herself again, but Lady Cassandra remained unnerved by the course of the story and her grandmother's mood changes. Nevertheless, she waited for Granny to continue. "What do you suppose happened to Carter?"

"I don't know," Lady Cassandra replied, but she had a pretty good idea of what was being implied.

"They all said it was an accident, but the servants whisper about their own opinion of things, you know. Carter often strolled in the high tower before the evening meal. Perhaps he wanted a moment to himself each day, and it is such an impressive view. He requested permission, and it was of no matter to myself or your grandfather. What would it hurt? People went up there so rarely, it was nice for someone to enjoy it once in a while, don't you think?" Grandmother asked, as her gaze moved from the jewel case to where the new puppy stirred on the rug near the hearth. Lady Cassandra followed her gaze and remembered the purpose of the dog was to provide the lonely old woman with a little companionship, but now she wondered if it might be better to hire a girl to come and be with Grandmother.

"Of course you know the story, these tragic tales have a way of lingering among the staff in the form of a ghost," Grandmother said, glancing at her granddaughter. "Carter fell from the high tower that night. It was just before we went down to dine, and I happened to look out the window when I heard a scream. I saw him there, twisted and broken on the ground. There was all that talk of him taking his own life, but I ask you this, Cassie, would a man who welcomed death scream on the way to his demise?"

Lady Cassandra felt coolness on her neck. She shuddered. Perhaps it was the question her grandmother asked of her, or maybe it was the stark eye-to-eye stare she received as the old woman spoke.

"Why are you telling me all of this?" Lady Cassandra asked, disconcerted.

"There is still more," Grandmother replied.

"But why?" the young woman wanted to know, "Why would you give me a gift with such a grievous history? This is a terrible gift, and I don't think I want it." She took the case from her grandmother, who instinctively reached for it, but let her granddaughter take it away. Lady Cassandra closed the brown case and put it on a nearby table.

"There is just a bit more, and it is important that you know, dear. I'm old, and someone must be responsible for that necklace and those horrible powers."

"I'm not sure I believe any of this, Grandmother, and I still don't understand why you want me to have it," Lady Cassandra said, again, taking her place on the divan.

"You must know the whole story, and then you will understand why the necklace is for you," Grandmother spoke gently, begging for her granddaughter to listen to the remainder of her tale.

"If you feel you must tell me, then so be it, but I'm not so sure I want anything to do with that thing," Lady Cassandra said.

"Listen to me, child. You've known me all your life. You know your grandmother as a logical thinker, the way her father taught her to be, just as I taught your father to be, and you grew up to be steadfast and wise. You, my darling, are an intelligent young woman. You are not superstitious, and you think for yourself. A rare gem of a woman, indeed. I have been in possession of that 'thing', as you called it, for a great many years because my father was amused by the idea that it had protective powers; perhaps he even thought it charming, coming from an indigenous people he encountered in his travels. In all my years, and in all the time I have had this necklace, I believe it has proved that it does something that is not quite logical. I shall tell you all I know, and you can decide for yourself if you accept my gift. Yes?" Grandmother was herself, unwavering and smart, sharp as can be.

"Then proceed if you must," Lady Cassandra asked, and she prepared for another grisly portion of the story.

"We brought on a new maid last spring, and she proved meticulous in her work; not a speck of dust on a thing in this household, I tell you. Of course, you've met Margaret, now," Grandmother said, Lady Cassandra nodded, recalling the plain young woman who had brought in the teapot that afternoon. "Early on in her duties, we went over the drawers in my vanity. She helped me sort my gloves and as we did so, she stumbled over that brown leather case, which was still stuffed at the bottom of the drawer. Before I saw what she was doing, she had the case open and she'd laid her fingers on the beads—"

"There's proof that necklace isn't cursed, then! I saw Margaret just today!" Lady Cassandra exclaimed, happy to have one positive outcome in the story.

"No, no, no, child. There's still more. Yes, I am alive, and Margaret is alive, but there is only one other person in this household who has touched that necklace since, and that was your late grandfather," Grandmother said.

Lady Cassandra's hand went to her lips. She recalled the events that ultimately resulted in the death of her grandfather. He'd been quite healthy, a man who had hunted the very same week he passed on. When she received the message, Lady Cassandra could hardly believe the words she read. A man who was vibrant and healthy well into the later years of his life had succumbed to injuries from a fall down the stairs in his own home.

"I know this is difficult for you to hear, but you must know the truth," Grandmother said as she reached to pat her granddaughter's hand. "I blame myself. It was thoughtless of me, really, to ask him to retrieve a necklace for me to wear that evening. I didn't know he was even aware that the piece was there in my glove drawer. Perhaps Margaret had mentioned it, or maybe he'd seen me reading my father's letter and looking at the necklace. Whatever it was, when I asked him to find me any old necklace to wear to dinner, he fastened that piece around my neck. At first, I thought it might be all right. Margaret had touched the necklace, and I'd worried endlessly about her for weeks after. Why wouldn't my husband also be spared?

I tell you this because it is the reason I am giving this necklace to you,

Cassie. It has caused such sorrow, it has done horrific things. My father said in his letter that the witch goddess refused to sell her jewels to my father; perhaps she was simply trying to protect him. Imagine, this witch goddess built an entire society around women; the men were merely servants. How do you suppose they kept these men from rising up and harming the women in an attempt to take over? The woman who traded the necklace to my father had said it was meant to protect a young woman, that the flower was the symbol of guardianship for young girls. So far, I have only witnessed the necklace having an ill effect on gentlemen.

Now, it may be faded, but I still see it there. Look at the bruise on your hand, my darling, and think of the bruises on your heart."

There was silence as Lady Cassandra looked down at the discoloration on her hand.

The young woman made a quiet decision. She picked up the brown leather case, and took it home with her that afternoon.

DEATH AND THE FAT MAN
Jessamy Dalton

They called him the fat man. The jolly, jolly fat man. He was six-foot-four in his oiled black boots, with a frame to match: broad, brawny, and rough-hewn. Peasant stock, made for use and endurance, not beauty. Of course he was fat. Where he came from, you worked on fat. Fat was warmth. Fat was security. Fat was ballast against the heaving tides of life. Every winter, when he came through, he looked with pity on all the skinny people hurrying down the streets, wrapped to the eyes and still shivering. No wonder they were unhappy. They had nothing. When you could grab your waist with both hands and shake, and watch the jiggle going around, then you had something. Then you could put your face into life, and whatever it might bring.

His face had a permanent glow: wind and weather, high altitudes, seasonal tipples. Capillary-laced cheeks rose from the full beard that had never seen a razor. The fur trim on his red boiled wool jacket was a little yellow with age. He had the arthritis in his back, from carrying that sack all these years. The cold weather played it up, and by the end of the day, he could barely get straight. He had thought about getting some kind of rig, straps, hang the damn bag from his shoulders like the postmen did, but no. People liked tradition. Without his shouldered sack of toys, and his big fur mitts, and his big round laugh, he would hardly be the fat man anymore, would he? Some things had to stay the same, the soul of the world depended on it. So he just humped the bag and kept on trudging.

Every winter it seemed like the snow got dirtier. Freshly fallen this morning, it was already clumped and churned with grime, crunchy under his boots. But still it took the mercury vapor of the street lamps and reflected it back with a blessing, making it warmer, softer, gentling the whole metropolis and giving the night the feeling of something out of time. It was

61

quite late. Parties still jingled and shimmied in buildings all over the city, but distantly, as though they were taking place inside a glass globe. Outside, all was calm. Clear and still. The air was so cold you could almost believe it was clean. He took a deep breath of it as he stamped up the steps to his next address.

"Merry Christmas, friend," he said to the doorman as he went by.

"Merry Christmas," replied the man. He would not remember the visit or the words, only the vague feeling he had had that someone or something had passed through his vestibule around midnight on Christmas Eve.

The fat man took the stairs. The building had an elevator, and the boy operator slouched on a stool beside it, pitching pennies to stay awake. But the fat man had always felt it was part of his contract to enter via the utilitarian side of things. The stairs in this building were well lit and clean. The furnace ducts hummed gently around him. He reached the door marked '6,' and opened it.

There was a light burning in the foyer, and this was not unusual, but there were also voices and activity, and people going in and out. Not partygoers. Not with their practical clothing and ungroomed hair. The fat man hesitated in the doorway. No one saw him, not the busy suits, nor the grim uniforms, nor even the waiting men in ambulance whites, sitting smoking beside their wheeled gurney. That they were sitting was not a good sign. The fat man thought he knew what this activity meant, and it meant this was no place for him. And yet, and yet, he had his obligations…

The fat man moved, unchallenged, through the hubbub, into the apartment's main bay. "Receptions rooms," the architect had probably called them, confident that anyone who purchased at *this* address would be the sort to require a dining room for thirty, a conversation pit, and a full service bar. The place reeked of money and style. It was done in creams and blues, and whoever had decked the hall for the season had gone for silver and gold, with touches of greenery. The focal piece was a large spruce, lit and trimmed in highly impersonal good taste.

It had been meant, anyway, to be the focal point. At the moment it was upstaged by the woman on the floor.

The fat man removed his cap. After all, like every adult in the world, she had once been a child. *A pretty one*, the fat man thought, *quick to laugh, easy to move to tears, everybody's friend.* A sweet, fair girlhood that was still just about visible on the battered face turned indifferently toward the ceiling. She was wearing a green silk dress from Dior's New Look, with sheer stockings, red garters, high thin heels, and a mink wrap. Her blonde hair was styled in a bouffant. Her lips and nails were the same shade of crimson, and her open, empty eyes had been outlined with kohl. It was a look she had probably worked hard on.

"Get the coffee table in a shot or two if you can," said a man at the fat man's elbow. But he was speaking to the photographer, who nodded, and shifted his tripod to include the low board of rustic French pine that stood above the dead woman. The man who had spoken sighed and rubbed his face. He was wearing an ill-fitting suit. It was harder to see him as a child; he would have been one of those youngsters who are born old, the conscientious ones with the worried expressions.

He plodded away from the technical business, back to the corner where he and his partner had set up, uncomfortably, on a pair of overstuffed chairs. In front of them was a matching piece of furniture, which the apartment's flamboyant male decorator had called, without a trace of irony, a pouf. Sitting on this pouf was a third man. He was wearing the remnants of a tuxedo, and his head was in his hands.

"After you struck her," said the man in the ill-fitting suit, picking up his notebook.

"I *didn't* strike her," said the tuxedo man. He wiped his forehead with the backs of both sleeves.

"So she's on the floor, out cold. Blunt trauma to the head. Skull fracture, cranial bleeding," said the man. Printed in fountain pen on the back of his notebook was 'Lt. F. Hanratty'. "You want to explain why you didn't call for a medic?"

The tuxedo man said, wretchedly, "I didn't even know she was here!"

"With the doorman putting her arrival around quarter to ten and yours at eleven, and the boy backs him up, that's at least an hour you were both in the same building, and we're supposed to believe you never saw her?"

"I *told* you, I went right to—"

"The powder room. You told us," said Hanratty's partner, the second detective. "You came in the door, hung a straight left into the tush, and sat there drinking Jim Beam from the bottle. It's a hell of an alibi."

"I just—look, don't you ever get sick of—of *Christmas*? The glitter, the twinkles. The *music*. I couldn't take it anymore. The hall toilet's the only place I wasn't staring a load of tinsel in the face. I just had to have a *break*."

"You know what I think you got sick of?" said the second detective. "I think you got sick of Miss Kronkheit. I think she turned into a problem for you. You've got deals, you know people, you're an important man. She was just a girl from Weehawken who wanted too much. She wanted to move up, didn't she? Wanted a ring, the whole nine yards. The way I see it, she's in here waiting for you, you get home, she's drunk, you're drunk, she starts in on you, you pick up that statue there, hit her on the head, she goes down, and you don't know what to do."

"I *didn't*—"

The fat man looked with interest at the ceramic figurine lying next to the dead woman. *It was intended*, he thought, *to be a reindeer.* Heavy, impressionistically molded, a crackle-glazed statuette maybe half a foot long, a foot high, not counting the antlers. The artist had been going for the spirit of the animal: a proud head, noble ruff, sinewy legs, shoulders bunched with power. *Damn propaganda*, thought the fat man, who knew the smelly beasts well. The statuette had two fellows, both still on the French pine table, arranged in a mass of loose white confetti meant to represent snow. Their heads were held in different attitudes, but they had the same body as their toppled companion, the same massive hindquarters, a muscular rump that almost palpably matched the indentation on the woman's head.

The first detective, Hanratty, said wearily, "Listen, Mr. Van Huesen, flat-out denial always seems like the smart option in these cases, but giving us the details could mean the difference between murder-one and manslaughter."

The second detective said, "Sure, you can get a good lawyer, but you're gonna find out some things money can't buy."

And then they were both interrupted by a new, smaller voice, saying, "Roger?"

There was a quick, subtle drawing together of all the busy people, screening off their work from view; against all odds they still believed in innocence. The tousled child in the pajamas could have been either gender, maybe four or five years old, but still, no lisping, no wubby, babyish pronunciation of the 'r'. "Roger?"

Hanratty looked at Van Heusen: "She doesn't call you daddy?"

"It was my wife's idea—before she left—some analyst she got talking to at her Method classes—supposed to encourage the development of independent identity..." The tuxedo man returned his head to his hands. "God, my wife. How am even I supposed to *reach* her on some producer's damn *yacht*?"

The second detective said, "Where the hell's that nanny?"

"She went back upstairs," said Hanratty, no less wearily. "She's got the Goldstein kids to think of, she was only looking in here as a favor—"

"And found a corpse. Merry Christmas."

"Shut up." The pajamas were padding over to the pouf.

Van Heusen raised a face with a ghastly smile. "Sweetie—sweetheart— I'm busy, I've got things to...to do. You need to go back to bed, honey."

The child gravely considered her father and then the gathered company. Only one figure seemed to make sense to her. She beamed all over her small face: "Santa!"

There were a few awkward smiles, and the attending doctor fingered his beard in embarrassment. So did the fat man, not that any of the others saw. They might believe in innocence, but they didn't possess it. Neither would this child, not for long, not now. The fat man shook his head. Not so long ago, it seemed to him, he'd been bringing gifts to girls on the eve of marriage, not so much younger than the woman on the floor. Now hardly anyone could see him.

Hanratty said softly, "That's what you've got to consider, Van Heusen. Standing right there. Think about it," and the man on the pouf gave a heartrending groan.

The fat man frowned. Something had been nagging at him, and he stepped over and picked up one of the model reindeer to confirm it. Yes: the sculptor had given the statuettes each four straight hooves, such as horses possess. Pointy tippy-toes, all the better to go tap-tap-tapping on the rooftops—*when everyone knows,* thought the fat man, *that reindeer have got cloven hooves, just like any ruminant; two splayed toes, buoyed up by fatty pads, flat, clumsy feet, nothing at all so sharp and keen as these figurines' feet, almost like chisels they were*—and the fat man straightened up, with a grunt, with an effort, to find the child's eyes fastened on him. Shining in expectation and delight.

And it was not his business, was it? And it was not his place, or his concern, but it *was* his night, and for a little while, all things were, in a way, at his discretion. And maybe he was just a foolish old man, who rewarded the nice and chided the naughty, a thankless task if there ever was one. There wasn't much that was nice about this situation, or the world at large, and the sooner the child learned that, maybe, the better off she would be. *But maybe,* the fat man thought, *the lesson didn't have to be tonight.* He filled his not inconsiderable chest with the tense air of the room, and blew it out in a long, silent huff.

His breath smelled of frost and apples, of pine, wintergreen, and wet wool. It was warm as a hearth and sweet as dried hay. It ruffled the hair and the suits of the adults in the room, who blinked, and wondered where the draft had come from, and it blew the snow-confetti off the French table and swirled it over the child, who squealed and leaped in glee. The two model reindeer were left standing on barren turf, with four skidding gouges revealed to show where their companion had stood—until something heavy had fallen against it and scored the marks of its hooves into the soft pine wood before carrying down it to the floor.

Hanratty and his cohorts stood silently, looking. Considering things like palm prints and bruising patterns, the scrape on the corpse's arm, the unstableness of a drunken woman in four-inch heels on a thick shag rug. The photographer measured the corpse with his eyes and calculated the trajectory and striking force of a falling human body. The doctor made mental notes to ask the pathologist to look for white confetti in the wound, the hairline, the mucous membranes of the nose.

The second detective, who had just seen his case devolve from an old, familiar story into a freak accident of the sort that enters legend precisely because it is true, pinched the bridge of his nose and said, "Van Heusen, you got a hell of a lot of questions to answer, but seeing as it's Christmas, we're cutting you a break. Get the kid out of here. Tuck her in somewhere, feed her a good breakfast in the morning, and I don't want you changing your shorts without letting us know about it."

"All right," said the tuxedo man meekly, and he gathered up his child, who was still sprinkled with white flakes and bore a look of sleepy satisfaction.

I am old, thought the fat man, *very, very old, and the world is not much better now than it ever was. But here and there, from time to time, a little goodness breaks through. It was enough to keep an old man walking,* he thought; and swinging his pack back up on his shoulder, with a wince, he waved to one and all, not that they would see it, and spoke, unheard, his timeworn benediction. Then he turned and trudged away out the door.

And all the suits and uniforms got back to work with slightly more hustle and bustle than necessary, because, for eff's sake, it wasn't like Christmas was anything to get sentimental about.

COAL FOR CHRISTMAS
M.R. DeLuca

The distinguished-looking gentleman stepped onto the train platform more confidently than any of his fellow passengers, of which there were few. He did not need even a perfunctory glance to know his clothes were the most fashionable, his stride the most graceful, his whiskers the most neat. He had been an outsider for the longest time, but he didn't mind feeling out of place. In fact, he welcomed the phenomenon—it meant he had finally left his roots behind.

Wintertime was difficult for most people around these parts; he remembered that much from his time as a coal miner. The white-capped mountains were breathtaking, but as he learned from his many years on the earth, beauty could be treacherous and not all was as it appeared. The snow had a way of settling into every nook and cranny of the hollers, piling high and heavy against rickety wooden shacks brimming with cold, half-starved settlers.

But the worst off were the bachelor shanties. As suggested by their namesake, they held the loneliest young men for miles around. They were orphans of the cosmos who worked to sustain a living and progress no further, having little motivation or means to abandon their secure loneliness for constant, aimless struggle toward an abstract goal. He revisited those memories too, sometimes, but not often. He never enjoyed staying in one place, be it physical or mental, for any substantial amount of time.

He had returned only for a couple days: to attend the funeral, pay the local attorney a visit, and promptly hop the railroad to his next destination. His position as a travelling businessman required his time and attention more than even any wife or child would, and he was glad for the distraction it provided in his life.

"I see you received the telegram," a voice called from the dwindling throng of people cheerfully escorting loved ones from the station.

The man swiveled his head toward the familiar inflection. It was one, he was surprised, that he was glad to hear, and that made him a little sad.

A taller, thinner man emerged from the crowd. He wore his Sunday best, which consisted of a simple black coat and trousers obviously worn from years of use. He rubbed the patch on his elbow—it was either self-consciousness or rheumatism—before smiling and approaching the traveler.

"Chester Braxton, as I live and breathe—if I hadn't seen it myself, I would've never believed you'd step foot back in this town again," he half-joked as he outstretched a weathered-looking hand.

Chester took it and noted, unsurprised, the comparative strength of the grip. "Good to see you, Rhett. It's been a while."

"Sixteen years is a long while," he responded cryptically.

An uncomfortable silence settled between them. Finally, after a chilling breeze swept over them, Rhett said, "It's too cold to stand out here like fools without proper coats or sense. My boy has the carriage—well, it's more like a cart, truth be told—waiting for us."

Chester forced a smile and waved his arms in show of good faith. "Then off we go."

They descended the platform's creaky stairs and hurried to a near-deserted road. A young man, the spitting image of his father, sat at the reins, futilely struggling to calm the restless horses.

As Chester motioned to hoist himself into the covered buggy, the smaller bay reared on its hind legs and whinnied agitatedly. Rhett pushed him aside and jumped into the makeshift carriage, yanking on the reins until both beasts stopped their protests and reluctantly obeyed.

"I'm sorry, Pa," the boy said between breaths. "They were still as night until a few minutes ago. Something must have spooked them terribly, but I haven't the foggiest." He turned to the uneasy man who had watched the whole ordeal. "You must be my father's old friend, Mr. Braxton. Pleased to make your acquaintance, sir. I am Daniel, the eldest son."

The sophisticated man tentatively climbed onto the seat and, with the crack of a whip, the three had started down the first of many rolling hills. They exchanged niceties and talked about the most neutral subjects they could garner: the weather, the heavy toil of labor, the titans of the day. Chester refused to mention he knew some of those prominent men personally—he did not earn his place as a shrewd businessman without possessing a good dose of knowledge of human behavior and psychology.

"I'm very sorry for what happened," he offered, referring to the telegram he had received days before.

"I know. And all this right before Christmas, of all times." Rhett clicked his tongue. "Mine explosion. There was too much gas in the air, and that side of the mountain just ignited before anyone knew what hit them. Fourteen men died, fourteen families torn to shreds, including that of the superintendent's. Remember Superintendent Kinsey? Lost a lot of money in stocks before settling here? He had that blind wife who was sweet as sugar; she died a couple years ago of the fever, bless her heart. He was gone first. Heard it was gruesome, that he was burned alive; thankfully she didn't live to grieve him."

Chester bit his lip. "Fourteen, you say? And Kinsey died? How curious."

"Why?" Rhett's son asked, watching the odd expression his father's childhood friend wore.

"Don't be rude to our guest, Daniel," his father chided.

"He's not going to be our guest if Mama doesn't let him in the house, springing a stranger on her like this. And on Christmas Eve, of all days. Even I didn't know he was coming until a few hours ago."

"Now you hush that trap of yours. The funeral's on Christmas, so he had to come in today. No helping that. And besides, they're not strangers to each other." He nervously turned to Chester. "His mother is—I married—you know Clementine."

He inwardly panicked but outwardly kept his cool. "As in Whitebush?"

Rhett refused to look at him. "Yes, but don't fret. I'm sure she'll let you stay. It was your cousin who died, after all. It'd be impolite to turn away a man who's grieving."

Chester didn't mention he wasn't grieving all that much, having met his much younger cousin from the other side of the mountain once or twice. Chester left shortly after Martin was born, and he wouldn't recognize him dead or alive. He wouldn't have come, but he needed to be present to hear the will read. The rest of the Braxtons had either died or moved west with the earliest pioneers, but Martin and Chester were the only ones who stayed in the east, for reasons halfway between choice and circumstance. Martin didn't have much, but maybe he left his final known living relative a monetarily valuable family heirloom. "I hope you're right."

"Worse comes to worse, I can always set up a place for you in a corner of the barn. It's only old plow parts, the two horses, and some chickens, so it shouldn't smell too bad."

He involuntarily scrunched his nose. He hadn't slept on anything but the finest sheets, in the finest rooms, for years. Every hotel room was grand and spacious: all that time working in narrow mountain tunnels during the day and returning to tight quarters at night had made him vow to never feel so closed in ever again. Even when he needed a sleeping car on the railroad, he would book their most spacious suite, which was still larger than the miner's shanty he had occupied in his past.

They arrived at a small wooden home on stilts, after passing a half-dozen just like it. "We're here," Daniel declared. He prepared to jump up and out, fueled by the exuberant energy of youth, but was sobered by his father's meaty hand weighing on his shoulder.

"Lead Petey and Hannah to their stalls, but keep an eye on them. Look at their tails; they're still jittery. I don't need them thrashing about. The roof could fall under the weight of the snow that's coming—" he pointed to the gray sky overhead "—and I don't need them knocking into the walls, too."

"Okay, Pa," he answered. "Good-bye, Mr. Braxton."

"Good-bye, son." He didn't know why he said that; he was usually cold and formal, and that was with people he knew intimately. He remarked to himself that the boy would've been his son's age, had he settled down and had one.

As they walked up the stairs, Chester heard a snap. Rhett chuckled as he motioned to the step that had broken in half underneath his own foot. "Water must have rotted the plank. We still get a lot of flooding in this neck of the woods. I keep warning Clem that we should put an ark on top of these stilts and live in that, because one day we're going to need it."

"Speaking of things that rot—or rather, ought to rot," said the tiny, stern woman at the top of the stairs, "I don't know why my husband thought he could bring the likes of you here, but you better get off my property before you learn how good I am with buckshot."

"This is why I didn't tell you beforehand," Rhett argued as he reached the landing at the top of the stairs. Chester stopped just short of it, wary that her threat might have credibility. "I wrote to tell him last week about his cousin Martin, and he wrote back that he was coming. The only family he had left here died in the blast, and the tavern closed up a while back, so where was he supposed to stay?"

"In jail, where he belongs."

"Clementine!" He stood to his full height, but still seemed to have less of a presence than his wife. "You have to stop blaming him for what happened almost two decades ago! It wasn't his fault; mining accidents happen more often than they should. I've been working underground long enough to say that for a fact."

"It wasn't an accident," she stated coldly. "They were the only two in that tunnel. Chester purposefully busted the weakest part of the coal seam to cause the roof to collapse. He made sure that he could escape in time, and that Sampson would be buried alive. He didn't even try to dig him out from the rubble."

"And how do you know all that?" her husband retorted. "This poor man felt so awful about what happened that he left everything he'd ever known and never intended to return. No one blamed him, except you and himself. You and I both read that note he left: he tried to save his mining partner, but couldn't. And I've known him since we were children, so I can vouch that he isn't the type to leave anyone or anything behind without good reason."

"The whole letter was a ruse to cover his hide." She glared at the subject of their conversation, who had remained silent the entire time. "Sampson told me what you were going to do. Some nights when Rhett and Daniel were working late up in the mountains and the young ones were asleep, he talked to me. He told me the whole story a long time ago, down to the last sordid detail." She pointed at him accusingly. "You might have left this area, but he never did. Sampson was a good man; he would never leave his home. And he would never do what you planned to do to the Kinseys!"

Chester turned pale as all the blood in his cheeks drained into this rapidly beating heart. "I have to leave." He ran quickly down the steps, taking care to skip the broken one.

Rhett started after him. In his haste, however, he slipped his foot into the cracked slot and had his leg caught. He yelped in pain.

His wife rushed to grab her husband by the waist and lift him as best she could. As she struggled she called out, "Stay away from us, Chester Braxton, or I will make sure you never harm my family again!"

Chester channeled all his focus into leaving town sooner rather than later. On foot, as quickly as his tired, unmuscled legs would allow, he followed the steep, long, snowy road back to the train station. His shoes were scuffed beyond repair, his jacket covered with a thin layer of ice, and to make matters worse, flurries were falling furiously. Forget the funeral and the will; he should have stayed true to his letter, and never returned.

After what seemed like hours, he wearily arrived in the cloak of night at his destination. Before he could climb the platform, however, he collapsed in the snow on the side of the road.

He awoke to find massive snowflakes caking his eyelashes. The ticket booth was closed, he noticed with a heavy heart—which soared when it heard the whistle.

A sleek, black train with blinding lights, the quintessential picture of the industrial age, emerged from the winter landscape. It spat thick clouds of smoke as it roared down the track. Finally it slowed to a stop and, without hesitation, the desperate man leapt on board. It started again promptly, as if it were waiting for him.

Chester searched the initial car for the conductor, but to no avail. He passed in between the cars, announcing his presence each time, but was surprised to find not a soul in sight. The train was deserted. He stalked his way to the front of the train and, alarmed, banged on the engineer's door.

"Engineer! Engineer! Sir, I must speak with you! The matter is urgent!"

The door creaked open. Chester nearly fainted when he saw the engineer leave his chair and turn around. "Sampson Whitebush?"

"In the flesh," he quipped with a straight face. He studied his own ethereal form. "Well, maybe not."

Chester felt sick to his stomach, which he clutched as his head spun. "This is either a dream, or I've gone mad."

"I can confirm you've gone mad, Chester, but that didn't occur recently." He crossed his arms and gave the same stern look his sister gave. "It happened the night you murdered me."

"I didn't murder you," he returned quickly. "The crumbling rocks above us killed you."

"Because you purposely triggered its collapse." Sampson's eyes became slits. "We were told that the area was vulnerable, liable to cave in. Don't think I didn't see you drive your pickaxe into that crevice. That night, you paid heed to make sure you weren't careful." His voice dripped with bitterness.

Chester saw he could no longer escape the truth. He took his next best option: to rationalize it. "But you knew I did what I had to do," he practically whispered. "I could no longer live the monotonous life of an impoverished miner. I was trapped in a cycle I could never leave, no matter how hard I tried. I thought you were a kindred soul with a disheartened spirit. But when I learned you weren't, I couldn't allow you to live and tell anyone about my scheme; you were set to ruin my life before it would even begin."

"You ruined your own life—not me." His aura emanated intense hatred. "You were the one who was going to rob the superintendent to get money for a ticket out of here. That night, you waited until we were alone in the mines, and then told me about your plan.

"Everyone knew Kinsey distrusted the banks. He lost his family's fortune when the stock market crashed in the Panic of 1873, and has since told everyone with working ears that the banks were doomed to fail next, that it would be foolish to do anything but stuff your mattress. So you wanted me to distract Superintendent Kinsey's wife the next morning while you ransacked their house, right in front of her nose. She couldn't see a blessed thing. You said if I kept her ears busy, you could find their stash of actual money that the company pays their officials, but not their miners. You were willing to give me most of it, all but fourteen dollars. Fourteen dollars to buy yourself the cheapest ticket out of town at the time. We could have been gone by that afternoon, long before anyone learned of what we did. When I told you I wouldn't be an accomplice, that all this was wrong, and that I'd turn you in if you actually went through with it—" He took a deep breath. "My fatal flaw was saying anything to you."

"They didn't pay us in real coin," Chester countered. "They gave us 'company currency,' scrip that we could only use in the company store. They charged us for our food, our housing, our equipment. At one point I was paying the company to work for them and live in that horrid little shanty. I'd die in bankruptcy. All that work I did, all those times I risked my life—for pretend tokens? I deserved real money that I could use to leave this soulless place."

"We all deserved more than scrip—but that still doesn't give you the right to do whatever you want to get whatever you want. You don't get to decide by your own self-serving whims who lives and who dies. That is not your domain. The deaths of those fourteen miners, including Martin's and Kinsey's, were calculated long ago. That night was their time. They were good men, and they will be treated well where they are going. But the night you killed me—my time wasn't up yet. So I was graciously granted my request to wait for your return and, as I wish, punish with impunity. Surely enough you were eventually led back by the greed that fuels your soul, and it will fittingly be your undoing. You—you are a sorry, repulsive creature, and it is my pleasure that I may deliver you to your fate."

Chester began to protest, but the look in Sampson's eyes silenced him. He scanned the room for an exit, even a window to jump out of, but to no avail.

"You cannot leave," the specter remarked, "and you cannot use your way with words to make a deal with me. For once in your life, you must simply stand there and listen."

Chester swallowed hard.

"This train will bring you to your afterlife. I am not at liberty to discuss the nature of such a realm; you will learn all about it when you get there. You will arrive when the fire turns to ash, and the train runs out of coal."

Chester mustered all the strength he could not to plead for mercy: it would not be well-received.

"But it is Christmastime, the season of generosity, as I am well aware. So instead of being brought directly to your final place, you were allowed to board this train. And you are given a choice, and a fitting one at that: as long as you continuously shovel coal—and you have an endless supply of it—you will remain on this train. If and when you stop, you will meet your fate—whatever that might be. And I think you know where you would go."

In one graceful turn, he sat back in the chair and melted into it, disappearing as a waft into the air. Chester had a decision to make, and quickly, lest it be made for him.

And so tirelessly, day by day, for the rest of his afterlife, the harried gentleman with the ragged, nice clothes, fueled his own train of misery with the coal he received for Christmas.

A MIDWINTER HAUNTING
Sammi Cox

I cannot say what madness drove me from the safety of my home that Midwinter night. Perhaps a momentary form of lunacy had descended upon me? Perhaps a dream that I can no longer recall persuaded me to open the door and flee into the night, with nothing but a shawl over my nightgown and woolen stockings to cover my bare feet and legs.

I do not know. That part seems hardly important now, unlike the rest. That which followed, I remembered. *Always*.

* * *

When I first became aware of what had happened, I was already outside at the end of the garden. How and why I came to be there, I could not guess. For innumerable minutes, I looked about me, bemused and confused, and yes, slightly afraid. I had never before suffered from somnambulism, for that was what this surely must be. I must have been sleepwalking.

Snow lay feet deep all around me, but the air was still and heavy with...I wasn't sure. Now, as I look back on it, I would say at once that the air was still and heavy with anticipation, but I know what is to come. Before hindsight gifted me this knowledge, I could only think that I somehow could sense that more snow was on its way.

The wind moaned softly, its voice muted by the winter air. And yet, there was something I could hear upon it, very quietly as if it was some distance away. I stared off into the darkness, straining to catch the words and at the same time trying to force my eyes to see through the shadows that were all about me. Nevertheless, the harder I listened, the more elusive the sound became.

That was until I felt a soft breath upon my ear and heard my name whispered into the night.

"Christina..."

I spun round, fear gripping my heart. And then I saw her. She was nothing more than a flash of white moving in the winter darkness at the edge of my vision.

"Christina..."

"Hello?" I called out to her in my disorientated state, but she paid me no heed as she passed beneath the archway in the old wall.

I turned away. I had no intention of following a strange woman through the night with nothing on my feet but a pair of woolen stockings. And yet, when I looked upon the house in the gloom, with its dark cold windows and brooding atmosphere, I realized that I could not return home. Something compelled me to turn back around and head towards the old wall. Something compelled me to follow the woman.

My footsteps were slow at first, protesting against what could only be described as my foolhardiness, rather than the icy paving slabs beneath my feet. Even now, many years later, I wonder that I didn't really feel the cold. I was somehow immune to its frosty bite.

When I reached the gate in the old wall, it was closed and locked. Momentarily I pondered how this were possible, when I had seen the woman pass through to the other side, and the gate could only be locked from where I was standing. Shaking my head, perplexed, I turned the key and passed under the archway. The gate closed behind me with an air of somber finality.

Before me lay acres of parkland, sprawling down towards the river, which meandered its way through the valley. It would be frozen solid this far into the season. To the west, looming in the darkness were the woods, but before it, between trees and river, was a hill, atop which stood the Tower, a folly built a hundred years ago or more. One round tower, which gave the ruins its name, stood tall and stark in the moonlight, like some terrible lone tooth protruding from an earthen jaw, whilst the walls to either side of it and the remains of other towers lay crumbling all about it.

It was to that dark and isolated place the woman was heading now, I discovered to my amazement, the whiteness of her dress illuminated against a canvas of black, tracking her direction. If I had arrived a few minutes earlier, I would never have seen her, so well camouflaged was she against the snow.

I set off in pursuit of her once more, though I still didn't know why. What business of mine was it if she wanted to wander the estate in the dead of night? Perhaps I was intrigued by her presence here. It wasn't unusual to find strangers exploring the many acres that surrounded the house, during the day at least. But how did she know my name?

It took me a little while to cross the open space to the foot of the hill. I tried not to look towards the forest. Although I could not see it clearly, I felt exposed before it, a thought which sent shivers up and down my spine. It also brought to mind all the frightening tales I had heard as a child, tales I had begged to hear, of ghosts and monsters and fairy spirits...

By this point the woman, who had been moving up the incline much quicker than I ever could, had crested the summit and was out of sight. I shivered then. For some reason I felt suddenly afraid. Something was amiss. I swallowed hard. Something dark, something terrifying, was to be found at the folly this night. I knew it.

Once more I wanted to turn back around and head for the safety of the house, and yet, once more something urged me on. Whatever was up there at the Tower, I could not let the woman face it alone.

And so I pushed on, breathing heavily as I climbed higher and higher, the drifts of snow making progress slow and painful. Once at the top, I was so weary with the exertion of the climb that I fell to my knees. When I finally managed to pull myself to my feet, the front of my nightdress was soaking with snow, causing it to hang heavy, weighing me down.

I looked up and tried to see through the darkness. There was something ethereal about the Tower, I saw. It seemed to glow ever so gently, making its dark stone appear a little lighter against the night. It was as if it wanted to be seen, to be found, a strange beacon in a sea of black.

It was then that I spotted her. Her white dress was fluttering in the breeze as she stood at the top of the Tower. My breath caught in my throat. She was too close to the edge, to which she had her back. I stepped forward, my arms reaching up to her even though I was so far away. She must have sensed the danger she was in, for she looked over her shoulder.

Now I knew she was not alone. Someone was up there with her. From my vantage point, I couldn't see them, but her behavior, her movements, told me they were there and that they were threatening her.

Without thinking, I started moving as fast as I could towards the ruins. Unfortunately, given the cold, this was not very quickly at all. The muscles in my legs were becoming increasingly stiff and sore. Gritting my teeth, and pulling my shawl tighter about me, I pressed on, my eyes remaining fixed on the woman standing precariously at the top of the Tower.

I was almost there when raised voices drifted down to me. However, the words were carried away on the wind long before they reached my ears. Automatically, I stopped. Horror filled me as I watched the woman's foot slip on the crumbling stone, before regaining her balance, but only for a moment. A shadowy hand, belonging to the unknown person arguing with her, reached into the air between them and shoved her hard.

Everything seemed to stop for a heartbeat, suspended as she was in mid-air. Then she was falling...falling...falling...

"No!" I tried to call out, but the only sound to escape my lips was a gravelly, hoarse whisper. I looked up to see a shadow retreat from the Tower's top. And then...nothing but the wind could be heard up at the folly.

I cannot tell you how much time passed before I could move. It was only when I decided that I should check to see if the mystery woman was dead—though how could she not be, falling from such a great height?— that I became aware of the tears streaming down my cheeks. As to the person who pushed her, I heard and saw no more.

I found her lying at the foot of the Tower, her legs and arms at impossible angles to her body. She was clearly dead.

"Oh, no," I whispered, still crying. I didn't know what to do. I wanted to lay her out neatly, to cover her over and restore her dignity. It was the least I could do. I reached down to pull her dress down over her exposed broken legs, when the fabric began disintegrating in my hands.

Instinctively, I recoiled, as the most horrific thing I ever saw started to unfold in front of my eyes. Only then did I grasp what was going on. What I was seeing, what I had seen, wasn't real. It was the replaying of a memory, of something that had gone before.

"I died here," she said, standing next to me, as both of our attention was given to the changing figure before us. "A few days before Christmas, it was."

Where a few moments before lay a dead woman in a depression of snow dyed red with her blood, now there was nothing more than bones that stood white in contrast to the scarlet. Soon, that too faded and the spot was bare, the snow unbroken.

"You will too, if you're not careful." Slowly, she turned to look at me.

"Who are you? What do you want?" My voice was quiet, but above all, it was sad.

"My name? Perhaps it was Annie. Or Katherine. Maybe Sarah. I cannot recall now. Can you help me remember?"

I looked up, meeting her gaze. "I'm sorry. I don't know how."

Panic spread across her dead face. "But you must. You must! I want to be remembered. I want to be mourned. But no one cared enough to miss me. I was all alone in the world, and they thought I would be easy to tame. I wasn't, and so they had no use for me. Now I am dead and nameless. Help me find my name," she sobbed as her bony fingers covered the face that could only partially conceal the skull beneath it.

Pity and sadness overwhelmed me. After all she had suffered, I didn't want to let her down. However, I had no idea how to find her lost name. "I will remember you. I will mourn you. I shall not forget," I whispered in earnest.

"Thank you, but there is more I must tell you," she replied. "Listen carefully and heed my warning. Do you know how to keep a secret? Your life depends upon it..."

I do not remember much of the return journey, only that a veil of sorrow had fallen across my heart and my eyes. It was as if crossing from one side of the old wall to the other had been like crossing a threshold. I had changed, transforming from the Christina-who-didn't-know into the Christina-who-knew-too-much.

I was met at the kitchen door by the steward. My absence had somehow been noted.

"Are you all right, miss?" he asked, with a look of suspicion—or was it fear?—on his face. He appeared not to be talking to me, but looking over my shoulder and into the grounds beyond.

"I am fine now. I couldn't sleep and decided to take a walk in the garden." I pulled my shawl tighter about my shoulders.

He looked me over. My nightdress was stiff where the dampness had frozen solid.

"Best get yourself back to bed, miss. The cold be frightful here, this close to Christmas." Still he continued to peer out of the doorway, as if looking for something or *someone*, in the garden.

"Yes, it is quite cold," I murmured. "Goodnight."

I walked the darkened corridors without the aid of a candle. It was only as I began to climb the stairs that I heard the kitchen door close shut and the bolts drawn.

In my room, I got into bed. But I didn't sleep.

* * *

Each winter she would come to me, though I was no longer required to make the long trek through the dark and snow to the Tower. I had already seen all that there was to see at the folly.

After that first meeting, I would wake in the night to find her in my bedroom. Sometimes she would simply be there, standing over me as I slept. On other occasions, I would stir to find her in the corner of my room paying me no attention at all, until I made to get out of the bed. Then she would slowly turn to me and smile as best as her dead face allowed. As my heart turned to ice, I would try my hardest to smile back, as I shivered involuntarily. It didn't matter how many times she visited, I could never quite get used to her company, though I missed her when she was gone.

Our last meeting was different to all the others. She arrived early that winter. I was sitting at my dressing table, brushing my hair before bed, when she suddenly materialized behind me and placed her bony hand on my shoulder. I would never see her again.

A few days later I would catch a fever, never waking from it. As I lay there in my sickroom, my mind lost to the delirium that accompanied the other symptoms of my malady, I would recall the words she shared with me at the folly. The words that had haunted me, more than she, poor soul that she was, ever could.

"They will deny it all," she had whispered. "Do not trust them, or you will end up dead and broken at the bottom of a ruined tower with none but *me* to mourn *you*. You were safe because you didn't know what they had done. But I had to tell you. I had to warn you. Only now can you see what they really are, but you must not let on. You must not tell."

There was something in her cold dead eyes that told me I would do well to take her advice.

And I did. I never said a word.

COFFIN JOE'S CAROL
Brian Malachy Quinn

If you had to walk by Coffin Joe, you kept your distance, for he was a black hearted man that even the devil would avoid. Joe was a sight to behold: his long dark greasy hair, the shade of wet grave dirt, hung in strands from under his filthy and worn gentleman's top hat, obtained through questionable means; his beard, a long unkempt tangle with bits of food and things that moved about. His waistcoat, shirt and trousers, were threadbare, his shoes worn down and full of holes, all the color of the muddy miserable, black coal dust sodden, fog choked streets of London's Blackfriars in which lay St. Anne's. His job? He was ferryman of the dead, escorting those from this world to the next and doing it with a smile of blackened, broken teeth. And, he did so in a churchyard, where a shrub and a patch of grass, as if sprung from the dead, were as rank as the iron railing enclosing them was rusty. The church tower itself was like a giant, indifferent to the gravestones looking on like the crowding ghosts of many miserable years, hemmed in by filthy houses on whose walls mold and rot climbed like a malignant disease.

He had appeared one day twenty years ago, fully formed like something loathsome from a sewer emptying into the Thames. Luckless John, the previous sexton, was lowering a bloated corpse into a grave when he suddenly gasped, coughing up blood, falling over, limbs twitching about. Joe, ever vigilant for an opportunity, simply jumped the fence, kicked John's legs into the grave with the rest of his body, picked up the shovel and covered him with dirt. Luckless to the end poor John, not yet departed from this world, started clawing his way out of the ground, to which Joe with a couple of strikes of the shovel to set the tempo, began his three step on John, singing:

"When the devil comes be ready
Life is hard and never steady
Hell welcomes all
Into its wide and gaping maul"

Now Joe was welcome at St. Anne's, for Unlucky John had not been a motivated employee, lacking attention to detail— leaving bones sticking out of the dirt and burying them in the wrong graves. Besides, finding someone dedicated to handle the dead was a challenge, especially when the Angel of Death was busy leaving bodies everywhere, as happened frequently in the largest city of Europe. The mortality rate in London was twice that of those that lived in the country. Sewers ran into drinking water, and death from water was more likely than death from starvation, and not by drowning but by drinking it. The poor lived packed together six to a room and millions of them packed into a couple of square miles, with a cough on Monday in Camberwill ending up being a full-blown killer contagion on Friday in Saffron Hill.

Joe, paid enough to keep a full bottle of gin in his pocket, the measure of his happiness, was always in some state of drunkenness. Being an enterprising good Englishman, he also found other ways to increase his worth, to engage in his passions and amass a small fortune.

His passions? Coffin Joe liked wagering and, more than that, winning. In the underworld of London there was "Slender Billy's", a house between Parliament and Millbank owned by William Aberfield, where bear-baiting and dogfighting kept commerce moving; "Harlequin Billy" ruled over bear and badger baiting in a cellar in Whitechapel every Monday, Wednesday, and Friday at eight o'clock, all year round. Mrs. Cummings, a fence, ran a cockpit on Bambridge Street with twice weekly fights, and in his own backyard, Mrs. Smith had a bear bait twice a week, Mondays and Thursdays in a shed in the back of the house. At these fights were butchers, dog-fanciers, and ruffians mixed with costermongers, coal-heavers, watermen, soldiers, and livery servants, and add in a few gentlemen with a sense of adventure. In a bear bait, chained to a wall by its neck, the beast stands on his hind legs as the dogs trouble him and bets laid as to how long a dog would last. Each time a dog retreats wounded, or dying, a new dog joins in until the bear collapses from his wounds or there are no more dogs.

With his winnings, Joe would meet up with an "unfortunate" in a back alley. "Unfortunates" or prostitutes made up five percent of London's population at that time, the destiny of many poor girls. Then after sating his most base needs, he would head to the local gin palace. Gin palaces flourished with the arrival of gas lighting and plate glass windows, they became wonders of light and warmth for many that had little of either. The poorer the neighborhood, the more splendid these places became. Joe was popular if he was buying after a big night of winning. This was London.

London was a city where wealth and poverty, vice and virtue, guilt and innocence, gluttony and hunger all crowded on each other as it had grown from a half million in 1820 to two and a half million in 1850. Growth that was not due to a longer life expectancy from improved conditions and a decrease in infant mortality, but from a deluge of people coming in search of employment only to become lost in the crowd and turmoil. Innocent people came for survival, which the city then destroyed. A city like a ravening beast capable of devouring all that entered. Food for the hospitals, the churchyards, the prisons, the river, fevers, madness, vice, and death; they passed into the monster, rearing in the distance and were lost. Suffer the mild miseries of elsewhere, rather than come here. As Charles Dickens wrote, "It is strange how little notice, good, bad or indifferent, a man may live and die in London, he awakens no sympathy in any single person; his existence is a matter of interest to no one save himself, he cannot be said to be forgotten when he dies, for no one remembered him when he was alive."

The cemetery at St. Anne's covered two-thirds of an acre with only space for about five hundred graves, but with over fifteen hundred corpses interred every year, and in the epidemic of 1842, twenty-one thousand. Coffin Joe had been at it for twenty years. How do you fit fifty thousand lost souls into a couple of holes? The industriousness and genius that had made England an empire and an industrial world power held the answer, and Coffin Joe did not disappoint. The original plan, lacking in subtlety, simply entailed burying the corpses one on top of the other. The top surface of the cemetery had risen from what was at foot level of the people walking on the street to throat high—to the bottom of the church windows. At St. Anne's the dead were elevated above the living. However, you could not go any higher, you could not cover up the windows—enter Coffin Joe. The old corpses were dug up, the coffins chopped into pieces and sold as firewood— there was nothing quite like the smell of burning corpse wood. The coffin nails and plates he sold to second hand shops. The bodies, if they were too recent to decompose naturally, were broken up and sold off to those that bought animal bones for fertilizer. All of this enterprise contributed to a jingle in Joe's pocket and a crooked smile on his wicked face.

One week before Christmas, Mary Elizabeth Whitley died. Only four years old, as delicate as a flower, always sickly— it was a wonder she lived that long, precious to her family, heartbroken by her loss. Now, Joe had been at Slender Billy's the night before. Cleaver, a bullmastiff, was undefeated, relatively untouched, a sure bet, but Joe had seen the look in Koenig, the German shepherd's eyes and knew a cold-blooded killer when he saw one, so he wagered all he had in his pockets on the Prussian. He had seen the same look in Roderick the Razor's eyes, right before he hung for the carnage he caused in White Chapel in '36 (Joe always attended the executions). The Prussian was quicker than the bull, and the favorite soon lay in a pool of blood. The payoff was ten to one, and Joe, after filling his pockets, celebrated his good fortune with more gambling and drinking and found his way back to his room behind the church late in the morning.

A layer of snow covered the frozen ground, and Joe had used a pickaxe the day before but only had gotten the grave two and half feet deep. *It would have to do,* he thought, as the body would soon be crawling with maggots anyway. The procession gathered in the Churchyard after the services and they placed the coffin in the hole, but it stuck up slightly above the ground. Much to the dismay of the deceased's family, Joe proceeded to jump up and down on the coffin to get it into the ground. The coffin collapsed, and the little girl, with blond hair in her eternal sleep, the touch of death beginning to show, lay in her red flowered dress and a white bonnet in the December dirt and snow. The mother fainted, and her brothers and sisters, some older and some younger, began sobbing.

The clergyman cursed most inappropriately, and the father of little Mary grabbed Joe by one arm and yelled, "Stop! What is wrong with you?"

"Got ta git it in the ground," Joe said, confused as to why he had to explain the obvious, and rubbing his grimy hand with its fingerless glove across his forehead, leaving a track of filth.

The father, taking a shilling out of his pocket, gave it to Joe imploring him, "Please, I beg of you, do it properly. That is my little angel," his voice cracking with anguish.

Joe liked shiny things that had value, so he pocketed the coin saying, "Cert'nly Gov'ner."

The father, with downcast head, walked slowly away with his family, not able to bear any more of it in the bitter cold, each step an effort. The clergyman said, as if a parent to a mischievous child, "You need to be more considerate of the grieving." Then he walked away quickly, wanting to get into the warmth of the indoors.

Joe waited until everyone was gone. He was feeling rather under the weather from the festivities of the previous night and wanted to just go back to his warm bed and sleep it off before he returned to the streets that night. He contemplated his options and decided quickly, with an evil grin that the devil would envy. He picked up the little body and dropped it down the neighboring house's well. He could not put it in the church's well for he drank from it!

In December 1850 in the Household Words Journal (Charles Dickens' paper) published a poem on the London churchyards' deplorable conditions:

"I saw from out the earth peep forth
The white and glistening bones,
With jagged ends of coffin planks
That e'en the worm disowns;
And once a smooth round skull rolled on,
Like a football, on the stones..."

The worst, Enon Chapel, not far from the Portugal Street burying grounds, halfway along the west side of Clement's Lane, a turning off the Strand, opened as a chapel in 1823. The burial vault underneath measured only fifty-nine by twenty-nine feet. Burials of up to twelve thousand bodies occurred over the next sixteen years, with nothing but a wooden floor between them and the worshippers in the chapel above. The children in Sunday school became accustomed to seeing 'body bugs', the flies that hatched in the decomposing corpses and flew up between the boards. Inside the vault, the air was so putrid that there was not enough oxygen for candles to stay alight. The floor seeped with reeking fluid, and the wells nearby became pestiferous as it seeped in the ground and became mixed with the drinking water. The neighbors complained of the continuous stench and of "drinking their dead neighbors".

Now Joe forgot about little Mary Elizabeth Whitley that night as he went about his gambling and drinking, but he would not forget her for long. At Mrs. Cummings cockpit, he lost five shillings in three fights. He went to Aubry's to drink off the ill luck and was poor company, as he had only enough money in his pockets for his own sorrows. After two hours of drinking, he stumbled out onto Bambridge Street, where black snow was falling—snow mixed in with the coal smoke that seemed perpetually to cover the city, with gas streetlights providing small beacons of illumination in the suffocating darkness. Hearing a noise behind him on what he thought an empty street, turning, he twisted his ankle and landed face first onto the rough street, tearing holes in his pants' knees, and peeling off some skin on his nose. Children's laughter filled the air.

"Who's there?" he asked.

More laughter answered him from out of the darkness.

"I'll git you all, you little bastards!" Joe grumbled as he rose to his feet.

It was then that the figure approached him out of the darkness, a young girl, red dress, golden yellow hair under a white bonnet. Joe in his drunken stupor vaguely remembered her but not from where.

"Go home!" he yelled at her.

As she came closer, her strikingly pale face shocked him, and then he saw her eyes— her eyes were black empty pits! "The Devil I say!" Joe exclaimed as he recognized Mary Elizabeth Whitley. He half ran and half lunged down the street, several times losing his balance and falling. By the time he made St. Anne's his clothes were torn and hands cut and bleeding, and he had lost his right shoe.

When he went to bed, sure that nothing had followed him, he did not extinguish the candle, constantly watching and waiting for his visitor from the other side, barely sleeping a wink, jumping at every sound. The next day he went about his business, distracted and watchful. By six that night, he was beginning to doubt what he had seen. For his evening meal, he went to the Red Boar, for a four-penny plate of red beef and a beer. The public house was a dark and gloomy den so full of dense tobacco smoke that it was difficult to discern anything. As he sat there with a glass of half-and-half, he convinced himself that he had dreamt it all. As his spirits rose, he heartily began to eat his meal until he felt eyes upon him. Looking up, the face of the girl formed out of the smoke, her mouth moving, condemning him. Joe jumped up and ran out of the building.

He knew he could not go home. "All I need to do," he thought, "is to win a few bets and my luck will change." At Harlequin Billy's he lost all the money he had in his pockets. After he had lost his last shilling in a cockfight, he came to the conclusion: "The whelp has cursed me!" He knew what he had to do, so he went back to the church, got a rope, and went to the well.

"Let me do this and be done with it!" Joe mumbled. "Bury the little devil and I will get my life back."

He tied one end of the rope around the wooden stanchion, threw the coils over into the well, and began climbing down inside. The light soon vanished and darkness engulfed him. Now the rope was old and badly cared for and began to fray under the tension and motion against the sharp edge of the stones. When Joe was halfway down it broke, and he fell, striking the back of his head on the other side of the well, landing with a splash into the water after breaking the thin layer of ice on the surface. Dazed, he realized that he was lying against something in the well. He put his hands down and felt cold hard limbs branching from a small tree trunk perhaps. Reaching around he found a little hand, Little Mary Whitley, exactly where he had dropped her body that morning.

Joe jumped to his feet and began cursing; bemoaning his bad luck, yelling up the shaft, hoping that someone would hear him. Standing in the cold water up to his knees, he began shaking. He tried climbing the walls, but the stones covered in a foul slime made it impossible and every time he tried, he slipped back down.

"Help me!" he yelled up, but without a response. The many nearby church clocks chimed three-quarters past eleven and in a cold dark December night, no one would be out at that time.

After the bells rang quarter-past one, he could no longer yell as the cold stole his strength. How unfair his life had been. He bitterly thought of his childhood; he never knew his father, and his mother died when he was only eight, leaving him an orphan in London left to fend for himself, begging and stealing to stay alive. His first job, at nine, was as a chimney boy where he developed an abject fear of confined places, then as a crossing sweeper, keeping the dung and the mud out of the pedestrians' pathway. *However*, he thought, *my mother did love me*, trying to remember her face, hoping to see her kind features again, but could not and began to weep. Though he was the coldest he had been in his entire life, his heart began to thaw.

His legs, having lost all feeling, gave out, collapsing into the water, sitting with it up to his waist.

Joe's breathing slowed, and then he felt painful pinpricks over all his body, then nothing at all. He thought of his companion in the well. "Poor child, I'm a mean ole bastard and this is my rightly pay— but not yours. Not yours. Who'll e'en miss me? No one!"

Resigned to his fate, darkness overcame him but his last thoughts were a plea, a forlorn hope, *If only…*

Just when all was nearly lost, a voice called from above into the abyss, "Is there someone down there?"

Joe struggled to find his voice. "Help me," he said feebly at first, then with his last strength louder.

Another voice asked, "How did you end up down there? Did you fall in?"

"Please get a rope."

They did so, and when they pulled him out he was holding the body of a little girl, clearly dead for many days.

When they began to question him Joe simply said, "Need to bury her, make it right."

When he regained strength in his legs, he carried the body to the back of the church. The men left him alone; they thought they should not have gotten involved in the first place. In this part of London bad things happened, this part of London harbored vice, crime and disease of all sorts, so mind your own business.

Joe brought the body into his room, covered it with a blanket, changed out of his wet clothes, and sat by the fire to get warm. When he felt he had recovered enough, he went out into the cold night and dug a proper grave in the frozen ground. With hands bleeding from the labor, he buried the body. He said a simple prayer between sobs and vowed to place a glorious marker.

He did not go to bed that night, but thought about what he would do to earn his redemption. Early in the morning, he filled his pockets with coins from his winnings. By 5:00 am, the day laborers began their journey to their work, at 5:30 street sellers were about, by 6 office workers filled the streets. At the working class stalls, there were thinly clad, gaunt, delicate looking factory boys and girls standing by in the freezing cold, hopefully. The popular belief among working men was that a fellow is never poorer for buying something hot for those even worse off than themselves, while the middle class had complete disdain for the poor— owing to increasing separation of the classes as the poor became poorer. Joe walked about the city, going from stall to stall, buying penny loaves, and at the coffee stands a cup of coffee and "two thin" pieces of bread and butter for a penny for those who could not afford it. The people, grateful for his kindness said, "God bless you, Joe," to which he said, "He already has, He's given me a second chance." At the docks, he bought stale pastries for half a penny for the workers. At the hot eel stalls, Joe bought half penny cupfuls of eel stew with a dash of vinegar and pepper. With a special place in his heart for the crossing sweepers from his working there as a child, Joe gave money to the old, infirm, and young, many hatless and some, even in the winter, coatless, enough money to buy clothes, used, but warmer than what they had. Joe went out almost every day and did the same thing. On Christmas Eve, he gave a few coins to the people that had children to buy gifts for them, while giving gifts himself, small gifts such as simple cloth dolls and toy tops to the small children who were orphans. Twenty years of wagering, winning more nights than not, had made him a veritable king amongst paupers.

And so Joe began to make things right. In February of 1849, Joe testified to a Parliamentary Select Committee of the conditions and practices of the burial business in London's cemeteries. The next year the Metropolitan Internments Act became law, enabling the Board of Health to supervise new cemeteries and to close churchyards that were full. Church officials all agreed that nothing of the sort could possibly have occurred, and St. Anne's was an aberration, but everyone had seen and smelt differently, for the cemeteries had made money for all their owners.

The blame of what happened at St. Anne's fell upon Joe, and in the spring he lost his job. However, God smiled down upon him, and when Mr. Whitley, the father of little Mary, saw the beautiful marker that Joe had paid for himself and placed, and heard of his plight, he gave him a letter of introduction to Lord Shaftsbury's Holloway district foundling's house for a groundskeeper position. Joe bought gently used clean clothes, went to a bathhouse, had his hair cut and beard shaved, and he vowed to never have another drink in his life nor place another bet. The next day he set out for his new life.

On the morning of his exodus, Joe hailed the Atlas, a gaudily painted omnibus, at James Street. The omnibus, a two horse drawn vehicle, with space to fit twelve passengers inside comfortably, sixteen uncomfortably, was the common transport of the middle class, costing only a fourth of the price of a short stage. Sixpence could get you to the end of the line. After hailing the driver, who stopped the bus, Joe climbed up the iron rungs at the back onto the seating at the top, which led to a knifeboard, a T-shaped bench where the passengers sat back to back, facing outwards. If it rained and you could not afford the more expensive seating inside, you were out of luck. The driver surveyed the world from his seat at the top, wearing a white top hat, a blue, white-spotted cravat, with high-collared shirt, dark green coat, boots polished to a sheen, and a rose in his buttonhole.

Joe had barely taken his seat, feet braced against the side railing, when the bus jolted forward. There were no general laws or conventions concerning street traffic, other than having to pay tolls at the bridges. Display advertising vehicles, buses, hackney coaches, and donkey carts clogged up the roads, some going to the left, some to the right, and others down the middle if the streets were wide enough. Add in a cat's meat man cart, who sold horsemeat to pet owners, surrounded by dogs hoping for scraps, and chaos reigned. Drivers cursed at each other, sometimes getting into fights, and three to four accidents a week ended up in human fatalities. Horses frequently fell in inclement weather or from exhaustion, and if they could not get back to their feet again, the licensed slaughterhouse carts were always at hand.

When it rained, the treading turned to mud, dogs indistinguishable from the mire, horses not much better, splashed to their blinkers, foot passengers in ill temper losing their footholds at street corners. When dry, dust coated everything and everyone in a dense suffocating cloud. The clip-clop of the horse hooves and iron rimmed wagon wheels on the granite paving stones, as well as the cursing of drivers, and vendors advertising their wares made busy streets a cacophony of sounds. The traffic and the frequent stops for passengers getting on and off could cause the bus to travel only seven to eight miles in two hours. Joe was in no hurry. He looked on with the sense of a man released from prison as they progressed out of the dull, melancholy streets where the two long rows of houses stared at each other.

The houses were overcrowded, ill drained, and badly ventilated dwellings, narrow, dark, and close, some falling into a state of damp decay while others wasting away with dry rot, occasionally one collapsing in a crash and cloud of dust. Black dilapidated streets avoided by all decent people, took to letting them out in lodgings for the working poor who could not afford to live in the suburbs. A swarm of misery, a crowd of foul existence that crawls in and out of gaps in walls and boards where the rain drips in comes and goes, fetching and carrying fever. Nothing to see but streets, streets, and streets and nothing for the spent toiler to do, but think of the weary life he led and slink home, after a hard day of distasteful work, to a miserable abode.

After several hours of going through the city and into the suburbs, the dark smog began to lift and in places the bright warm sun shined through. The air was fresh and the flowers in full bloom. The bus stopped at the George and Vulture in Holloway, and Joe got off. After getting directions, he made his way along the path. At the top of a hill, surrounded by a blue sky, was a large brick house covered in ivy and climbing vines, braced by sheltering trees. A proper home, formerly of a family of wealth, very orderly with round top door and white steps, a most cheery and comforting place, wonderfully inviting but with signs of gentle disrepair in want of fixing.

Next to the house was an expansive garden of flowers, now gone wild with weeds interspersed and a fountain with begrimed surfaces and fouled water damned up by fallen leaves and branches, but a place that still had a glimmer of what it once was and still meant to be.

Joe heard joyful voices as small children came from the side of the house playing a game that would hold their attention for hours. They smiled at him. They seemed healthy and well cared for, with gently mended clothes. Following them was a woman, of middle age, with a most charitable look about her. As he approached her, he saw behind her gold speckled frames, kindly eyes.

"Pardon me, is this the Foundling House?" Joe said taking off his hat. When she nodded her head, he took out the letter of introduction from the pocket of his waistcoat, handing it to her.

She read it and smiled at him, "We cannot offer much, Joe." She folded up the letter, handing it back to him.

"I need little, some food, a place to sleep ... a little happiness", he said shrugging his shoulders, the last said with downcast eyes. "Don't you want to know what I did before?"

"You are here and that is all that matters. We could use your help."

Joe pointed to the fountain, "Does that still work?"

"My husband took care of things around here." She shook her head sadly. "Buried him five months ago. Things have kind of been let go since."

"If only the children could hear the water laugh," Joe remarked and went to the fountain, stuck his arm in all the way up to the shoulder, cleared out handfuls of debris, and the water began to flow.

"There now, Joe, you were meant to be here," she said smiling.

Joe stayed there for the rest of his life, not only keeping the place maintained, but returning it to its former glory, as he became a sort of jack-of-all-trades. The garden became famous for its beauty, and Joe, who so loved the sparrows' twittering, became Joe Sparrow to everyone. He loved the children like his own and brought smiles to their faces, often showering them with gifts paid for with what remained of his winnings from his previous life. There, he atoned for his wasted life and proved despite all the days of his drunkenness, self-indulgence, and debauchery, he was capable of an inexpressively noble, ineffably touching compassion and kindness. Little Mary never haunted Joe again, for she most approved of who he became and the joy he brought others. Years later, as he lay on his deathbed with some of the people that had been children in the foundling house gathered around him, their heartfelt warmth put a smile on his face, and just before he passed, he thought, *I believe possibly, the world to be a better place for me having been in it.*

THE BLACK COACH
OR
THE VISITATION AT WAKWAK CREEK
R.C. Mulhare & I.M. Mulhare

December 24th, 1898. Northern Territory, Australia.

Christmas Eve, and Sheilagh Donnelly had tucked her youngest boy into bed next to his brother Cillian, who lay there pretending he had already fallen asleep.

"Will Father Christmas find us out here in the bush?" Micheleen asked as Sheilagh smoothed the summer-weight coverlet over his side of the bed.

She smiled on her wee boyo, black haired and with a face tanned from playing in the sun, a chip off the sturdy block that was her husband, Big Michael. "Sure, he'll find us out here."

"But there's no snow for his sled run upon, and how will his reindeers take the heat?"

She had to smile at how he'd woven in the story of St. Nicholas that he had heard from Dutch Pieter, the bluff, blond German who kept an eye on the family's sheep station and bossed its hands around while Himself and a few men had gone out into the further parts of their lands, looking for the stragglers strayed from the herds. Somehow her boy had mixed Father Christmas with the German's stories of Sankt Nicklaus.

"When Father Christmas comes this far south, he changes teams, even changes his sled for a wagon, and he hitches up six big, white 'roos, like the wee lost joey that Black Tom found, to pull it," she said, weaving a tale on the spot fit to make her Da, Kelley Maguire— God rest his soul, gone to Paradise these fifteen Christmases past— beam from ear to ear.

Micheleen's eyes grew big, shining in the light from the candle in a crockery pot on the windowsill. "But he can't come 'til you've gone to sleep," she said, rising and creeping from under the nets against the fever-flies.

"Will he bring Da home when he comes?" Micheleen asked.

"He might even give your Da and the men a ride in his wagon, bringing the sheep with them," she said, straightening the nets with a practiced hand.

"Will he leave a lamb with the Baby Jesus at the church?" he asked.

"Perhaps he will," she said, stepping out of the room. "Now go to sleep, boyo."

Micheleen yawned and settled on the pillow. "I will," he said, snuggling down and earning a sleepy rumble from Cillian, now with his head burrowed under the other pillow.

No fire on the hearth of the main kitchen, on a warm night like this. The only light came from the tall white tallow candles set into crockery pots full of sand, into which she and Fiona, her oldest girl, had arranged sprigs of green leaves from the gums and acacia trees down by the creek, which cast the hearth into shadow. In the darkness about the hearth, a larger shadow moved, as if it had come down the chimney, before it stepped toward her and stood up, the light of the candles revealing Dutch Pieter as he reached to straighten the five bulging stockings hung there— one for each of the children, even Cillian who insisted he was too old for a stocking, but that had not kept him from hanging one up with the rest of the clan.

"I almost took you for Father Christmas," she said.

"I must look like a strange Sankt Niklaus, in bush hat and brogans," Dutch Pieter replied, looking down at himself.

"Will you be coming with us to Christmas Mass tomorrow?" Sheilagh asked.

"Ja, so long as Herr Donnelly comes home by then," he replied.

"I shan't keep you from riding out to meet him then," she said.

"Will you keep watch for him?" he asked.

"As long as I can stay awake," she said.

"Like a little girl waiting for Vater Christmas," he said, with one of his rare smiles.

Once Dutch Pieter had gone on his way, and once she had added more trinkets and treats to the stockings, she went out to the summer kitchen to pour herself a cup of tea, then returned to the house, up to the porch, before sitting down on the cane-bottom rocking chair to the right of the front door. There she kept watch over the gravel walk that ran through the rock garden before the house, leading down to the dusty track that ran between Wakwak Creek and the land before the house. Overhead, ragged clouds scudded across the yellow face of the moon as it sailed above the tops of the gum trees and acacias that lined the banks of the creek. Birds, likely the galahs and grass parrots she'd seen hanging about the horse paddocks earlier, twittered and murmured sleepily in the treetops, and night bugs buzzed and chirped in the long grass close to the house.

She could hear hoof-beats in the near distance, three riders approaching on the dusty track from the station hands' bunkhouse and the stables beside it, heading for the bridge that spanned the creek, Dutch Pieter riding in the lead, as they went out to meet their master.

The dog flap beside the door opened and Bluey, the blue heeler that Big Michael had given to the family when their middle daughter Bridget was born, let herself out, her nails ticking on the floorboards as she approached Sheilagh's chair. The dog turned herself around three times before laying down for a long summer's nap.

Not a single sound now, aside from the breeze in the treetops; at least they had a breeze to stir the air this warm summer's night, so different from the Christmases she knew as a girl, with a coating of snow on the sleeping fields around her family's home, and awakening to find her mother's donkey looking forlornly at the coating of ice in his water bucket. That first Christmas she spent with Michael Donnelly as his wife, they had planned to emigrate to America. Then word came from Down Under that his uncle, Sean, had died and left him a sheep station near Wakwak Creek and the village that shared the name. They had shipped out on the first steamer they could find passage on, and en route, found that Cillian had joined them as a stowaway beneath her heart. A better life than they might have made for themselves in the States: they could call themselves their own master and mistress, with a thousand head of sheep, while Sheilagh tended her lavender plants in a field close to the main house.

And on the morrow, they would celebrate their sixteenth Christmas together, Father Murphy visiting the village below as he did twice a month. T'would be good to have the clan together for Christmas, going to Mass and taking communion, then home in the late afternoon, with their Christmas dinner of roast goose awaiting them.

Bluey lifted her head, rumbling low in her throat, before rising to her feet. "What is it, Bluey? Dingoes down by the creek?" she asked.

Not another sound beyond the dog's warning growl. A cloud passed across the face of the moon above as if it hid from what stirred below. The birds stopped chirping, the night insects no longer shrilled. Even the distant murmur of the creek seemed hushed. A wagon approached over the bridge, but without raising a sound, no rumble of wheels, no creak of the harness or the axles, no hoof-beats or the husky breathing of the horses. Bluey growled again, louder this time, as the wagon came closer, coming around the bend and onto the road before the house. Sheilagh felt her blood turn cold, even on this warm night, and the teacup, all but forgotten, fell from her nerveless fingers to crash on the decking. What she had taken for a wagon, she saw was an enclosed coach, of the kind she had seen on the streets of Dublin and again in Sydney. Four horses pulled it, their dull eyes red in the dim light, their black harnesses stark against their white hides. Four skulls perched on the four corners of the coach, the eyes lit from within with candle flames. A coachman all in black held the reins, not turning toward her, not that he would if he could, for she saw that he lacked a head.

Sheilagh backed away, grabbing Bluey's collar with one hand while she crossed herself with her other hand. Reaching for the door, she pulled it open, hauling on Bluey's collar as she rushed inside, though the dog tried to dig her claws into the floorboards and scrabble away. She had to grab the dog's collar again, the moment she released it, on closing the door behind them both, as Bluey tried to duck out through the dog flap.

"Bluey, stay, lie down," Sheilagh said, voice wavering. The dog looked up to her mistress, letting out a querulous whine, as if objecting and insisting that her mistress let her loose to chase the intruder. "No, Bluey, sit yourself down." Obedient but reluctant, the dog flopped down on the floor, but kept her snout toward the dog flap, head raised, ears lifted.

Granny Peg had told her stories of the Cóiste Bodhar, the Coach-a-Bower, the death coach, which came betimes from the realm of the dead and never returned there without a passenger on board, and often the soul of a person who possessed some link to the person who beheld it, if not the one who saw it with their own eyes. She could not tell if the coachman's head sat beside him on the driver's box, much less than if it had turned toward her: if it had, she would need to start making a sincere act of contrition and warn her children.

She went to the children's rooms, the two boys in their room and the three girls in the next. She could hear Micheleen breathing, and Cillian grumbling in his sleep, as his little brother had shoved his head against his neck. She heard the two older girls, Fiona and Bridget, whispering to each other, then shushing each other as the bed creaked, trying to keep quiet as they heard her approach. Eileen lay quiet on the trundle bed at the foot, breathing softly.

"I must be getting tired, and my mind is wandering to Granny's ghost tales," she murmured, thinking of those Christmas Eves when Granny Peg would share her chilly tales with the grandchildren clustered about her hearth. Time she went to bed herself, fright or no.

* * *

She awoke to voices in the kitchen that abutted the bedroom that she shared with Himself, but Big Michael had not crept in to join her under the covers. His pillow lay undented and the covers on his side lay smooth. Someone tapped on the closed door to the chamber. She arose, reaching

93

for her shawl, and draped it about her shoulders before going to reply.

She found several of the men who had gone out to meet her husband gathered in the kitchen. Full morning sunlight shone outside the kitchen window. Hettie, the kitchen maid, brought in a pot of coffee from the summer kitchen, filling mugs to pass among the men, but while they took the mugs, not a one tried to drink from them. Black Tom, Dutch Pieter's right hand man, stood in their midst, his bush hat in hand, his dark face grave.

"Mrs. Donnelly, I got bad news," he said, not lifting his eye to her face.

"Is it Michael?" she asked.

"He's dead," he replied. "A black snake came out the rocks, when we had stopped after a horse threw a shoe. He put his foot right on it, and it fanged his ankle above his boot." He paused, his jaw working slightly. "I tried to suck out the poison, but it hit his heart."

"I think I knew," she said, her mind going back to what she had seen on the road before the house. "Where is he?"

"We left him at Johnson's ice house," Dutch Pieter said. "We could not bring him here, der Kinder..."

"You chose wise, Pieter; let the children have their Christmas," she said.

Pieter nodded his head slowly. "Shall I ready the horses and the wagon?"

"Yes, I'll wake the wee ones," she said, going to fetch what she still had of her family.

The children needed no coaxing to get up. They fairly flew to the hearth to find their stockings, the nuts and oranges, the wooden animals that Dutch Pieter had carved for them, a whittling knife for Cillian, the amber ear-bobs that had belonged to Granny Peg for Fiona, now big enough to treasure them.

"Where's Da?" Micheleen asked. Hettie, who had brought in the fry bread and milk for the children's breakfast, looked to Dutch Pieter, who looked to Sheilagh.

"We'll see Da tomorrow," she said. On St. Stephen's day, no less, the first saint to shed his blood for the Lord, and the day of Burying the Wren back on the old sod. "He's hurt his foot and had to spend the night in town." Not a lie and half the truth; they would get the rest of the full truth only too soon enough. Let them have this Christmas without the shadow falling over it. The darkness would come and grow them up too soon...

FIGGY
Wendy L. Schmidt

The pudding, the pudding, but the Figgy had flopped.

Susan's eyes opened wide. "Why is it—moving?"

"Forgive me, my dear," Mildred said, "but isn't Figgy Pudding supposed to stay on the frigging, figgy plate?"

It all started innocently enough. Figgy Pudding seemed like such a sweet, sentimental idea for the holiday dinner dessert. It was Grandmother Edna's specialty. As the story goes, Edna had hidden ancient family recipes deep inside her very old, very odd house under antique lock and key.

The day after the will reading and subsequent house viewing, Margaret was supposed to take what was basically everything. She was one of the few relatives with any true interest in Edna's estate. Most of the others were too far away to make the trip or simply not all that interested in what might have been considered room after room of distressed junk. Margaret was the sole recipient of the house and all its contents. Whatever this might imply was not fully understood by its benefactress.

"Some of the British-made furniture is fabulous!" Jenny exclaimed. "At least it will be, once it's cleaned up a bit. And, oh my, that silver tea set is simply scrumptious!"

Margaret inspected the pot. "It was used, by my mother's account, at formal gatherings with ladies of rather selectively strange societal standing. Most of this stuff will fit right into my eclectic decorating scheme. Fred will be annoyed, of course."

Jenny laughed, "Poor Freddie, your place is pretty full up already. Is there any room for him in your home or has he been relegated to a corner?"

95

Jenny was Margaret's nearest and dearest friend. She'd happily agreed to help with the sorting and stacking duties. A full professor at Clayton College, Jenny taught Women's Studies. But, her true passions were collecting antiques, analyzing and transcribing Old English text, and growing unusual herbs and flowers. She particularly liked the kind used in medicinal mixtures during medieval times.

Margaret was bequeathed the whole lot of Edna's objects, but they'd had no luck finding the infamous recipes.

"Mmm...now where could they be? Perhaps they're up in the batty attic or down in the castle dungeon?" Jenny quipped.

"I hardly think there's a dungeon, though I wouldn't be surprised to spot a moat. I remember Edna mentioning an old well on the property, or was it a creek? Grandmother's house was always a little damp and dicey," Margaret replied.

She knew the recipes must exist. Margaret's mother, Mary had talked about them for years. She'd extolled the virtues of their magical properties and the fact that they were cooked in the old world way.

"Divine and sometimes deadly, if not handled by an expert," Mary would say. "Our ancestors knew their way around a pot, pestle, and English pudding."

Mary died when Margaret was 12 years old. After that, Margaret's father rarely allowed his daughter to visit her maternal grandmother. In fact, she hadn't seen Edna for years. She missed the extravagant meals Edna and Mary presented to the family every December.

The holidays always felt empty without them. Margaret would forever mourn her mother's premature passing. Adding to this deep sadness was the hard fact that she could not bear a child. All of the family's precious traditions would now be buried with these two strong women.

The month of December strengthened that strong longing for a child. But, Margaret was forty-five years old now and had put herself and Fred through the wringer trying to conceive. It was enough heartache for one lifetime.

"I remember my mother sent me off to bed around 11," Margaret explained. "It's hard to recall all the details of the December dinner. I was so young. But the decorations were elaborate and nature-made. Fruits, nuts, and pine branches were woven together to form wreaths and centerpieces. I helped light all the candles. My grandmother was always cooking something in a pot. The scent in the house was heavenly. I hated going to bed."

"Why were you put to bed before the celebration was over?" Jenny asked.

"I don't know. My mother simply said, 'When you're older you will understand.'" Mary glanced forlornly at the tea set. "But, of course, she died before that happened and my father didn't want to talk about it. I wonder where those recipes could be?"

Jenny looked doubtful. "We've been through the whole house. Perhaps she never wrote them down, and they existed only in her memory. I wonder what she meant by, 'you will understand?'"

"I hope you aren't disappointed if we don't find anything beyond the normal ingredients," Margaret said. "I mean, Grandmother's recipes were wonderful but I'm not sure they were anything out of the ordinary."

"Are you kidding?" Jenny smiled. "The tea set alone was worth my time."

Margaret sighed, "I can't think of any other place to search unless there's a hidden hallway." She suddenly snapped her fingers. "Wait a minute, I just remembered."

Jenny jumped on her last word. "Remembered a hidden hallway?"

"There's a room in the basement. I noticed it when the estate lawyer was guiding me through the house. The door is bolted shut by a heavy lock, and he didn't seem to have the key. But, it's the only room we haven't searched. Though why recipes would be in there makes no sense. The basement smells musty and feels damp. It's definitely moat material. And, the stairs are pretty treacherous. Maybe we should wait for Fred."

Jenny put her hands on her hips. "Wait for Fred?! I love Freddie dearly but he is a klutz when it comes to any kind of handyman help. A hammer or crowbar should do the trick if we can't find the key."

They both smiled at each other and said in unison, "Poor Freddie." Then they started laughing as if they were back in college pulling an all-nighter. It was fun, doing something that felt slightly dark and a little dangerous. Margaret missed those days.

"Let's go!" Jenny said.

Even with bare bulbs lighting the way, the basement still seemed murky. There were huge cobwebs hanging everywhere.

"I expect to hear a gong and Lurch to step out at any second. It's got all the earmarks of a mansion gone mad! Your grandmother probably never ventured down here in her later years."

Margaret wiped a sticky web from her face. "She was a hardy woman. She took daily constitutionals into her 90's. At least that's what her friends at the funeral said. But, these stairs are difficult for even me to manage." Margaret dodged another giant web. "She certainly wasn't big on dusting."

"No, I should say not," Jenny replied.

"Oh well, I've always found cobwebs kind of cozy, like black cats and worn woodwork."

Jenny eyed the nearest dark corner. "If a cat flies out at me, I'm gone."

"No cats, at least none currently in residence. I believe her friends took possession of them."

"That's an interesting choice of words, took possession." Jenny grinned, then her eyes widened in excitement. "I think that's the entrance."

They followed a very narrow hallway past a row of old shelves filled with canning jars. The jars were thick with dust. It was hard to see their contents. Jenny promptly started searching through the lot.

"AHH!" she screamed.

Margaret jumped. "What! What is it?"

"Spider! I hate spiders! I know, I know, how can a woman who loves gardening and old houses hate spiders? It's a visceral fear thing. Damn, these jars seem to have nothing but nails and screws and stuff. A bit of a dead end. Sorry, no bad pun intended."

Margaret aimed the flashlight at the back of the shelf. "Let me give it a try."

She couldn't explain why, but she had a strange sense that something of value was inside one of the jars. Each was filthy with dust and grime. But, for an instant, she saw a glint of gold.

"What's that?" Jenny asked.

Margaret pulled out the last jar. She gripped its tight lid and heard a pop. A stash of old hardware went clanging onto the floor.

"That should scare any errant cats or spiders," Jenny said.

"Check this out!" Margaret held up an ornate key. It still held some of its original brass color.

"Like magic!" Jenny exclaimed. "You knew something was hidden in that jar! You must be psychically connected to this old house. And, while I'm musing, might that key be *the one*?"

"Let's try it." Margaret felt a shiver of excitement run down her spine.

The lock was old, older than any lock she had ever seen before. And, it was intricately detailed with some kind of ornamental design.

"Give me the flashlight for a minute, will you Margie?" Jenny examined the lock more closely. "This is rather special. I need to see it in better light but it's certainly an antique; the design is Celtic in nature, maybe a cross or family crest. Does the key fit?"

One small click answered her question.

"Eureka! We hit pay dirt!" Margaret said. "Well, at least dirt."

The door groaned as if complaining of neglect. Both women pushed until it finally let loose and allowed them to enter. The room was pitch black. There was no sign of a light switch.

With the flashlight, Margaret bounced from wall to wall getting a feel for size and shape. She spotted a high shelf lined with candles set in pewter holders.

"Got a match?" Margaret asked.

"Think I saw a box in one of the jars outside," Jenny replied.

In a moment the room was eerily lit. The flickering of candlelight against the stone walls was unsettling. Moving shadows advanced then receded. There were many bottles scattered around the room. Each was different in shape and color. Both women saw oddly shaped objects, but they were unidentifiable especially in such poor light. The bottles seemed to be labeled, again unreadable under the dim conditions.

"Hey, look over there! That desk is magnificent. I bet it's worth plenty!" Jenny exclaimed. "The carved legs alone tell me it's probably late 17th century, burled wood, Louis XVI-style bureau desk? I have to see it in a better light. This is a fabulous find!"

"Oh no," Margaret groaned. "The front panel seems to be locked."

Jenny ran her hand along the top. "Ahh, here's the key."

Click, it turned easily, almost by itself. The panel dropped into a writing area. Inside there was a myriad of pigeon holes, slots, and drawers. Several books, glass containers, a mortar and pestle, a finely carved pen, and rolled up loose pages were stashed into the compartments.

"Recipes?" Margaret murmured. She felt the strange need to keep her voice down.

"Maybe, this smaller book looks ancient. Bring both upstairs so we can get an idea of what we are dealing with here. Take a few of the bottles too. I'd like to examine what's in them, maybe seeds or roots," Jenny ordered. She was in her take charge state. Nothing could deter her when she turned archaeologist, not even the threat of spiders.

As they were heading up the stairs Jenny asked, "Did you taste any of her dishes?"

"Oh sure, she let me dine at the table until dessert time. I wanted to try the dessert too, but, wasn't allowed. My grandmother told me, in no uncertain terms, to go to bed. The food was so good, I mean really good like nothing I've ever had before or since…" Margaret trailed off.

"Since?"

"I don't know what I was going to say. A wisp of memory hit me just then. I swear I smelled something sweet for a second."

Jenny stopped and stared at her friend. "That's interesting. You know, scent memory is a powerful reminder. It can take you back in time. So, let me get this straight. The group was all women, no men involved?"

Margaret cleared a space on the cluttered kitchen table to set down Edna's books. "I think they sent the men out to a local pub or something. All I remember is mother telling me the dinner was meant for womenfolk only."

"Intriguing. Turn on the overhead, will you?" Jenny grabbed her glasses out of an overstuffed purse. "Look at this metal clasp on the oldest book. And, this medallion in the middle. The cover is made out of fine leather."

"What about the newer, bigger book?" Margaret asked. But Jenny was completely engrossed in the small, leather-bound one.

"I think these pages may be parchment!" Jenny exclaimed. "And, it's written in Old English! The loose pages look to have your grandmother's script, this is regular paper. She could have been transcribing the Old English into modern and slowly adding the contents to the bigger book. See, this one says, 'Figgy Pudding.'"

"Margaret grabbed the book. "Did you say Figgy Pudding? These must be her recipes!"

"Margie! Careful, careful, they are fragile. Let me see the larger volume. Yes, recipes."

Jenny skillfully opened a page written in Edna's beautiful script.

"So they're both recipe books? One is very old, one is newer? Jenny?"

Again, her friend was lost in thought. "Mmm…yes, no, not exactly. This bigger book has cooking instructions, of that I'm quite sure, but the other one. I mean, there are ingredients for…"

"For what?" Margaret asked.

Jenny scowled, "For medicinal purposes? Mint and fennel and…" Now she was getting excited. "Mugwort! Your grandmother wouldn't have used that in food preparation."

"So?"

"Margie, don't you get it? These aren't all about making meals."

The two women spent most of the afternoon searching through the books and poking at strange looking seeds, pods, and dried roots inside several bottles. After a little tea, they agreed that Jenny would take the oldest book to the university and do more research. Margaret was longing to try out a few of her grandmother's recipes.

"Maybe I can have that December dinner I've been missing for so long," she said.

"Oh wouldn't that be a hoot. I'd help with the decorating and certainly with some of the more unfamiliar ingredients. We could invite the whole gang! We could do just what your grandmother did and send the men away for the evening." Jenny smiled. "Are you up for a challenge, Merry Margaret?"

"Yes, M'lady."

And, up for it they were, on what started out to be an intriguing adventure. But, now Margaret was wondering what she'd gotten herself into while trying to mix several of the stranger parts. It was so much work. And, the recipes were hard to read. Some of the words made little sense even in modern English. She reluctantly took her nose out of Edna's recipe book and the big cooking pot for a much needed break.

Margaret scanned the living room and dining room. With this, at least, she was extremely satisfied. It felt like a captured memory from the old days. The house was decorated to perfection with fresh fruit and bowls of nuts, dates, grapes, and olives set in ornate dishes on the table. Candles were lit and fragrant teas wrapped as presents.

Jenny and Margaret had found the whole description of how-to on one of the loose pages:

Hold the dinner on the night of December 21st. Fill your home with kindred spirits. Early in the eve send menfolk to the pub. Off to bed the wee ones go for the hour is drawing nigh. Pine tree and branches spread about, mistletoe hung at the entry, white candles, yule log burning bright, bowls of fresh fruit, nuts, dates, olives. A hardy goose and mince meat pies and plenty of wine to bewitch the lusty women. Figgy Pudding turned out on a silver serving tray. Settle the suckling. Then, set ablaze and listen to its cry, repeat this prayer:

Oh Lord and Lady, Mother and Father,

we sing to the starry skies.

On this night of all nights,

shall a child be conceived,

we seek your sacred blessing,

give us the gift of life.

Margaret wasn't at all sure about the last part concerning the suckling and crying. Again, they were Old English cooking terms, hard to interpret for today's kitchen. But both women thought the prayer was a lovely addition. It covered the Christian idea of Christmas as well as a simple blessing for the season.

Once the dessert has been served and consumed, each woman was to receive a wrapped package of homemade tea to share with her husband or lover.

Jenny hadn't yet translated the entire contents of the small leather-bound book. Margaret refused to hand over any loose pages written by her grandmother.

"I want some of her ingredients to remain a family secret," she insisted.

"Oh, come on! Just reveal the ones in her dessert and teas!" Jenny begged.

Though, the teas were a simple combination of vanilla and hibiscus, the Figgy Pudding was much more mysterious. Figs and dates, nutmeg and cinnamon, rum and cognac were common ingredients. But, there were other things she wasn't so sure about adding. She had found a few jars labeled with strange names on the shelves in her grandmother's basement room. At first, she was hesitant to put them into the pudding. But, when the lids were popped the herbs smelled so fresh and sweet. "Bewitching", was that the word used in Edna's description? Margaret felt a bit bewitched herself. And, before she realized it, she'd brought them upstairs and sprinkled them into the pudding pot.

The dinner was going well. Her friends raved about the decorations and the food. They ate and drank, hardily. In fact, Margaret was a little surprised at the amounts consumed. Each asking for seconds and even thirds. Then came dessert serving time. Margaret plopped the pudding onto its lovely silver plate as the instructions had said to do.

"Ta da!," Jenny cried. "Ladies, enjoy your Figgy Pudding!"

But, the pudding immediately began to move, twist and turn, and make a squealing sound!

Mildred and Susan and Julie and Jenny all looked perplexed and more than a little frightened.

"Is it supposed to do that?" Julie asked.

Margaret sat staring at her masterpiece. "I...I don't know. What is it doing?"

The pudding began to take form, and its form was increasingly disturbing.

Susan gasped. "It looks like a—like a..."

"Fetus!" Julie blurted out.

All five women simply sat mesmerized while the thing squirmed slowly off its silver serving cradle.

Jenny glanced at Margaret. She could see the panic in her face. This whole evening had truly been magical, and she did not want her friend's efforts to be ruined by a blob of deformed pudding.

"It's good luck," she stated. "It's like those tea leaves that take different shapes, and you read the future. This shape means the night is young. We have spent this evening learning to love the child living inside all of us. Didn't this whole celebration make you feel like a kid again?"

The women cheered and each raised a glass of wine. "To feeling young!" they shouted.

"Now, let's have some pudding!" Jenny said.

Margaret pushed it back onto its bed, poured alcohol on the top and lit a match. "To wise women everywhere!" The dessert, set aflame, stopped moving, but there was now a high-pitched cry coming for the center.

Susan, shocked out of her drunken stupor, said, "It sounds like a—"

Jenny stopped her in mid-sentence. "A delicious dessert, just what we need to top off the fabulous dinner."

The flames died away as did the creepy crying. Margaret served the pudding and then said, "Before we consume it, a chant written by my dear old Grandmother. Everyone, please read and repeat out loud the little parchment paper prayer rolled up by your pudding while I take the first bite."

"Together now ladies," Jenny instructed.

"Oh Lord and Lady, Mother and Father,

we sing to the starry skies.

On this night of all nights,

shall a child be conceived.

We seek your sacred blessing,

give us the gift of life."

Margaret ate a spoonful and suddenly felt a little dazed. "Oh my goodness, this dessert is really incredible!"

Seeing her delight, they all lifted their spoons in unison and consumed the pudding.

"Wow, this is, wow!" is all Susan could manage to say.

"Oh my heavens, this is like the best thing I've ever, eaten, ever!" Mildred exclaimed.

"Better than Chocolate Mousse, better than chocolate anything!" Julie agreed.

Jenny shoveled the spoon into her mouth nearly nonstop. They all did, and as they did they became aware of a kind of energy force connecting the circle of women around the table.

They knew the pudding, or perhaps Margaret, was doing something magical, and it felt incredible.

As soon as the last bit of Figgy was finished, each woman suddenly stood up and said goodnight. Each dutifully took the gift of tea bags. They had promised to go home and share a cup with their husbands that very evening.

Margaret sat down on the couch and waited for Fred to come back from the pub. She did not feel her usual urge to pick up or do any dishes. She simply wanted, no, needed to see Fred and share a cup of tea with him.

"Honey, how did it go?" Fred asked, as he walked into the room smelling a little of beer and cigarettes.

"Fine, great it was great. Now let's have some tea, Freddie"

"Whoa, what? Freddie? You never call me that unless you want..." A lightbulb went off over his head. "Let's skip the tea, baby."

"NO! Tea or no me."

"Okay, okay just lemme take off my coat and sit..."

Margaret grabbed his hat and coat, threw them on the floor, sat him at the table, filled his cup with tea, and ordered him to drink it.

"Hey, don't I get some sugar?"

"Drink," Margaret ordered.

"Oh, I get it. You're gonna serve me my sugar in the bedroom. I think I like this dominatrix side of you, Margie."

"Shut up and sip!"

Fred drank as he was told, trying to comprehend this new, demanding woman. Then, he watched as his usually modest wife stripped off all her clothes and strode into their bedroom. His eyes nearly popped out of his head. What was happening?

"DRINK IT ALL DOWN AND COME TO BED!" Margaret shouted.

"Yes ma'am!" Fred gulped the rest of the contents, burning his tongue in the process. He barely noticed the pain as he ran for his waiting wife.

Two months later Margaret was still a little foggy about that night. She vaguely remembered the dinner and pudding and Fred jumping onto the bed. But, the rest slipped away with the pudding and tea. Her cell phone shook her out of her hypnotic state.

"Hello? Margaret? It's Jenny. I have to talk to you! Do you have some time to meet me? I can come over right after my last class."

"What's wrong, Jenny?"

"I can't talk about it over the phone. See you in an hour." Click, the line went dead.

Exactly one hour later, Jenny rushed through the door with Edna's leather-bound book.

And, in her other hand was a paper lunch bag.

Margaret leaned on the kitchen table feeling a little sick to her stomach. It was the third time this month that her own lunch hadn't set right. But, Margaret hated going to the doctor after all the years of fertility treatments and disappointment. If she was truly honest, the aversion to doctors had started following her mother's accident. The vague memories of hospital waiting rooms still gave her nightmares. She could deal with a sour stomach, she couldn't deal with more doctors and bad news.

"What's so urgent?" she asked.

Jenny gestured towards the table. They both sat down.

"Listen Margaret, I've been doing some research on your grandmother's herbal recipes. You realize this book was probably handed down through your mother's side for centuries. It's that old. And, once I transcribed the language I realized it was much more than simple recipes. Some of these pages contain potions for medicinal remedies. Some of them contain concoctions for charms and divination spells and how to invoke supernatural creatures. As far as I can, tell she dealt in natural magic to help people with any and all kinds of problems."

Margaret stared at the book. "What are you saying exactly?"

"I'm saying this book is what they call a Grimoire. Many Wise Women wrote their ideas down and passed the books to the next generation. Each woman would add to the book. These Wise Women were sometimes called cunning folk or, well, witches." Jenny took Margaret's hand. "Don't think this is a bad thing. It's actually quite a wonderful discovery. The book is a part of history, your history, specifically. But there is more. Do you want to hear it?"

"I might as well. First, let me grab the pot. I need to settle my stomach." Margaret reached for the tea pot whistling on the stove and poured herself a cup.

"I'm curious," Jenny asked. "What made you use ginger tea for your sour stomach? Did you read somewhere that it was a good remedy?"

Margaret thought for a moment. "No, as a matter of fact, I think my mother told me to use ginger for stomach upset."

"My guess is your mother knew about the family history. Perhaps she decided not to pursue it so passionately. Perhaps your father didn't approve." Jenny looked into her friend's eyes.

"What are you thinking?"

"I'm thinking," Margaret paused. "I suppose it makes sense. I mean, I've always thought there was something different about the women in my family. And, I remember feeling it the strongest when we had our December feast."

Margaret had been wondering ever since the night of her own dinner. Something strange had happened between the women. Recently, two of her dinner guests announced the surprising news that they were expecting. In fact, she had been meaning to call Mildred just to see if it was three. But, why would it be? Why would that thought even enter her mind?

"Margaret? What are you thinking?" Jenny repeated.

"What's in the paper bag? Is it a pregnancy stick with a plus sign?" Margaret stated.

Jenny sat back on her chair. "How in the world did you know? I haven't told anybody except Charles. He's over the moon. We wanted another child at some point, but I kept putting it off and putting it off. I didn't know if I should say anything. I mean, I know how hard this kind of news can be for you."

"Nonsense! I'm happy for you Jenny, I truly am. But, I'm also very troubled."

"Troubled? Why are you troubled?" Jenny took her friend's hand again.

Margaret didn't know what to do with her suspicion. She didn't know how Jenny might take it. She certainly didn't want to cause her any concern or throw a shadow of doubt over her good news.

"Have you talked to any of the other women that were at the dinner in December?"

Margaret asked.

"No, I haven't. Classes this year have been a bit overcrowded and overwhelming and now, with this new baby on the way...Why do you ask?"

"Well, counting you, that makes three pregnancies since that night."

Margaret paused. "I suspected something weird was going on even then. Until you came here today to tell me about my grandmother, I didn't really want to believe it. I think that dinner was more than a dinner. I think it was some kind of ceremony. I mean, I felt a powerful energy pass between us when we were eating the pudding."

"So did I! Oh, my, it's sort of a relief to know I wasn't the only one. But, what are you trying to say? That we did some sort of spell without realizing it? That somehow this ceremony caused the pregnancies?" Jenny sat for a long time going over the dinner in her mind. "Oh my GOD! Do you realize that everything, the decor, the food, the drinks, the...wait, what was in those tea bags?"

"Vanilla and hibiscus," Margaret replied.

"Lust and potency. The entire dinner was a fertility ritual. And the Figgy Pudding was the final ingredient. Figs and dates are fertility fruits and whatever else you put in it to add to the pot."

Margaret's stomach was feeling a little bit better. She popped in a piece of toast and set out the butter.

"Jenny, do you remember what happened to the Figgy Pudding?"

"No, wait, yes, I do. The shape was of a fetus and that weird crying sound it made when you lit it on fire. It sent a chill down my spine. We all started eating the pudding as if we were..."

"Under a spell," Margaret finished the thought. "Maybe we were. Maybe we were under my grandmother's spell. Or maybe, maybe somehow it was mine as well. I mean, isn't it possible that I inherited some of my ancestor's magical abilities?"

Jenny watched the brown bread pop up. She had always been interested in magic and medieval medicine, but this was no longer history, this was happening now. It excited her but scared her too. She brushed her hand protectively over her stomach.

"What about Mildred?" Jenny asked.

"She's been out of the country since the end of January." Margaret buttered the toast and took a bite. "I haven't had breakfast this morning, and I'm starving. But, my stomach is just off lately, really off. I thought I had the flu but I...I..." She suddenly bolted from the table and out of the room.

Jenny was startled. She wondered if she should follow her friend. Margaret came back looking profoundly pale.

"Gee, honey, you don't look so good," Jenny said. "How long has this stomach bug been biting?"

Margaret tore a paper towel from the roll and wiped her mouth. "Several weeks, it's weird because I've never have problems along this line. Fred always jokes that I have an iron gut."

Both women sat in silence. Jenny had a feeling about her friend but was extremely hesitant to say anything. She knew if it wasn't true it would be hard for her to bear. Instead, she suggested a doctor visit.

"I know you hate the idea, but I'll go with you for moral support. I know a great doc at the university, who could see you today."

Margaret sighed, "Fine, I'm sick of feeling sick. Let me get my purse."

The little white room reminded her of all the things she hated to think about: sickness, medical tests, needles, disappointment. How many times had a doctor told her the hormones hadn't worked? The embryo wasn't viable, her uterus was tipped, and it made conception nearly impossible. How many years had she tried until Fred said it was enough and time to give up and adopt? Emotionally, adopting was not an easy thing for her to accept.

A doctor with a kind, concerned face walked into the room.

"So, your stomach is sour. Any other symptoms before we take some blood?" he asked.

Margaret thought for moment. She hadn't been paying that much attention to her body lately. She was 45 and knew menopause was not far away. She didn't want to think about it, but now that she was forced to think, she suddenly realized that her periods had stopped a few months back. Margaret started to cry. It was over. She felt foolish but she couldn't seem to stop herself.

The doctor patted her shoulder. "What is it, Mrs. Wilding?"

"Oh, it's just that I haven't had my period in two months. I think I might be starting the change early."

"Let me be the judge of that," he said. "Anything else?"

"Yes, but I think it's all part of the same thing. My breasts feel tender."

The doctor looked in her eyes with a small light. "You are a little young. When did your mother go through menopause?"

Margaret nearly lost any composure she had left. "She died before it happened."

"I'm so sorry, Mrs. Wilding. Why don't we take a bit of blood. Just relax. Be right back."

A cherub faced nurse came in and grabbed a needle. "This won't hurt much." But it did hurt. The whole idea hurt. No babies, no chance of ever having a baby. Her body had betrayed her in the cruelest way for the last time.

Yet, something nagged at her. Some small voice inside kept telling Margaret to be of good cheer. Be of good cheer? What a strange old expression.

"Be of good cheer?" she said. "Where the hell did that come from?"

"Are you okay Mrs. Wilding?" The doctor walked in and patted her shoulder.

"Yes, yes, I'm not crazy, doctor, just talking to myself," Margaret laughed. "Is that your idea of okay, or am I having some sort of menopausal mental breakdown?"

The doctor sat on a sterile looking chair and smiled.

"Not menopause, in fact, just the opposite. I'm happy to say you're a few months along."

Margaret looked confused. "A few months along what?"

This time the doctor laughed. "You're pregnant, Mrs. Wilding. I don't know how or why it happened now after all this time of trying, but, you are going to have a baby!"

Margaret sat bolt upright, grabbed the nearest waste basket and barfed. The doctor looked concerned.

"This is good news? I mean, usually a new mother doesn't vomit when I tell her."

"Oh, it is! It is the most wonderful news in the world. It's just that, I've had morning sickness for several weeks when I thought it was the flu!" Margaret stood up, feeling shaky but so happy she wanted to jump in the air.

On the ride home Jenny kept shaking her head and saying, "It's incredible!"

Margaret had a smile so wide she thought it might stay glued there. "I owe my ancestors another big dinner. This time to celebrate the coming of new life!" Just then her cell phone rang. Was it Fred? Adorable, klutzy Freddie, she didn't want to tell him over the phone. She wanted to wait until he came home. But, as it happened, it was her friend, Mildred.

"I've just come back from overseas, and I have big news. You'll never guess. You'll simply never guess!"

THE TWELFTH PAIR
Bill Dale Grizzle

To Carlos Calderon it seemed as though there were a million stars out on this dark and moonless night. The lush and thick mid-calf high wild grasses gave way to his carefully placed footsteps; his eyes continually searched the lighted circle given by the oil lantern he held in one hand. His other hand held firmly onto the hand of the woman he loved.

"Step carefully, Francini, we have disturbed two of those nasty ones just this week. One today was in an old tree stump we pulled out of the ground. It almost got Paco when he slipped down trying to get out of its way. I'm sure glad I was there, or you would have seen Paco at the hospital. That Fer-de-Lance is not a happy serpent when his nap is interrupted."

Carlos could feel Francini's shudder travel through her body, down her arm, and from her hand to his. "We have treated seven bites from the Fer-de-Lance at the hospital just this year, Carlos. I don't know why we have so many nowadays. It worries me, your being out here at the coffee plantation all the time."

Carlos stole a glance and flashed Francini a reassuring smile, his teeth glowing white against his brown face. The soft light from the lantern made him look even more handsome, and the young woman's heart skipped a beat. They had loved one another since they were teenagers; they had worked together to help each other with their educations and had always known someday they would become a family.

"You shouldn't worry about me," he answered sweetly. "I'm not going to let anything happen to me, not now, now that you have your nursing degree, the plantation is doing so well, and we have the rest of our lives ahead of us."

At that moment he led her into a small clearing that was surrounded by coffee trees. A familiar spot, they'd often been here to picnic, to study their lessons, or just to have some quiet time together. This time, however, the clearing was different. Instead of just a clearing, there was a blanket spread upon the ground, an ice chest, cushions, and flowers.

"My goodness," she exclaimed, "you have brought romance to our spot."

"Indeed," he flashed another toothy smile, "along with wine and bread and some of that delicious Gouda cheese my cousin brings back from St. Maarten." Carlos held both of Francini's hands, gently lowering her to the ground.

Things had changed for the better during the past few years. The 48-acre coffee plantation Carlos Calderon had inherited from his father and his uncle was producing some of the finest coffee in the world. This 50-square kilometer area along the banks of the Rio Sarapiqui in the central valley region of Costa Rica had always produced some of the finest coffee in the world; the world just didn't know it. Now that the secret was out, the demand for these bold tasting beans had skyrocketed, and in turn put wealth into the pockets of a few that once could only dream of it. Carlos was one of those fortunate few, and now he could finally see a way to give Francini Rojas the life she deserved. Tonight, he would ask Francini for her hand in marriage.

"For the lady." Carlos handed a glass of wine to Francini, they made a toast, and were suddenly and without warning blinded by a slender streak of light that crossed the sky before them and disappeared into the valley below. There was no impact noise, only a low hum for a second or two.

"*What was that?*" exclaimed Carlos, as he leapt to his feet.

"I don't know," answered Francini almost in a whisper. "Maybe a falling star."

"Whatever it was, it seemed like it was just right there." He held his hand out like he could touch the air the streak of light had penetrated.

Settling back down on the blanket, he noticed Francini was shaking; she was obviously frightened. Holding her snugly in his arms, he soothed her fears with tiny kisses delicately placed on her pretty face and soft reassuring whispers.

"That really unnerved me, Carlos. I don't know why, but it did." She tried to laugh it off and soon turned her attention to slicing bread and cheese. "I wonder if anyone else saw it?"

"Surely someone else saw it," Carlos replied. "It *was* bright. As bright as a flash of lightning, I'd say."

Soon the subject changed to more cheerful topics, the all-important question was asked, tears were shared, a wedding date was set, and happy laughter echoed across the ridges and through the valley. They even danced to their favorite songs as they played on their cell phones. They were young, they were in love, they were happy, and as they rested on their backs, holding hands, gazing up at the star-filled sky, they fell asleep. The soft glow of the lantern that had been hung on a limb some feet away was soon chased away by the velvety blackness of the night.

Carlos opened his eyes with the movement of Francini's hand. For a few moments he was disoriented; the wine and the total darkness that surrounded them were more than his sluggish mind could handle. The stars above them, however, came into focus within several seconds, and he squeezed Francini's hand. "We fell asleep, sweetheart, the lantern has gone out," he whispered. "Look at all those stars, Francini, aren't they beautiful? It's so dark it seems as though you can see forever."

"Yes they are beautiful, Carlos, but I have to be at the hospital at six in the morning. We must go home. What time is it, anyway?' Francini scrambled to her feet, located her smart phone and switched on the flashlight feature. "Ten after two," she muttered and began packing everything back into the ice chest.

"I'll get all this tomorrow," said Carlos. "I have another flash....." His words trailed off as he stared down the slope into the night. "Look, Francini, fireflies, or something."

A small group of, for a lack of a better description, points of light floated among the coffee trees. Francini switched off her flashlight as the floating white dots of light emerged from the trees and came closer to the couple. They stood perfectly still as all but one of the cluster floated silently a few feet over their heads. The one hovered at eye level within arm's length. Out of curiosity Carlos reached out and with a forefinger touched the motionless dot of light, then jerked his hand back as it instantly disappeared.

"It tingled," said Carlos, rubbing his forefinger with the tip of his thumb. They both turned and watched as the remainder of the cluster vanished into the vegetation.

"Did it sting you?" inquired Francini.

"No, not really," he answered. "It just tingled, and then it disappeared." Carlos shrugged his shoulders, grabbed his flashlight, caught hold of Francini's hand, and cautiously led her back to his house.

* * *

Less than seven hours from the time the mysterious light streak had lit the night skies of central Costa Rica, five United States Air Force C-130's had touched down at an airfield just outside San Jose. The first plane to land carried 75 highly-trained members of a Special Forces Unit and their equipment. The existence of this unit was known to only a handful, as their sole mission was to respond to national and international threats of grave magnitude. The second C-130 carried another unknown group of men and women; 30 individuals to be exact, from at least nine different countries, the most experienced and well-versed in bio-chemicals and bio-weaponry the world had to offer. This plane was also laden with several tons of equipment used in the detection, collection, elimination, and or transportation of any and all known bio-hazardous materials in existence. The other three air craft were stuffed with transport vehicles unlike anyone in Costa Rica had ever seen. The citizens of this fine country surely must have thought they were being invaded; they gawked in disbelief as the convoy of unmarked, tan colored machines commandeered their roadways and raced northward away from the city.

An hour later they did in fact invade. They invaded the peaceful little valley just east of San Miguel, targeting every coffee plantation in the area, including Carlos Calderon's. As soon as the battle ready, heavily armed troops saw Carlos they took two steps back. Within a second a monotone voice could be heard summoning others. Carlos didn't know which of the three had spoken; their helmets with dark tinted face shields prevented him from seeing any facial features. He did not like what he saw. Growing up in a part of the world that had seen more than its share of internal strife had taught him not to be so trusting; he was poised to flee into the nearby jungle when one of them spoke in his native tongue.

"We mean you no harm," said that same monotone voice that Carlos had heard a few seconds before. "We simply want to ask you a few questions."

"About what?" Carlos had found his voice, and now stood more erect.

"Sir, it's about last night."

"What about last night?" questioned Carlos. Then suddenly it occurred to him that something may have happened to Francini on her way home from his house. "Is Francini alright? Has *something* happened to her?" Carlos took an anxious step forward, prompting the troops to take a step back.

One of the trio held up a hand as if to say, *calm down.* "We have no knowledge of that, sir, please remain calm for just a few moments. Who is Francini? Was she here last night?"

Carlos nodded, but before he could speak four more troops emerged from the coffee trees along with three other oddly-dressed individuals, each carrying an aluminum case.

"What is this about?!" demanded Carlos. "What are you doing on my plantation? You have no business here!"

"Please, sir," said a different voice this time. "If you'll give me just a few moments, I will explain. Did you happen to see the light streak that came through this area last night?"

"Of course we did," answered Carlos, "it was just right here." He waved his arm in the direction of the river.

"By, 'we,' do you mean you and Francini?" The first voice again.

"Yes. We were up on the ridge a way, in our little clearing."

The second voice spoke again. "Did you happen to see any other strange lights after you witnessed the light streak? Anything that seemed out of place?"

Carlos shivered as an involuntary chill ran through his body; fear began to grip him. "We thought they were fireflies or some other kind of insect."

"How many were there?"

"I didn't count them, several, maybe ten. *What* is this about?"

"Did you come into contact with any of the lights?"

"I think I touched one and then it just disappeared. At least I think I touched it." Carlos reached out with his forefinger extended just as he had done the night before. "We just thought they were fireflies," he said again.

"Did Francini touch, or come into contact with any of the lights in any way?"

"No," replied Carlos, "we watched all the others float over our heads and into the trees. Are you going to tell me what this is about? We didn't do anything wrong. You all need to leave now, I have work to do."

"Carlos, please trust us, I have one more question. Where is Francini now?"

"*How* did you know my name?" yelled Carlos. "*Trust you?* I don't know who you are, *how can* I trust you?"

The person who had been doing most of the talking slowly removed his helmet and face shield. His eyes met those of Carlos. They were kind eyes, feeling eyes, in spite of belonging to a person who must make decisions that would forever haunt a normal member of humanity. "Carlos, we have been watching that light streak for several days, we knew it would come down here. We know everyone in this area, but somehow we don't know Francini. For her wellbeing, please tell us where she is at this moment."

Full blown fear now consumed him; he shook uncontrollably. Still something in him said he must put his trust in these strangers. The three oddly-dressed ones with the cases stepped closer. "She's a nurse at the little hospital in town."

The helmet-less troop who'd been doing most of the talking nodded his thanks to Carlos, and the next thing he felt was a slight pressure on his forearm. Carlos collapsed into the arms of two of the oddly-dressed persons and was gently lowered to the ground. A device was quickly produced from one of the cases and a type of scan was performed. In a matter of seconds the results were known.

"He's been invaded, Colonel. One-hundred per cent positive results."

The colonel dropped his head in sadness. "The first human; let's pray that the surgery works on us as well as it does on primates. Find Francini, and let's hope she's okay."

"They have her already, Colonel Ray. She's clear. Her scan was one-hundred per cent negative. She'll be at the LZ when we get back, they'll wake her then so you can question her."

Colonel Ray cast his eyes upward and whispered a thank you. This was the twelfth time in the same number of months that Colonel David Ray's unit had been deployed for this same type of threat. Much to his relief, the higher-ups at the International Agency for Deep Space Observation had assured him they were not monitoring any more light streaks headed in the Earth's direction. At least not in the foreseeable future. It would be good to be back to business of the craziness of humans here on Earth; he'd had enough of the craziness an unknown deep space could throw at our world.

Francini fluttered her eyes then opened them wide.

"Francini," said the colonel in a calm and reassuring voice, "you're alright. No one is going to harm you."

"Where am I?" she asked, trying to bring herself to a sitting position, but the restraints wouldn't allow her. "*Why* am I tethered?"

"Just for your security while you were waking up," said the colonel, he then turned to someone behind him and directed them to remove her restraints.

"*What* do you mean, waking up? I'm supposed to be at work. *Who* are you people and *where* am I?"

Colonel Ray offered her a hand. "Let me help you to that chair, and I'll answer all your questions, to the best of my ability, anyway." With that Francini took his hand and allowed him to steady her as she crossed the room and took a seat in a folding, but comfortable chair. The colonel placed an identical chair facing her a few feet away. "Please allow me to introduce myself. I am Colonel David Ray, commanding officer of MM1. We are a Special Forces unit that responds to biological threats to humanity worldwide. Us along with a team of some of the most brilliant men and women in the world. I'll get Doctor Kellson in here to talk to you as soon as she's available."

Francini was confused. "What does that have to do with me?" she demanded. "And where am I? This is obviously some kind of portable building; I'm supposed to be at the hospital. And what are you talking about: a biological threat?"

"I'm getting there, Francini." The colonel couldn't help but chuckle at this fireball of a young woman. "Do you remember the streak of light that you and Carlos saw last night? And the cluster of little lights that floated in your direction?"

Suddenly fear replaced her wondering what this was all about, and she sprang from her chair. "Is Carlos alright?" she almost screamed. "Do you have him, too?"

"Yes, yes, Carlos is in good hands. We should have a report on him very soon." The colonel encouraged the young lady to reclaim her chair. "You are a nurse, I understand." She nodded yes. "Then you may very well understand this better than I do. The light streak you and Carlos saw last night was a conveyance mechanism for a colony of microorganisms from somewhere in very deep space. Honestly, no one has a clue where they come from, but we do know what they are capable of. These microorganisms are like nothing we have here on Earth, they are not carbon-based like all living things on our planet; they are seltavane-based. Seltavane is the name scientists have given to this previously unknown element. The single cell organism is about a thousand times smaller than a typical human cell, and they are called SLV's. They always travel in pairs, called SLV2's. Those were the small lights you and Carlos saw last night. A colony is always twelve pairs, called SLV12's. There are a million questions that have not been answered concerning these organisms, but here are a few things we do know about them: they exist and reproduce using a modified binary system. They start out as two, but once they've chosen a host things change somewhat. That's the 'modified' part of the binary system. It's still a numerical thing, and it just happens to be our number twelve. The pair, within a certain time period, will reproduce by a multiplication factor of twelve, and in that exact time frame will reproduce again by the multiplication factor of twelve. The organism will repeat this reproduction pattern twelve times. The time-frame from initial invasion to the first reproduction varies with the size and physical shape of the host. The organism will only survive in warm-blooded mammal host. According to our studies, we should have an eighteen-hour incubation period with humans. Thankfully we are well within that time-frame."

Francini had been trying to follow along with the colonel's explanations, but his last few words were more than she could stand; once again she sprang from her chair. This time, however, the colonel had on his hands a young woman on the verge of hysterics. Colonel Ray had tried to be delicate in his explanations, but apparently twenty-two years as a Special Forces officer in the Army had roughened his softer side.

Francini screamed so loudly and fast that the colonel failed to understand much of what she was saying, in spite of being very well versed in the Spanish language. "Please, Francini," the colonel pleaded, "calm down, slow down, please, and hear me out." Finally, she settled down enough for Colonel Ray to continue. But still she stood. "Carlos is in surgery at this very moment. The organism will be removed, and I have complete confidence that he will be just fine."

"You mean to tell me that Carlos has been infected by some kind of organism that looks like a light, and comes from outer space?"

"Basically, yes, but he has not been infected, he's been invaded. The organism leaves no ill effects on its host. To the best of our knowledge, that is. Carlos is the first human to be invaded. We have done extensive testing on primates and other species of mammals. They have all survived and lived normal lives after the organism is removed. We are convinced that the SLV2's select their host at random and out of convenience. It is simply a coincidence that you and Carlos were there just when the colony arrived; otherwise, we would be searching for all twelve of the SLV2's in the wildlife. Francini, you can rest assured you were not attacked; these organisms simply want and need a host in order to reproduce. They don't need a food supply, or water, in fact they absolutely cannot survive in a wet or even damp environment. It seems as though their sole purpose of existence is to produce energy, and there is speculation that they may have had some kind of symbiotic relationship with another species, wherever it is they came from." The colonel shrugged his shoulders, "that's about all I can tell you right now."

Just then the door opened and a tall, slender lady entered. She removed her surgical garb from her head allowing flowing auburn hair to fall upon her shoulders. "Francini," she offered her hand, "I'm Doctor Kellson. Spanish is not my strongest language, so please excuse me if I have to ask Colonel Ray to help me out. First of all: the surgery was a complete success, the organism has been removed and contained, and Carlos should have no lasting effects other than a sore neck for a few days."

"*Neck?*" questioned Francini. "He touched it with his finger."

Doctor Kellson smiled. "Yes, the organism always migrates to the neck area. We are going to keep Carlos for a couple of days just to make sure there is no infection from the surgery, but you can see him in about half an hour." The doctor smiled again, nodded a single nod to the colonel and then left.

"See?" said Colonel Ray as he watched Francini slowly sit back down. "I told you he'd be fine."

"What would have happened if you had not come here? If you had not removed that *thing* from Carlos?" Tears flowed freely from her big brown eyes. "Carlos had just last night asked me to marry him. I was so afraid I'd lost him." She rose and crossed the room to the farthermost corner where she could weep in relative privacy and give thanks that her Carlos had been spared.

David Ray took this opportunity to slip out of the sixteen by sixteen feet portable structural unit, or PSU's as they're called. He shook his head as he had trouble getting the door to close properly. *It's a wonder they work at all*, he thought, *the things have been hauled all over the world this past year*. But his thoughts quickly went back to the young lady inside. He was thankful that Carlos would be alright, and that they could go forward with their plans. He was also thankful that she had not pursued the line of questioning of 'what if.' He would not have wanted to explain to her that in nine days Carlos would have had a spherical mass of some one hundred and eighty trillion single cell organisms attached to his neck. Every single one of them existing for two common goals: to produce and release a new pair capable of reproducing, and to produce energy. Sure, Carlos would have been fine walking around with a reddish-purplish, metallic-looking sphere the size of an ordinary grapefruit; the problem is, up to now at least, the uncontrollable energy they are capable of producing. Testing had shown that a mature pair that had completed their twelve reproduction cycles could produce enough energy to run a half-dozen average American homes. Disturbing the pair is the touchy part, and being attached to mobile creatures such as primates or humans would surely result in them being disturbed. Reactions range, depending on the perceived threat, from a flash of light to a small scale violent lightning storm with laser-like light streaks capable of inflicting severe damage or even death.

Well, we've avoided all that, he thought, just as a fellow officer stepped up to report that all but one of the SLV2's had been located and contained. Only two had found host, the remainder were caught up in the thick vegetation at the edge of the coffee trees belonging to Carlos Calderon. "It started raining up there just as we located the SLV2's, three perished before we could get them into protective containers," said the junior officer. "The last one must have perished before the scan could pick it up. It rained pretty hard for about fifteen minutes, Colonel, everything is drenched."

"You're probably right, Sam," said the colonel, "but just to make sure, go ahead and run a phase two scan and to be double sure we haven't missed anything, run a phase three scan, also."

"Yes sir, Colonel." The lieutenant gave him an unnecessary, but respectful salute before he retreated.

"Francini," Colonel Ray called through the doorway, "let's go see Carlos, I'm sure he's beside himself worrying about you."

* * *

Young Joel Ramon, well hidden in a brush pile, watched everything that happened at the Calderon Plantation that morning. He'd been there on a mission; the same mission he undertook every time a tour bus passed through their little town. Tourists, especially American tourists, loved their souvenirs. What better souvenir from the prime coffee district could there be than fresh from the tree coffee cherries? For the past couple of years, the fifteen-year-old Joel had pilfered small cuttings from coffee trees, stuffed them into sandwich size zip-lock bags, and sold them for a buck each to the tourists in San Miguel. Joel made his rounds, visiting all the plantations in the area, never taking so much that it would cause alarm for the plantation owners, and always taking care not to damage the trees or property. This day was his turn to visit the Calderon Plantation. Normally he would visit with Carlos for a while. On this land, he had never been scolded for his little escapades; Carlos understood that the boy was only doing what he had to do to survive.

Silently, Joel watched as the scene unfolded, some fifty yards away. He didn't feel afraid at first, but as Carlos suddenly collapsed into the arms of the strange-looking men surrounding him, Joel almost panicked. He was certain he had just witnessed a murder. Ever so quietly and quickly, he slipped from the brush and made his way to the crest of the ridge. He then ran as fast as he could to San Miguel, reaching the center of town just as a tour bus pulled to a stop in front of the local coffee shop. Time to go to work, then he would report what he had seen to the authorities.

* * *

The plane touched down at Logan International on schedule in spite of the late December snowstorm that had moved in overnight. Carl Stevens practically dragged his over-stuffed, over-sized carry-on from the overhead bin onto the lady seated in front of him.

"Pardon me, lady," he muttered to the glaring face of the offended woman. "I'm in a hurry. I don't even want to be here." She heard him swear under his breath as he bulldozed his way toward the exit door mumbling additional obscenities with every step.

"Of all the rudeness," exclaimed the lady. "Well, Merry Christmas to him," she said to the young woman who'd been seated by Carl a few moments before.

"I'm sorry," said the young lady. "I'm embarrassed to say right now, but he's my brother. And trust me I'll give him an earful when I catch up with him. Not to make excuses for him, but we both have to use our Christmas vacation time to get a piece of property in Salem ready to put on the market."

"Oh," said the older lady, "that sounds like you've lost a family member."

This kind lady seems so compassionate, thought the young woman, *even after my jerk brother almost took her head off.* She nodded. "Our aunt. She never had children, Carl and I were her closest relatives, outside our dad, and he's a bigger jerk than Carl. Dad and Aunt Mary haven't spoken in twenty-three years. Actually, they were in-laws, and Dad always blamed her for the car accident that took the life of his older brother. Twenty-three years ago."

"I'm so sorry, dear one. That's a hard thing to have to do right here at Christmastime." The old lady managed to turn far enough in her seat to pat the young lady on the hand.

"Thank you. By the way, my name is Abigail Stevens-Tomms. I guess I should introduce myself if I'm going to share my life's story with you." Both ladies laughed, and then noticed that the plane was virtually empty.

"Well, my name is Shirley Watson," said the elderly lady, pulling herself from the cramped economy seat, "and would you happen to be the niece of

Betty Jane Stevens?"

Abigail was caught completely by surprise. How could this lady know her aunt's name, as far as she knew she'd never met her before?

Ms. Watson laughed softly. "I live right down the street from Betty Jane. We used to share gardening ideas on a regular basis. I'm really going to miss her come springtime, that's when we spent most of our time together. I met you once, just after you finished college, although I'm sure you won't remember, it was almost just in passing. But I do recall your aunt speaking very fondly of you."

The two ladies made their way off the plane, through the jet-way, and into the busy terminal, all the while laughing about what a small world it is.

"Say, young lady," exclaimed Ms. Watson, "have you made arrangements for transportation to Salem, and where are you staying?"

"I would imagine Carl is already at baggage claim and working on that. We have reservations at the Lane House Inn."

"Well, call him on your cell phone and tell him not to bother with transportation, my Grandson is picking me up in one of those Hummer things, and you two can ride with me. I don't think your hotel will be very far out of the way."

"I don't know," hesitated Abigail, "Carl is weird, and he almost brained you with his bag, you know."

Ms. Watson laughed again. "Sweetheart, I knew your aunt, so weird doesn't bother me, and it might do that young man some good to suffer the discomfort of riding in a car with me all the way to Salem."

"You are exactly right, Ms. Watson, that would serve him right. Are you sure it won't cause you an inconvenience?" So with the kind old lady's insistence, Abigail called her brother and informed him that travel arrangements to Salem had been made.

* * *

"I'm still not happy with you for tricking me into riding with that strange woman and her loud-mouth grandson last night, you know." Carl had complained about it all through dinner the night before, not even for a second considering how rudely he'd treated Shirley Watson, or that he'd failed to thank her for the ride *and* saving him a couple of hundred bucks. *"Abigail, are you listening to me?"*

"No," Abigail answered rather flatly. It had been eleven years since she'd been in this house. Even longer for her brother. If anything had changed, it was simply an updated version of the strange 'stuff' Aunt Betty Jane liked around her. There were dozens and dozens of books about witchcraft and the witchcraft history of Salem, Massachusetts; old paintings of morbid scenes hung on every wall in the place, and where there was no painting, strange masks or playbills from the scores of macabre plays she'd attended, found a home. Abigail stood close to the center of the living room shaking her head. As far as she knew Aunt Betty Jane was not a pagan; she did celebrate Christmas, albeit, in her own odd way. She'd died on the twenty-first of October, but there in the corner near the fireplace stood the Christmas tree, fully decorated with orange lights, black cats, jack-o-lanterns, bats and rats, and a silver star on top. On every flat surface there was a volume of Charles Dickens', "A Christmas Carol." Four of them were beautifully illustrated, and each one of these opened to one of the four visiting ghosts.

"What a way to spend the week before Christmas," complained Carl. "I'm losing a week's vacation time for this *and* had to change my skiing trip reservations in Vail. My new girlfriend was furious *and* it cost me a ton of money. Abigail, you'd better hope we clear a lot of money on this dump to make up for all the trouble this has caused me. I don't know why you couldn't have taken care of all this without me. I never liked the old hag anyway, and this place gives me the creeps. Betty Jane was without a doubt the weirdest woman in Salem. Wouldn't surprise me at all if she were a witch, herself. I mean, look at all this weird stuff."

"Carl!" screamed Abigail. "That's *enough* of your complaining. I know you think the world revolves around you, but it *doesn't*. Aunt Betty Jane left everything she owned to *us*, and *we* are going to deal with it."

Abigail had already done most of the leg-work; she'd contacted a local estate sale specialist and contracted for things to be sold at auction. Her aunt's clothing and most of the household items had already been donated to a shelter for the homeless. Still in this modest home, however, remained a lifetime of antiques, artwork, hundreds of books, and boxes of photographs, both old and new. Even with the help of the donations and the estate sale, Abigail knew this was going to be a monumental task, and her partner just might be a bigger hindrance than help.

"Look, Carl, I know you're unhappy about being here. I'm not so thrilled myself, and neither is my husband, but we'll both just have to do the best we can."

Carl glared at his sister. "Don't expect smiles from me."

"Whatever, Carl. The lady from the estate sale place, Erin, put a stack of boxes on the dining room table; mostly pictures. Let's start there. Sort through them, and if we know who's in the photos we'll box them up and send them to Mom and Dad. Everything else, trash."

Carl nodded, and then turned toward the dining room.

Many of the photographs were black and whites from who knows when or where and within a few hours, years' worth of memories were reduced to a neat little pile inside a dark green plastic bag destined for the landfill.

"Wow," muttered Carl, "these were taken in Rome. I never realized

Betty Jane did anything or went anywhere, besides the theatre to see "Phantom" for the hundredth time. But here are photos from all around Europe and Great Britain."

"Yes, Carl, for the past seven or eight years she traveled quite a lot. There're a couple of senior groups here in Salem she toured with. She's sent me postcards from all over the world. In fact, I got one from Costa Rica just a couple of weeks before she died.

"Well I guess that explains this." Abigail glanced up to see him holding a small zip-lock bag. "Looks like coffee beans. They were in this envelope with these pictures; must be her Costa Rica pictures." He held the zip-lock bag up to the light for a closer look. "Why would anybody bring something like this home?"

"That was Aunt Betty Jane, Carl. That is why she was who she was, different by all standards." Abigail turned to a new box of photographs.

"Ho-ly!" yelled Carl. "Did you see that?"

His sister looked up. "See what?" She did see that Carl had removed the little cluster of coffee cherries from its zip-lock bag, and was holding it with one hand while rubbing the end of his thumb with the other hand.

"That flash of light. Almost like a static spark." Again he asked, "Did you see it?"

"No. Did it shock you?"

"No, it was more like a tingle, but the light was so bright, but for only an instant, then it disappeared." Carl then shoved the coffee beans back into their bag and tossed them into the trash.

Abigail tolerated her brother's constant complaining and bashing of their aunt for two more days. When she could stand no more, she hired Ms. Watson's grandson to deliver him to the airport. "Merry Christmas, Carl," she said as he tossed his bag into the back seat, then crawled in with it like he was being chauffeured. Abigail shook her head disapprovingly, and then noticed him scratching the red, swollen place on his neck. "Got a pimple?" she asked.

"I guess," he answered flatly. "Probably stress from being here at this horrible place."

"Then by all means, go do something that makes you happy." Again she wished him a Merry Christmas. He simply waved her off as the car pulled away.

Merry Christmas indeed, Carl Stevens, you don't have a clue what's in store for you. While you were driving your sister to misery, belittling your aunt mercilessly, and being the royal pain in the neck that you are, you were invaded by The Twelfth Pair. Good luck with that.

A SLIGHT MATTER OF CONTRACT
Larry Lefkowitz

The study was all leather and oak, except for the mounted animal heads which testified to the hunting successes of its lone occupant. Wreathed in the smoke of his favorite pipe, he reclined in his favorite chair, a robust figure in a smoking jacket. The picture of a contented man, but the personage described—he *was* a personage, his face known to every newspaper reader from his successes in the games of politics, hunting, and finance—was not content. There was one competition in which he had been a woeful failure: the contest of finding a woman worthy of him.

By his own standards he has failed; by anyone else's he has been a roaring success. Linked to a string of movie stars (and starlets), princesses, and heiresses, a brace of which he married, he did not remain linked to them for very long. Although their pretty heads did not line his study walls, he had bagged their hearts as surely, and their continued affection for him was attested to by the prompt and unremitting arrival of birthday and holiday cards. Unknown to their senders, they were promptly deposited in the refuse bin. Had they known, these former trophies would have excused this discarding even as they excused in their "memoirs" their own discarding: "One woman cannot satisfy *him*," they invariably said, or something similarly admiring and forgiving at the same time.

No, he had never found the perfect woman he could worship. A patient stalker, he had hoped to find her before his own Stalker struck; now he had come to the reluctant conclusion that there was simply no such game—the perfect woman did not exist.

It was the Christmas season, as confirmed by the sprig of holly that thrusts itself determinedly from a fifteenth century Florentine vase, his only concession to the festive season. But in his heart it was not Christmas. People were receiving gifts they cherished; for him the one gift he has sought is not forthcoming. He placed his pipe, still half-filled with his favorite blended tobacco, on the African ivory table next to his chair; smoking it afforded no solace in his present mood. He grasped his head in his hands, a rare gesture of despair for a man who has always prided himself in not surrendering to despair. "I would give everything I possess for the perfect woman," he sighed—and he was a man who abhorred sighing. "I would give my very soul."

A noise like curtains being rustled caused him to raise his head and look behind him. The curtains were unmoving as a tomb. He had given the maid off, in fact all the servants, for the holiday season. It was not the maid, however, who appeared suddenly before him in the place where a moment before there had been no one, leaning an arm casually on the Louis XIV writing desk.

An arm—the term does the arm thus reclining an injustice—it was *the* arm from which all other womanly arms imperfectly derived, just as all other womanly attributes imperfectly derived from the rest of her. Encircling the arm's perfect wrist was a jade bracelet, which matched the jade Buddha squatting in a corner on the other side of the room. He was amazed in a thousand ways at once. He dug his nails into the palms of his hands to confirm that he was awake and not dreaming. Although smitten (no other word will do) by the beauty of the apparition, he nonetheless, as a connoisseur, managed to observe that her taste in a bracelet could not have been more perfect.

"Of course," she said, replying to his thoughts. "It is your own taste."

Despite his state of shock, he did not fail to note that she met all the criteria of his ultimate desire, and that her clothes and jewelry were the fitting complement to her perfect face and figure.

"You formed me," she said in a voice that covered him like ambrosia.

After staring, hypnotized, for some moments, he stammered, "How did you get in?" It sounded inadequate, even ungrateful, in his ears.

She raised her delicious arm in a simple gesture. "You sent for me."

"In my dreams, yes, but—"

"No, not only in your dreams," she purred. "Just now."

"Just now?" He uttered a nervous laugh. "You don't mean—"

"Precisely."

"But I always pictured the Devil as a man."

She tossed her head in a magnificent gesture which sent her long hair flowing, giving off sparks of fire from its own deeper russet. "Not for you, my dear."

He smiled in spite of a hint of fear which he suddenly experienced— for him a rare feeling. He recalled that the last time he had such a feeling was on the occasion of his bringing down a charging rhino on the Endegi plain with his last bullet. But now he was faced with something quite different, far more threatening, for which a gun would be of no avail. He had difficulty grasping what she had intimated. "*Are* you the Devil?" he asked, for one of the few times in his life open-mouthed and not the master of a situation.

For answer, she bowed ever so slightly.

"And you are a woman?"

She pirouetted smartly in her diaphanous gown which showed off her celestial figure to advantage. "Do you doubt it?"

"No," he said simply, for he did not.

"And if I told you that the Devil was a man for others, would it affect your feeling for me?"

He knew it wouldn't. The truth stood in front of him, the dream metamorphosed into reality. None of his precious artifacts—and he loved them dearly, had spent his best years amassing them—amounted to a hundredth of what he felt toward her. She would be the greatest of his possessions. For possess her he must.

Until now he had been unable to rise from his chair. Now desire had replaced amazement, welling up within him from somewhere deep in his bowels. He stood and advanced hesitantly toward her, feeling, oddly, that he was, despite his slow progress toward her, the rhino that had charged him. No, not a rhino, something else—a satyr, a minotaur. He was surprised boiling steam did not spurt from his nostrils.

"Not so fast, my enamored," she intoned deliciously, if tauntingly. "Aren't you forgetting something?"

He hesitated, and then realized what she meant. It stopped him as effectively as he had the rhino. "Oh, the contract—my soul in exchange and all that."

"'All that', as you phrase it. For 'all this'." A sweep of her hand encompassed her.

He bestowed upon her the smile that had helped him in many a conquest, pleased to note that despite her intimidating presence, he was able to function in his accustomed manner. "Do I have to sign in blood?"

"Certainly not—that's no longer the fashion."

"What *is* the fashion?" he inquired. "Should I summon my lawyer—or rather the whole firm since I have three?"

"No need for one, less a trinity. Simply your word. Do you give it freely?"

The word "freely" was a mockery in his present state. He knew he could not resist. Not only because she was irresistible, but because that gambling instinct that had been heady challenge to him all his life had now to react to the greatest challenge of them all. Bowing, he said, "I give it willingly."

She extended her hand to seal the bargain.

"Not so quickly," he countered. "I like to savor the fruit before I bite into it."

"So did Eve."

"On the subject of immortal women, were you really Helen of Troy to

Faustus?"

She tossed her head once more. A chain of sparklers climbed from bottom to crown. "I am much more to you than her," she purred.

"I cannot argue with you there. Nonetheless I would very much like to behold Helen."

She tapped a lovely foot on the oriental carpet as if in impatience. "Nothing could be easier. I am your servant," she said, a hint of mockery in her voice.

Small wonder, he thought with some disquiet, *I will soon be yours.*

"Now, now," she chided. "Don't adopt a negative attitude. How many men receive everything they want in life? Even the famous Helen. Shall I summon her now?"

Something about Agamemnon and pride swept through his mind in warning. Yet he must see her. Suddenly he raised both hands to stop her. "Wait, wait—at no extra cost!"

"You don't need a firm of lawyers," she laughed playfully, adding in a more subdued voice, "Relax, love. You have only one soul."

A short young lady, rather snub-nosed in appearance and entirely too squat for his own taste, stood where the vision had formerly, assuming the formal pose, in profile, of a Greek statue.

"Ugh, you're joking," he said. "*That* can't be the face that launched a thousand ships!"

"Actually considerably less," answered a voice an octave higher than his vision had had, which he assumed to be Helen's voice. "Eighty-five, to be exact—including beacon vessels."

"Even a beacon wouldn't make me believe that you are Helen of Troy—excuse me, I don't mean to be insulting."

"Think nothing of it—your tastes are simply not classical," she answered, still in Helen's voice and with a gentle rebuke, he mused, that would please the real Helen's shade.

"Have you finished with Helen?" she asked, pirouetting in that way of hers, so that her Grecian robe flowed sensuously over her legs which, he had to admit, weren't so bad even if short.

"Yes—wait a moment. Isn't there anyone else—say Cleopatra, who would match her reputation for ultimate beauty?"

"You would find Cleo a bit too voluptuously vulgar for your taste."

He was curious about another woman—one whose rejection of Dante had caused him to create a Hell of his own. "And Beatrice?"

"You wouldn't care for her, either. But Dante was a queer one. His precious Beatrice was red-faced like a scullery maid."

"I rather thought you would have fancied the color red," he said casually.

"Darling, the wearer makes all the difference. There *are* such things as pale imitations, you know."

"Speaking of which, I would like to have *my* inimitable back."

A second view did nothing to diminish what the first had shown. It seemed to him even to enhance it. She was once again *there* as she had always been there in his mind. Without lightning or thunder, she just materialized in his study, once again leaning nonchalantly on the Louis XIV.

"Yes, for you, I was always there. For you, I will always be there."

"I believe you. Nonetheless a residual caution besets me."

"Yet," she said in a dismissive tone, "I think it will evaporate if I sit upon thy knee."

"No doubt. Nevertheless, I still worry about my fate."

"I am no grim reaper. Thou art the reaper, and I the wheat." As if in confirmation, her body rippled like sheaves of coruscating gold.

"Blake's innocent Devil. Beguiling creature," he murmured helplessly.

"For you I am more than beguiling and not so innocent, which is the way you desire me. Come. Take."

"Damn you!"

"That's usually my line."

She would drive him mad. Her wit—clearly his own—added to her beauty made her irresistible. He had tasted her wit—what remained, not yet tasted, obsessed him. Suddenly another thought prevented him from seizing her. "*There* you won't appear to be as a man?"

"For you, I will be a woman, always."

"The same woman? The one I see in front of me? Not a crone you will assume with your cunning? I want the same woman!" he shouted.

"The one you see in front of you," she purred softly.

Her assurance quieted him. "Having you for eternity sounds like paradise," he said in a more subdued tone. "Yet I wonder. I am somewhat fickle."

"Yes, or I wouldn't be here. You have quite a reputation, you know."

He ignored the compliment. "The same woman," he repeated, trying to make absolutely sure on her part, while at the same time musing on the prospect.

"Relax. You will enjoy me—for the first thousand years."

"And after that?"

"Why think so far ahead?"

"And if I don't go for the deal?"

"You will. You find me irresistible."

He nodded. "Yes, I do. I am trying not to, but I really do. You are fiendish."

"Thank you."

He attempted to turn his back on her, to pry himself loose from her grip, but he could not.

She leaned toward him and beckoned with a perfect finger. Despite it seeming the serpent summoning Eve—which his mind urged him to reject—he could not. With a movement that was like the wind in his ears, he closed the distance between them, and she was in his arms, their lips joined. Something delicious, which was at the same time enervating, shot through him, undercut with an arpeggio of mounting danger which sounded like the notes of a flute far off. He was about to abandon himself—to seize that of which the kiss was a hundredth—when the notes of the flute were submerged in a ringing of bells. The clock on the mantelpiece struck the hour. The angels who moved in a circle when the hour struck sailed by before his eyes; their golden wings seemed to fan his face.

He saw it as a warning. His final one. Later he would wonder if it came from Above or was merely chance. That it was the most significant sign he had ever received in his life, he had no doubt. Fortunately, he was to reflect, he had an old-fashioned taste in clocks.

"Go to Hell!" he cried from the depths of his soul, thrusting himself from her.

Her face turned furious, her body seemed to suddenly glow with reddish-golden scales. But only for a moment. "You're much too obvious," she laughingly taunted. "Be not influenced by metal angels. For you to be in heaven is to be with *me*."

"The agreement wasn't sealed. We did not consummate it. You have no claim." From somewhere he felt the truth of this assertion. And the fact that she did not contradict him confirmed it.

She was still boiling with anger. He sensed this clearly. Yet her exterior was as calmly beautiful as ever, though now with the beauty of ice, as if chiseled out of a glacier in the bowels of the earth. She said quietly, confidently, "You will summon me back, you cannot do without me. I am the consummation of your perfect woman."

With a sticking out of her tongue—now forked—she disappeared, seeming to plunge through the oriental carpet like a fallen angel, without a whiff of sulfur—only a hint of her delicious perfume remaining like a beckoning finger.

Would he hold out? Had he seen the last of her? He was assuredly not the same man that he was before she came. Who would be? The test would come next Christmas when he got to feeling lonely and sorry he lacked the gift he wanted then. For he was not the kind of a gentleman who ever stops seeking. If not the perfect woman, it will be the perfect something. And the Devil—who takes many guises—will be willing to provide it.

For the usual price.

HOME BY CHRISTMAS
D.J. Tyrer

"I wish you would stop sniveling, girl. It is not your husband who is headed off to war," sniffed Lady Margaret, waving her kerchief as a farewell to Lord Montfalck as he strode away down the drive.

The statement was factually correct, but betrayed Lady Margaret's inability to see her staff as people in their own rights: As far as she was concerned, Beth was upset because her master was going off to war, when her stifled sobs were really for Bert, the boot-boy, who had signed up at the master's behest.

Lady Margaret turned and swept back inside the house in a regal fashion, chin up, lips stiff, her expression betraying no emotion. She might as easily have been waving her husband off to a session of the Lords.

Beth followed her mistress in, her shoulders slumped, save for the jerking movement of sobs.

Mrs. Grant, the housekeeper, slipped her arm around the girl's shoulders, saying, "There, there, my dear. It'll all be over shortly, and they'll all be home by Christmas. Be brave."

Beth nodded and resolved not to cry. If the mistress could be strong, then so could she.

* * *

The telegram came the week before Christmas. The butler carried it to Lady Margaret on a silver tray, which he placed upon her side table. She looked down at it as if he had placed something noisome there, then her expression resumed its neutrality. He stood silently beside the door. He knew as well as she did that telegrams seldom brought good news.

Lady Margaret picked it up and slit it open with a letter knife. As she did so, she told him, "You may go."

"Milady." He bobbed his head and stepped out of the room. As he closed the door, he heard her begin to sob.

* * *

"I can't believe she's going ahead," commented Cook over a large brandy liberated from the Christmas supplies.

Mrs. Grant shrugged. "Christmas comes every year, whatever comes to pass. Her ladyship understands her *noblesse oblige* and her responsibilities. She sets the example we all must follow."

"Still seems callous. Her husband's dead and her son's still in the trenches somewhere. It seems wrong to be celebrating while he's mourning and fighting."

The housekeeper shrugged again. "We're keeping the home fires burning: That's what the boys are fighting for."

A muffled sob interrupted their conversation, as Beth entered the kitchen and threw herself down on the table.

The women exchanged a look, and Cook murmured, "It's such a shame about Bert..."

"Shh!" Mrs. Grant had had to break the news to the girl, once it had filtered back to the house from the boot-boy's family: Bert had died in one of the myriad of failed advances on the German lines, but she doubted the mistress was even aware. What did the likes of her care about a boot-boy?

* * *

Although she wore a mask of stately indifference during the day, Lady Margaret allowed it to slip at night. She would cry herself to sleep, and dream of her husband: not as a corpse in the Flanders mud, but as he had been when they first met all those years before, young and dashing in his bright-red uniform, a hero in her eyes.

"So handsome..." she murmured as she drifted back into wakefulness.

Something, a sound, perhaps, had wakened her. She opened eyes glued shut by the patina of sleep and pushed herself up on one elbow.

Then, she screamed. There was a figure at the end of her bed.

A moment later, the door to her room swung open, and her maid rushed in on a tide of warm, syrupy gaslight, summoned by her cry.

Lady Margaret blinked her eyes. The room was empty, except for her and her maid. Yet, she knew she had seen someone standing there, at the foot of her bed. Someone with a gas mask over his face.

* * *

Lady Margaret had no doubts: the man she had seen in her room was her husband. He had come back to her from where he had died; for what

129

purpose, she had no idea. All she knew was that she was desperate to see him again, one last time, to say goodbye.

To that end, she resolved to stay awake, to wait for him.

In spite of herself, she began to doze in the early hours of the morning, the romance novel she had been reading slipping from her fingers to flop shut on her chest.

Then, she heard it, although, again, what it was she heard, she couldn't say. She opened her eyes and saw him.

The figure was, as she had thought, a soldier in the dark, mud-and-blood-stained uniform of the trenches with a tin hat upon his head. His face was concealed behind a gas mask, but she knew it was her husband.

"Oh, Ranald, I'm so glad to see you. I love you," she said, sliding from her bed, the book slipping from her to land with a thud on the floor as she stood.

Then, he was gone, and her heart broke again.

* * *

"Parcel for you," called Mrs. Grant as Beth entered the kitchen. Normally, such an announcement would have been cause for excitement, but the girl didn't seem to hear.

"It's from Bert," Mrs. Grant added, wondering if passing it on was a good idea or not. The caveat did at least catch the girl's attention, and Beth took the small cardboard box and headed for the privacy of her room to open it and discover what her beau had wanted her to have.

It was, Mrs. Grant thought, as if the boy had sent Beth a final Christmas gift.

* * *

Mrs. Grant had attempted to arrange for Beth to have Christmas Day off, despite being unable to find a replacement at such short notice, but the mistress had seemed not to hear her.

"She hasn't been quite right since her husband died," she commented to Cook over late-morning Sherries. "Not that you can blame her."

"That poor mite, too," said Cook. "Bert's death has hit her head."

"I wish we could let her have the day off," Mrs. Grant sighed, "but, with so many of the men gone, we're too shorthanded and her ladyship insists on a full celebration."

The day passed in a flurry of activity for the staff and the irksome necessity of playing host to her guests for Lady Margaret, who found her only interest, now, lay with her dead husband's ghost.

Beth had served at table, face pale and mask-like, much like her mistress, but while moving stiffly, as if in a trance, had done all that she was called upon to do well and without complaint.

"One can only hope she'll get over it," Cook said, as she and the housekeeper shared a nightcap. "Unlike her ladyship, she's young..."

Mrs. Grant nodded. "It's always difficult to lose your first love like that..."

"I just hope the poor girl's heart heals."

"Hear, hear," said Mrs. Grant, raising her glass.

* * *

Lady Margaret was grateful to finally escape the inane wittering of her guests and go to receive Ranald.

A maid slipped out of her room as she approached, but she barely noticed her: to her, the staff was little more than walking furniture. Had she noticed, she wouldn't have known it was Beth, nor that the girl was suffering an emotional wound as deep as that which afflicted her.

She went into her room and lay down, waiting.

While she fought against her tiredness, once more she began to drift off until a sound woke her. A rifle crack? A sigh?

There he was, once more.

Lady Margaret bounded out of bed and over to him, more spry than she had been in many years.

"My love!" she cried, halting before him, uncertain whether she should, whether she could, embrace him.

Her husband stood motionless before her, as stiff as if he were standing to attention on parade. He looked at her through the thick, murky glass of the gas mask visor.

"Oh, I miss you so much," she whispered, reaching out to touch his arms; he felt solid beneath her fingers. She could feel the coarse texture of his uniform as if the cloth were real. She smiled: this was the perfect Christmas gift, if they were to be apart in the flesh.

Slowly, a little fearfully, she raised her hands towards his gas mask to remove it, to gaze once more upon his face. Was it marked? The telegram had said nothing of how Ranald had been killed, and it seemed his body lay alongside those of his fellow fighting men who had died in their thousands in Flanders fields, never to return home.

He didn't resist, and she took hold of the mask and slipped it up off his face.

She gasped: The face that grinned madly at her was not that of her husband. Lady Margaret did not recognize him, having never noticed Bert as he went about his chores, but, now, he laughed mockingly at her.

"Who...?" She stumbled back towards the bed, not understanding.

There was the sudden insistent sound of an alarm clock that, momentarily, served to perplex her more, as the gift Bert had sent his girl from the front, along with instructions on how to prime and place it, did its deadly job.

In her attic room, Beth heard the thunder crack as the grenade detonated. Her Bert was avenged. Yet, the hole in her heart remained unhealed, and she knew she would never celebrate Christmas again, as long as she lived.

How she wished Bert had been home by Christmas.

She lay down and cried, wishing she might have seen him just one more time.

A BROTHER'S GIFT
Gabriel Barbaro

The winter of 1891 was the bleakest of my young life. Icy winds blew, howling over Hampstead Heath, while my elder brother Edgar and I watched through ruddy windows. Though we were on school holiday, our parents would not let us leave the house, fearing the unusually intense winter of that year. And so we played games inside. At the tender ages of seven and five, Edgar and I had full use of our imaginations. And oh, how we employed them! We pretended to be renowned archaeologists and famous professors adventuring on sabbatical. We were Gentlemen Explorers, as we liked to call ourselves and our game. Off we would go on expeditions throughout the house, our trips always leading up to our cavernous attic, where we were surrounded by objects from the past. That was when the real work began. We foraged through layers and layers of family history, finding objects of interest, and conducting lectures around them. Our young minds ran wild with imagined histories: an old coin discovered in an ancient Egyptian tomb, a compass that pointed towards ancient Incan gold. There were countless antique objects for us to play with, for our house was large and old. My father loved it there, as he too grew up under its storied slate roof as did his father and his father before him.

But the winter of that year was different. Day after day, the winds howled through the Heath, like tortured souls of the damned. Snow fell upon snow, until all my brother and I looked out into was a frozen world of white. Our door could only open wide enough for our father to leave in the morning.

Each holiday season, our father had a Christmas tree delivered to our home, and my brother and I cheered upon its arrival. Christmas was our favorite holiday. We trimmed the tree with garlands of popcorn and walnuts and adorned the branches with Christmas crackers. My parents placed small candles on every branch, which when lit, made the tree glow. We stood looking with appreciation, for the candles cast warmth over the room. It was a hopeful sight.

Up in our bedroom, Edgar and I kneeled over our beds, begging St. Nicholas for exploring equipment for use in new expeditions.

Mornings found us up in the attic. One day, as I examined an old pewter mug, I heard Edgar coughing behind a pile of trunks. "It's only a bit of dust," I heard his muffled voice say. But soon the cough grew worse. When he emerged into the light, I noticed his face was flushed. I put my hand to his forehead, and it burnt like hot coals. Panicked, I ran down to tell Mother.

As the fever worsened, the doctor was summoned, and to our horror, Edgar was diagnosed with the Russian Flu.

During the long nights leading up to Christmas thereafter, instead of praying for presents, I prayed for my brother's recovery. He lay quarantined in our room upstairs, and I could not see him nor speak to him for days on end. So it was that on Christmas Eve 1891, after a fortnight of heroic struggle, my dear brother Edgar took his last breath. Although I was young, the tragedy of his passing stung my heart. That Christmas morning was filled with despair. Mother cried silently in her bedroom, Father locked himself in his study, and I sat alone under the tree staring at our unopened gifts. I would have given them all back to have my brother living once more.

Days later, a simple funeral was held at our parish church. I remember the high-necked, charcoal lace dress my mother wore. I remember my father's grim face, as we sat listening to the priest's kind words of condolence. He tried to comfort us. His gentle words could not reach us, however. What I wanted so dearly was to speak with Edgar, to tell him I loved him.

A month passed and the snow fell with cruel vengeance. Now when I looked out the window I could no longer see the Heath, only indistinct forms, where the snow had covered the brush, its weight bending them to the frozen ground. Frost encrusted each pane of glass so that there was hardly space to look through. London was engulfed in the flu epidemic, shutting down the city, including my school. Traumatized by Edgar's passing, Mother forbade me to leave the house, terrified I would contract the illness and suffer the same fate. Locked within the house, isolated from the world outside, I was so very lonely for company. Dressed in black, Mother knit and read by the fire, wiping tears from her pale face, her gaze hardly leaving me. Father kept his own counsel in his study, rarely emerging. He no longer smiled at me.

The absence of Edgar's laugh impressed upon me the loneliness of my isolation. Desperate to reconnect with my brother, I decided to adventure up to our attic once more. I climbed the three flights of stairs, tracing the dark wood banisters with my finger. I imagined I was hiking behind Edgar up a huge mountain in Nepal. Up in our attic fort once more, I rediscovered our favorite treasures: sacred wooden marbles from Africa, enchanted leaded soldiers from India, a toy gun which had been used to stop a killer elephant. Soon I found myself distracted from the pall of sorrow below.

On the third night of my solitary adventures, I read in my bed by candlelight. My parents had gone to bed hours before, but I had trouble falling asleep in the room Edgar and I had once shared. It was lonely with no one with whom to whisper. I closed the book, snuffed the candle, and settled deeper into my bed. It was always chilliest down by my feet, and I rubbed them together to create heat.

I began to slip into a soporific state, my eyes half-open, when I noticed something beyond Edgar's empty bed, in the darkness by the window. At first, I was not so much frightened as doubtful. After all, I knew logically, I was alone in the room. I shut my right eye but kept my left eye slightly open to observe the thing, and noticed a gray haze floating towards the foot of Edgar's bed. Formless and wispy, it seemed to drift upon an invisible breeze. It rounded his bed. As this realization entered my brain, my curiosity perished and fear stabbed my abdomen like a palpable thing. I forced my eyes shut and clutched the blankets tightly, willing the room to revert back to its prior state. After several moments, I felt collected and decided I was a fool.

I opened my eyes and peered carefully down to my feet. I cannot forget what I saw. It was Edgar. I swear upon the Holy Bible it was him, right down to the last detail of his neatly combed black hair. Although partly in shadow, I could make him out in his best suit. The dim light from the window caught his silver pin. A favorite of his, it was a miniature steam ship, that my grieving parents had pinned to his lapel, before they closed his casket forever. For several moments I could not breathe. My heart raced.

"Edgar!" I exclaimed, sitting upright.

He gave me a familiar smile, but indicated with a finger to his ashen lips that I should not be so loud. I noticed then how thin and bony he was, the effects of the illness that had taken his life apparent on his wasted face. Slowly I nodded in agreement. My fear paired with excitement, and I wanted to pester him with questions, but thought it best to maintain his wish for silence, lest he vanish. He gestured and I followed, throwing back the covers and slipping into my sheepskin slippers. The floors were freezing at this time of night.

Edgar turned and walked silently into the hall. I found that my eyes were surprisingly accustomed to the dark, and soon we were ascending the second floor staircase. His form gave off a dim gray light, and I was mesmerized by the way his feet did not touch the steps, although his legs still made the motions. Soon he stopped at the door to the attic. He paused, then turned and grinned. Although his smile was recognizable, I noticed that his eye sockets were hollow, and it frightened me. However, I made the effort to smile back, which seemed to satisfy him. He turned to open the door, and I followed. Just as in life, we marched through boxes and trunks, amid antique furniture, to our fort. All our treasures lay where I had left them that day.

"I love you dear brother, how I have missed you!" I exclaimed, for I could no longer hold my tongue.

Edgar nodded and smiled, bringing a finger up for silence. I noticed again how gray his flesh was. How wrinkled. His finger was so bony that it seemed the flesh was all dried up. Fear seized the muscles in my arms and legs, paralyzing them. *How could Edgar be here?* I thought to myself. He motioned for me to stay put as he moved back through the clutter and into one of the darkened eaves. Stricken as I was with fear, there was no way I could move had I so desired.

As if to assuage these fears, my brother reappeared from the dark eave. He glided to the clearing of our fort, his legs simulating the motion of his old gait, unaware they no longer had any use. I became aware of two facts. First, my brother was indeed fluorescing, his gray form enveloped in a dimly glowing light. Second, was that he now carried an old photo album. It was bound in worn leather with faint gilt lettering on the front and locked with a tired brass clasp. I looked up into his sallow face and noticed seriousness in his visage. He set the book down with purpose on the floor and opened it. A slight tilt of his head signaled me to join him. His glow illuminated the pages of the album, revealing portraits of our family. Albumen prints and daguerreotypes, dating back to our grandfathers' time, filled each page. Edgar kept turning the pages until he reached his and my portraits, taken just one year past. I looked up and smiled at Edgar, remembering just how still we had to sit in front of the camera. He looked at me and I noticed again the utter darkness where his eyes should have been. His mouth moved to form a sentence, but he did not make a sound. Try as I might, I could not understand what it was he said, but I saw him point down, and I looked where he indicated. He was pointing at his own portrait, again mouthing words I could not comprehend. Then I lost all consciousness.

When I awoke in the attic early the next morning, Edgar was gone. I searched the house for him, and when my parents inquired what I was about, I told them of Edgar's visit. My mother burst into violent tears as my father grimaced. Dismissing my story as delusional grief, they left me to eat breakfast alone. However, I was not put off from my mission, and I continued my search, eventually ending up at the attic door. I had decided that if I could not find Edgar, I would at least find the album, as proof that I had not been imagining things. Sure enough, in my haste to find him, I had overlooked it. The album lay open, right where Edgar had left it. Gazing once more at his portrait, I noticed something clumsily scrawled under it, in what appeared to be dirt. A date: 24th December, 1891. The day my brother had departed this world. I recognized the scrawl; it was Edgar's handwriting. Penned with his dead finger. I picked the album up, and it was then that the weight of all that had happened washed over me: Edgar's death, his return and his sudden departure once more. I wept until my eyes ran dry, muffling my sobs with the cuff of my shirt.

Fifty years since his death, I still think of Edgar. What had he tried to tell me? How can one ever truly pay tribute when someone they love is delivered unto the Kingdom of Heaven before their time? I tried to show my parents the album, but they would not believe me. And who could blame them, for it was a story too fantastical for this world. So I hid the album away. Over the years, I have discovered dates written in my brother's hand under other portraits in that book. The writing seems to appear several days before the subject's passing. It appeared under my mother's portrait days before she succumbed to pneumonia. Likewise, the scrawl forewarned of my father's passing, due to a train derailment. It became clear to me that these dates were death dates. Try as I might, I have not discovered a way to change them. My brother's accuracy is terrifying and final, but I have come to realize that this phenomenon has advantages. Over the years the album has grown, and in all of these years I have never once lost the chance to say goodbye.

However well I live my life, I will always fear the day when I consult the album and discover my brother's scrawl under my portrait. Who will say goodbye to me?

THE SIXPENCE IN THE PUDDING
Callum McSorley

Of course there were stories. All old families had stories. And whether you gave credence to them or not said a lot about your character, so thought Annie Jones, and as head housekeeper for several renowned families in the past, including the Hadleys, the Smith-Westertons, and the Ashburys, she had done her utmost to quash such idle gossip among her staff.

The Idleweathers were no different, and when she first heard the tale related in a conspiratorial whisper by a silly young scullery maid called Marcy, she made her disapproval felt. However, she couldn't resist a shudder whenever she passed the black-veiled portrait on the second floor, as if her body would not obey the stern ethics of her mind.

It was two months prior when Marcy told the story, during the second week of Annie's appointment. Despite the tingle on her neck produced by the covered painting on the wall of the second floor corridor, she had put it almost completely out of her mind until the early afternoon of Christmas Eve. The snow was falling heavily outside, the garden already completely buried under thick sheets, blinding in the winter sun, and lying on the leaden crossbars of the windows.

"Do wrap up well Marcy, it'll be bitter cold out there even with the sun, and the snow will be knee deep by the time you reach London."

"I will do, thank you, ma'am. I've got this good woolen shawl of mine and the warmth of Christmas cheer in my heart." Marcy was visiting her family for Christmas dinner, and in the spirit of the season Annie had let her go a whole day early. The girl was quite giddy with excitement.

"Christmas cheer won't banish pneumonia. Do be careful, girl."

"I will, thank you, ma'am. You be careful too, ma'am."

"Me? Why I shall be perfectly warm and dry here in Idleweather Hall. I assure you I don't plan on doing any gardening today!"

"No, ma'am, I mean you being alone here this Christmas Eve."

138

The small staff had already been dismissed for the holiday and all were traveling back to be with their families on Christmas Day. Marcy, her family living nearest to the Hall, had been the last to go. Annie had no family and would spend Christmas Day waiting on Mr. and Mrs. Idleweather and their two children, Jean and Maisy. She had already begun to prepare the lunch, soaking peeled potatoes and carrots in pots and wrestling the goose into a slightly-too-small baking tray. With the Idleweathers out for Christmas Eve service she would indeed be alone in the Hall until they returned well after midnight.

"What do I have to fear from being alone, except a rare chance of peace and quiet?"

A small flicker of a smile passed over Marcy's face and disappeared. "It's just they say that on Christmas Eve *she* is even more…agitated…than usual."

"They? She? Whoever do you mean, girl?"

Marcy replied with silence and a look that said, *You know exactly who I mean.*

"That's enough nonsense; you'd better be going before I change my mind."

"Sorry, ma'am, I meant no harm, ma'am." Marcy headed out into the snow with her shawl wrapped around her head, the icy wind plucking strands of hair loose from under it. She stopped halfway down the path and turned back to face Annie, as if hesitating. Her face, at first screwed up either with worry or from the reflection of the sun on virgin snow, broke into a wide smile. "Merry Christmas!" she called and carried on out the gate.

Annie watched her disappear down the path towards the train station, a black slash in the snow getting smaller. Soon her small tracks were completely covered again, the landscape around the house once more pure, flat, and featureless.

* * *

With great care Annie tied the twine around the Christmas pudding, ready to go in the pot first thing in the morning. Mrs. Idleweather herself had made the pudding. It was her only venture into the kitchen during the year, and it would not do to ruin the lady's work with clumsiness, even if it was a tough old tooth-breaker of a piece. When Annie finished wrapping the muslin around it and had bound it up she tied the loose end of the string to a wooden spoon and gave it an experimental lift, barely an inch off the counter, to check if it could bear the load.

That's when she heard it: a tinkling of piano keys.

The girls were always messing around on the old thing. Mr. Idleweather would be sure to give them trouble soon for disturbing it. *But the girls aren't home.* The thought jerked Annie's head to attention and the pudding thudded onto the counter (lucky it was sturdy).

She held her breath and strained to hear. Annie was used to the grumbling characters of ancient houses, with their creaks and groans and shifting, crumbling brick. Idleweather Hall shuddered in the wind, its aged shoulders slumping under the weight of snow. But there it was again, the soft trembling strings of piano wire and the crystal clink of ivory keys. Annie breathed deeply to still her heart.

She followed the sound out of the kitchen and into the main hallway, where a grand sweep of stairs led up to a gallery on the second floor with corridors taking off into the north, east, and west wings. She climbed the stairs as the tentative twinkling began to form into a melody. It wasn't only the house that was creaking, decades of service having ground away at Annie's knees. *Didn't deaf old ladies hear music?* she thought. She remembered how Mrs. Bothwell, the mother of Mrs. Hadley—her first appointment as head of staff—had often complained about hearing choirs. "The angels are singing again," she'd say. And she was by no means a mad old bat. Hard of hearing, yes, but her wits were sharp.

Annie began to recognize the tune. It was being played well below tempo, and with a gentle touch at the high end of the scale, but it was definitely *God Rest Ye Merry, Gentlemen.* It got clearer as she headed down the north corridor towards the bedroom, with every step making Annie less convinced that it was just age playing tricks on her. *A trick.* Could it be some sort of joke being made at her expense by one of her own staff? She had definitely upset a few of them with her stern position about telling silly stories, and this would be a clever way to get back at her. But no, she had seen off every member of the staff and there were certainly no returning tracks in the snow. She had seen off the Idleweathers this morning also, the girls wrapped up tight for their day in town. "We shan't be back until late, Ms. Jones," Mr. Idleweather had said, "but do keep the fires burning, it'll be dreadfully drafty in here otherwise."

The black-veiled portrait hung forbidding across from the bedroom door, and Annie felt the familiar tingles on the back of her neck. For the first time, though, her body seemed entirely reluctant to go near it. Underneath the veil was a picture of Mrs. Idleweather—the first Mrs. Idleweather. Across from it was the bedroom that now contained her belongings, the ones Mr. Idleweather could not throw away. These included a beautiful Bechstein pianoforte, now languishing under a dust sheet. The young girls held a certain fascination for the instrument, and again and again braved awful verbal lashings from their parents just to tap away at the keys for a handful of stolen minutes.

Annie now recalled the stories told by the gossiping maids. The Idleweathers were old money, heirs to hidden fortunes of gold. When

Richard Harrow married their only daughter, Iris, he took the distinguished family name. They met with tragedy early on when they lost their first child during labor, and poor Iris died of a broken heart, having never left the bed where she had given birth. The elder Idleweathers followed in the months after, succumbing to illness, and Richard was left alone in the big house. He spent long years in mourning dress before remarrying and having two children, much to the delight of those who knew him and were pained to see him living out a cursed and lonely life. The ghost stories were obvious, sightings common, and every foolish maid misplacing items during dusting was quick to put the blame on the supernatural.

During the time Annie had spent hesitating on the threshold of the bedroom the music had stopped. She could hear the wind in the chimneys and the tick of the antique grandfather clock in the hallway. No music. No Christmas carol.

"Silly girl," she said, admonishing both herself and Marcy, and headed back downstairs at a step quicker than her old bones cared for.

She took a circuitous route through the ground floor rooms to the kitchen, hoping the cheer of the lounge with its ceiling-scraping evergreen and stockings hung over the fireplace would calm her nerves. The presents beneath the tree were beautifully wrapped in printed parchment and tied with silk ribbon. Of all the sights of Christmas—the tree, the decorations, the snow on the grounds—these filled Annie with pure delight. *What lucky little girls Jean and Maisy are,* she thought.

Annie returned to the kitchen in good spirits, humming snippets of *God Rest Ye Merry, Gentlemen*, ridiculous notions of ghosts pushed to the back of her mind. She was lifting the great pudding into the dry cupboard when the thundering sound of piano keys exploded from upstairs—not the mournful jingling of before, but an awful crash of all the keys being mashed down at once. Annie jumped as if jolted by lightning. The pudding flew up in the air and, frozen, she watched it crash down onto the floor. As sturdy as it was, it couldn't survive the fall from such a height, now a heap of sponge and fruit smashed and flattened on the tiles.

* * *

She cursed herself, then she cursed Marcy—that silly girl should have been here helping her with the preparations. The shame of leaving an old woman to lift that damn bowling ball of a cake! She bit her nails and tugged at her hair. She desperately tried to pull the thing back together, but it was crumbled into great chunks all across the kitchen floor, she'd be sweeping up raisins well into the New Year. Among the debris was a silver sixpence—good luck for whoever found it in their slice of pudding and didn't crack a tooth on it. She searched desperately through the larder but

Mrs. Idleweather had used up all the ingredients on this one monstrous confection.

Once the shock had worn off, it wasn't fear of piano-playing ghosts that made tears run down her face. Mr. and Mrs. Idleweather had been so understanding. She'd been desperate for work, and with no reference from the Ashburys...

She kneeled on the floor with her head in her hands, a high wave of despair bearing down on her.

One of the servants' bells began to ring out and panic shot through Annie—*they were home early!* It must have been the weather, the sensible decision being to return before it got any worse than it already was. What would she do? What would she say to the lady? However, when Annie looked up at the rows of black iron bells above the doorway it wasn't the hall bell, or the lounge bell, or even the dining room bell. The string on that particular bell which was ringing led upstairs to the bedroom in the north corridor. The bedroom across from the black-veiled portrait. The late Iris Idleweather's bedroom.

The bells usually struck Annie with a sense of irritability and duty, years of conditioning making her back snap to attention whenever their impatient clamoring disturbed her quarters. This time it filled her with a dread she had never experienced before, and she rose unsteadily to her feet.

As suddenly as the ringing started it stopped, and again she was left to the whistling of the wind and the ticking of the grandfather clock which traveled through every chamber of the Hall like a heartbeat.

In tentative steps she left the kitchen and entered the main hall. As she neared the bottom of the staircase it struck her how dark it was, the former airy brightness of the sun and gleaming snow no longer spilling into the entranceway through the high windows, replaced now by murky shadow. The winter sun—brilliant but cold—had set while she'd been sobbing on the kitchen floor.

Dear God! She hadn't lit the lamps. The bottom of the drive outside was almost completely invisible from the porch. In all the drama, the tearing back and forth from panic to despair, she'd forgotten another task. First the pudding, now this. How would the Idleweathers ever find their way back from the station without the lamps to guide them? "Where would the Wise Men be without the star over the stable in Bethlehem?" She berated and chastised herself as she scrambled around getting her coat and boots, the piano and the ringing bell forgotten again.

She got a shock from the cold as it bit at her exposed face, and a further shock from the depth her boot plunged into the snow, sinking almost up to her knee.

She left the front door open behind her, the electric light from the hall casting a short path onto the garden, beyond which she had only the sputtering flame of a spirit-burning candle to guide her. The snow was still falling, though now that she was out in it, she no longer admired its beauty. Oaths were carried away by the wind.

She struggled her way to the front gate through flurries of snow which tumbled down on her in directionless spirals, the wind blowing every which way. The lanterns sat atop the mercifully low wall, one on either side of the spiked iron railings of the gate. They lit without much trouble, even with the wind, and threw their inviting orange glow over the garden and down the country road towards the station.

Maybe there really was some attractive magic in those gently lapping flames, Annie thought later, once she'd gotten over the surprise of the figure emerging from the night into soft haze of the lanterns.

"I'm so sorry to alarm you," the woman said, "but would you do me the greatest courtesy this Christmas Eve and let me take rest here for a moment?" The face wrapped in the shawl was young. Her petite nose and full mouth were commonly pretty, but her eyes gave her face a startling beauty, one that would be undamaged by age or experience. With a strand of hair hanging loose from under the shawl, Annie had almost taken her to be Marcy until the woman spoke. "I will not stay long, I promise," the stranger continued, "I just need a little break from the cold. Just a minute."

Annie's first instinct would have been to turn her away, but with mention of the season of giving and her recent thoughts of the kings crossing the desert to see the baby Christ—not to mention her now ardent desire not to be alone in the house—made her reply, "Well come on then, dear, if it's just for a minute."

As they approached the light of the entrance hall Annie noticed that the young woman's hunched posture wasn't just an attempt to shield herself from the wind and snowfall, but was also due to a large knapsack she carried on her back.

Annie led her through to the kitchen. It was still early, only just past dinner time, so it would still be long before the Idleweathers returned (barring an early appearance due to the weather), yet having the stranger in the house still made Annie uneasy. What made her more nervous still was the way in which the young woman dropped down her bag, threw off her hood and coat, and took up a seat by the kitchen counter, making herself comfortably at home before being asked.

"Would you like some tea, dear? Get the heat back in you?"

"Yes, please, ma'am. Very kind, thank you." Those wonderful eyes surveyed the kitchen, her gaze skirting like fingertips over the counter, the cooker, the blackened pots, the servants' bells, and the small gas fire where Annie was boiling the kettle. They alighted on the mess on the floor (Annie had yet to clean up properly, having first been disturbed by the ghostly bells, then the lamps, then this stranger conjured from the dark) where the destroyed Christmas pudding lay in a heap among the open muslin cloth and loose twine.

"If I may ask, where is it you're heading to in this weather on Christmas Eve?" Annie said, handing over a steaming cup.

The stranger's eyes didn't leave the floor and, as if she hadn't even heard Annie speak, she asked, "Whatever has happened here?" Her tone was not admonishing but both curious and even a little amused.

A flush of anger passed through Annie but quickly became the tremor of dismay from earlier. *What would she do?*

"A little accident is all," Annie said, doing her best to calm herself and master her emotions. "Clumsiness on my part, I'm afraid."

"Gosh, how dreadful. I'm very sorry for you, ma'am. What will the lord and lady of the house say when they find out they have no Christmas pudding on Christmas Day?" There was definite laughter in those stunning eyes, and just a hint of it playing on her lips.

Who is this awful young wretch? Annie thought in another quick snap of anger. "I'll simply apologize. It was an accident, after all, and Mr. and Mrs. Idleweather are gracious people—"

"They won't be upset?" The unrelenting gaze of her eyes was now focused on Annie, boring into her.

"Well, I'd say they'll maybe be a trifle put out, and more than a little irritated at my clumsiness, but..."

"If I were you, I'd be in fits of panic just now."

It was as if she were looking right into Annie's mind and reading her thoughts. Indeed, worry was beginning to overtake any hospitable feelings Annie had left towards the girl, it was like poison in her sick stomach, and she almost reached out to strike her. She restrained the urge and said, a little more sharply than intended, "Well, I'm not some foolish young maid driven to hysterics by a little crumbled cake, or silly noises in the night for that matter."

"Silly noises..." the girl repeated under her breath, tilting her head to get a different view of Annie, who was feeling thoroughly exposed and unable to move or speak. Even the wind outside was silenced. Annie held her gaze, unable to look away. "I think I can help you," the girl said, finally looking away, to Annie's relief. She opened the knapsack at her feet and began to rummage around in it. She was up almost to her shoulders in the sack when she shouted, "Aha!" and came back up like a swimmer from water. She held out a round parcel, wrapped in muslin, tied with twine.

"Oh, Good Lord, no, I couldn't—"

"It's no big thing, really, and you've been so...*kind* to me, letting me escape the cold."

"But don't you need it?"

"I think you need it more. Come on, you can consider it payment for the tea."

The young woman held out the Christmas pudding in front of her in two arms. It was smaller than Mrs. Idleweathers, *but if I serve it already in portions she won't know*, Annie caught herself thinking.

"No, it's too kind; it's altogether too much—"

"Please, ma'am, please take it. I'd hate for such a kind woman such as yourself to be in trouble. There aren't many who'd go out of their way to help a stranger."

No, Annie thought, *there weren't*. After being dismissed without reference by the Ashburys, the Idleweathers had taken a chance on hiring Annie. Luckily for her it was at a busy time for the family, and they were desperate, their head of staff having fallen suddenly ill and died. The chances of her finding another job so easily were slim. She'd only spent a fortnight in the poorhouse but it was enough to make her vow never to return. Better to die.

"Thank you, thank you so much," Annie said, taking the pudding, tears on her cheeks again. "So kind, you're like Father Christmas himself!"

The stranger let out a musical laugh. "Call me 'Mother Christmas', rather!" With that she tied up her knapsack, swallowed the remainder of her tea, then slung the sack up onto her shoulder. "Ho! Ho! Ho!"

Annie was swirling and giddy with a rush of compassion and relief, and guilt at her ill thoughts towards the woman. *What a beautiful young woman!* she thought.

The woman left through the service entrance and shouted "Merry Christmas!" as she headed into the night.

"Merry Christmas!" Annie cried back. "Wait!" Annie hadn't even asked the kind young woman's name, and here she was letting her walk out into a snowstorm. *For shame!* "Where are you going?"

"Home for Christmas!" she called over her shoulder, then without another backwards glance was gone, hidden under the veil of darkness. The snow soon covered her prints and all trace of her disappeared except for the pudding in the kitchen.

Annie tidied up the mess in the kitchen, tucking the silver sixpence into the pocket of her apron. She was fearful to be alone again but was ashamed to admit to herself that she was also relieved to be free of the stranger's penetrating gaze. The night passed without any more haunting piano melodies, ringing bells, or visitors, and the Idleweathers returned from church just after one o'clock in the early morning of Christmas Day.

* * *

Despite their late night, Jean and Maisy were up early and could be heard charging all over the house, squealing in fits of excitement. Annie had been up even earlier to get the goose in the oven and the pudding in the pot—the sight of it struck a chord of nervous tension in her but the little girls' gay laughter and merriment helped push it to the back of her mind.

She watched them tear into their presents, and the whirl of colorful ribbon and delicate parchment paper filled her with joy, so much so that she wished dearly to be among them, rather than an intruder in the corner of the room, waiting to pour tea, coffee, hot chocolate, and sherry.

The living room was lavishly decorated for the season and the fir tree a spectacular sight to behold. With the girls sitting among torn shreds of wrapping paper, bursting with excitement over new toys and chocolate treats, it was a picture perfect Christmas card scene.

The Idleweathers sat down to lunch around one and gobbled their way through goose, roast potatoes, mashed potatoes, honey-soaked carrots, Brussels sprouts fried in pork dripping, lashings of rich, thick gravy, and balls of sage and cranberry stuffing.

For Annie, moving the food, plates, crockery, glasses, and cutlery in and out from the kitchen to the dining room by herself, it was all over in a flash and with some trepidation it was time to serve the cake. She soaked it in sherry and lit it, watching the blue flame lick the surface of the steamed pudding before burning out. She then sliced it up on a serving plate and wheeled it through to the dining room on a trolley.

"Oh, Ms. Jones, you've cut up my pudding?" remarked Mrs. Idleweather.

"Yes, ma'am, are you not wanting it right away?"

"It's not that, Ms. Jones, it's that usually we put the pudding on the table and light it for everyone to see. I thought you understood that?"

"I'm dreadfully sorry, ma'am, please accept my apologies, it must have slipped my mind."

Mrs. Idleweather fixed her with a glare. "Please listen carefully to my instructions in future, Ms. Jones. At least we can still enjoy the taste of it if not the spectacle."

"My sincere apologies again, ma'am."

Mrs. Idleweather dismissed her with a look, and Annie placed a plate of steaming pudding in front of each of the diners. As she suspected, Mrs. Idleweather didn't even realize it was not her cake they were eating and warmly accepted the doting compliments of her husband and children, with Maisy saying it was best Christmas pudding Mummy had ever made, and Jean one-upping her by stating it was the best cake she'd ever eaten, full stop.

Mrs. Idleweather basked in their admiration until she bit down on something hard. "Oh, I must be the lucky one this year," she said, fishing into her mouth for the coin, but what she drew out wasn't a silver sixpence at all. "What...? What on earth is this? Richard—" Her eyes began to widen, confusion turning to understanding and fear. In her hand she held a thick, gold ingot, the stamps on its faces worn nearly smooth. "Richard, how did—Richard? Richard!"

Mr. Idleweather was gagging and clawing at the collar of his shirt.

"Oh, Mr. Idleweather, do you need some water?" Annie asked.

He stood up, his chair tipping backwards onto the floor and, still tearing at his neck and chest with his fingers, wretched onto the table, a torrent of half-digested goose and potato and gravy and stuffing pouring out of him onto the white linen tablecloth and the remainder of his Christmas pudding. Still being violently sick he fell to the floor. Annie and Mrs. Idleweather were and up and moving towards him, but before his wife could cry out she too began to vomit, her stomach aching and groaning and erupting. The girls screamed for their parents before they too hit the floor, overtaken by the sudden illness that had ripped through the Idleweather family. Annie fell back against the wall and slid down until she was sitting, curled up, her head in her hands and sobs racking her body, unable to look upon the horror in front of her, the twitching, gurning bodies…

* * *

Annie's eyes were still shut tight. The ringing bell had been going on for a long time, but it was only now that Annie began to register it, piercing the bubble of silence that lay over the room and the dead bodies on the floor. They were undoubtedly dead. No doctor would be needed to tell Annie that.

In a daze, she scraped herself off the floor and wandered through to the kitchen where, inevitably, it seemed, the servants' bell for the bedroom in the north corridor of the second floor was ringing. She took the stairs slowly, unhurried. The incident had bled all emotion out of her, she was numb with shock, and she moved towards the bedroom without dread of what she would find.

The door to Iris Idleweather's bedroom was open and, with only a cursory glance at the black-veiled portrait on the wall opposite, Annie stepped inside. The room was sheeted—wardrobes, bureaus, a bed, the piano, all supporting a fine film of dust, even more of it floating in the air, caught in the light of the winter sun that sliced through the gaps in the curtains. On the floor in the center of the room was a large present, wrapped in paper printed with a pattern of Christmas trees, green silk ribbon tied in a bow on top. Annie kneeled and ran her fingers over the smooth, expensive wrapping paper. The tag read: "To Annie Jones xxx".

Annie pulled carefully at the loose tails of the ribbon, untying the bow. Part of her wanted to tear into like the children, but she'd never received a gift so beautifully parceled, and it seemed a shame to destroy the delicate wrapping. Inside was a wooden chest, ornately carved and varnished to a dull shine. She lifted the lid and the glow from inside filled the room—a treasure trove of gold ingots, their markings nearly smooth but still every bit as bright as the sun.

She heard a sound like curtain runners being drawn, and she turned to the open door. On the opposite wall the black veil over the portrait was being drawn aside, and the face of a young woman looked out at her. A woman with a petite nose and full lips—commonly pretty—and a pair of the most stunning, absorbing eyes Annie had ever seen: Mother Christmas.

* * *

The square was alive with revelers and grill smoke, the wonderful smells of hot mulled wine—cinnamon, cloves, and vinegar—and sweet roasted chestnuts filled the air and made Annie light-headed. A train car, every compartment empty, had carried her for the short trip to London, where the streets were bustling with merry-makers and carolers and families doing the rounds or going to and from church services. The sound of church bells themselves were beautiful music and fitting accompaniment to the groups of singers. She caught a snippet of song as she passed by: *"Tidings of comfort and joy! Comfort and joy! Oh..."* Also going door to door were charity collectors—London's many wealthy businessmen being in a somewhat more generous mood this year after having Mr. Dickens's *Christmas Carol* unleashed upon them—and Annie meant to slip a couple of gold coins into their buckets once she had got herself something to eat and drink, having missed dinner entirely while serving others. The gold coins were piled in the traveling bag on her shoulders, hidden under a small selection of modest dresses she had packed. She let her nose guide her and gravitated towards the grills and their perfumed smoke.

"Hello, ma'am, how nice to see you! Merry Christmas!"

Annie spun round to find Marcy, her thick woolen shawl wrapped around her neck and head.

"Oh, hello dear...Merry Christmas to you, too."

"I never expected to see you here, ma'am, I thought you were looking after the lord and lady today?"

"Are you here with your family?"

"No, they're back at the house. I stepped out for some fresh air—"

"And have you had a nice day, dear?"

"Yes, ma'am, lovely thank you, it has been wonderful."

"Good, dear, that's good. Me too. Would you care for some mulled wine?"

NOCEBO
E.W. Farnsworth

Winston Featherwell hated the Christmas season. He was repulsed by the commercialism, the fake jollity, and the vapid displays of bows, presents, and evergreens. When others wished him, "Merry Christmas," it was all he could do to refrain from replying, "Bah, humbug!" It did not help that he lived in Kensington near the park. Carolers haunted his neighborhood knocking on doors and singing from sundown until ten o'clock at night each of the twelve days. In the run-up to the season, he braced himself. During the critical days, he did a lot of drinking. After the New Year's Day festivities, it took him almost a week to settle back into his curmudgeonly routine. This Christmas was going to be no exception to his rule.

Sondra Islington took Featherwell to task for kvetching about the holiday. She was, in his view, inordinately cheerful, one of those born with the "happy gene." She smiled at everyone whether she knew him or not. During the Christmas season, she burst in on those who hid their souls under leaden bushels with a glee that, she thought, would raise the dead. If there was an opposite of Featherwell, Islington was the operational prototype. Attracted to Featherwell like a magnet, she decided to make him happy this Christmas in spite of him. She made it a protracted campaign. Her plan might not have stood a chance of success except she had the same shift as he on the same floor of the Druid's Curse department store two blocks from Harrods.

Druid's was an unlikely venue for Christmas displays. It was situated in a venerable, dreary stone building with expressive gargoyles looming from each level above the first floor. Rumor had it that Druid's was actually under a curse—hence the full name Druid's Curse. One Christmas Eve a grisly murder had been committed on the top floor of the building. The ghost of the victim haunted the building, complaining it would remain excluded from the afterlife until the murderers were found and punished. Many employees at Druid's had strong opinions about the ghost. Only high

149

wages and bonuses, as well as job scarcity, kept them on the job. Throughout all of London in the 1830s life was hard and meaningful jobs required references. From the eligible maiden's point of view, the vetting was an advantage. Islington had no fear that Featherwell was a truly evil man because he had passed muster in the hiring process. He dressed as a gentleman should. He was distantly polite. Featherwell's only problem was his constant whining around Christmastime.

At Druid's, the change of tone in decor occurred on December 8th. Autumnal displays with their berries were taken down in a single night and boxed. Then from the top floor the Christmas things were fetched, and evergreens were set up to transform the dreary interior into a fairyland of highly decorated Christmas trees and wreaths. Ironically, Featherwell and Islington were charged to distribute the Christmas decorations to every floor. They oversaw the staff unpacking and setting out the ornaments and displays.

Under his breath Featherwell huffed out, "Humbug," while each time Islington answered, "Merry Christmas to you, too!" in her sweetest voice. He knew she was baiting him, so he ignored her. She was emboldened by his detachment.

Standing in front of him, like a human-sized egg cup with a broad skirt below and an enormous bust above her crossed arms, red-cheeked, beady-eyed Islington asked, "Mr. Featherwell, do you have a family to share the Christmas season with you?"

The mustached man, standing on tiptoe in his three-piece suit with cravat and pin, sighed in exasperation and pulled at the two tufts of hair that stood out on either side of his round head. "No, Miss Islington, I do not. And if I did have a family remaining, I wouldn't celebrate Christmas with them. Do you have to be so confoundedly cheerful at the prospect?"

She was happy to have any response at all from the misanthrope. "It's the season of joy for the whole world!"

He frowned. "Miss Islington, are you aware of what happened in this very storage closet where we're sorting out the flighty baubles of the season?"

"Mr. Featherwell, whatever do you mean?" She eyed him warily and rocked back, searching his brown eyes for any sign of human sympathy.

He shook his head. As if he was reluctant to impart an evil vision, he stated, "I mean a man was not only brutally killed in this place, but his disembowelment left his intestines strung like the decorations of a Christmas tree on hooks the murderer affixed to the walls. The killer was never found. The ghost haunts the place even now." As he said this, Featherwell lifted festoons out of a box and weighted them between his extended hands as an example of how the guts had been hung from point to point with the entrails hanging down between the points.

She nodded, tears forming in her eyes. "I've heard the sad, gruesome stories." Then she had an inspiration and asked him, "Have you actually seen the ghost?"

"I have, indeed, seen the ghost—in fact, more than once. I saw it last Christmas in this very room." His eyes scanned the large floor as if looking for a sign of the ghost. Then to add a vivid proof of what he had seen, he said, "It looks like a white flame the size of a man. When it speaks, it glows." His hands moved inward and outward in front of him as if representing the resonance of the glow.

"The way you say it, a chill runs up my spine. What did the ghost say?"

"First it moaned as if it was suffering great pain. Then it said it was trapped in this building until its murderers had been found and punished. The Bobbies long ago abandoned the heinous case as unsolvable, so the ghost will never be freed, I suppose."

"It must be horrible for the ghost to know it'll never be able to get on with things until others do what can't be done. All the same, we can't help. So we might as well be cheerful about what we're doing." She lifted a box of blue and silver ornaments and carried them to the lift. He carried a large box of festoons in her wake. Down they descended to the ground floor so the staff could integrate the decorations into their growing displays arranged tastefully throughout the space.

When the two returned to the top floor, they searched for the box of candles. Featherstone replaced the white working candles on the floor with huge red decorative candles. Islington looked on approvingly. "That's the spirit."

Featherstone looked doubtful. "See how the red glows and casts gules of red like blood? What can be cheerful about that?"

She shook her head. "Mr. Featherwell, it happens I brought a small bottle of cheer. Maybe a drink will lift your soul from its doldrums." She uncorked and took a swig from her bottle. She handed it to him, and he drank too.

"We'd best be careful not to drink too much, Miss. Mr. Oldface will sack us, to be sure, if he catches us drinking on the job. I, for one, would not like to lose my job during the Christmas season." He frowned.

Islington blushed and put the bottle back under her skirt. She had another idea and said, "Mr. Featherwell, why are you always so glum? We're helping remake this store from a dour and hopeless venue into a bright and cheerful customer haven."

He hesitated, considering how to answer her highly personal question. "If you must know, it's because I've known such tragedy that my heart can't rejoice as yours evidently does without great effort."

"Will you tell me about your troubles?" She leaned towards him as she sorted through a chest of nutcrackers of all sizes. She smiled a crooked smile and cocked her head to indicate she would need help lifting the chest. "Take your time and think about it. We've got a lot yet to take down to the floors. Here, pick up the other end of the chest. Let's move it to the elevator."

He dutifully did as she requested. They lugged the chest to the elevator. Then he walked back to fetch the box of candles. They descended to the first floor and offloaded the containers so the staff could use their contents. As they ascended in the elevator again, Featherwell began to tell Islington his story.

"Since you asked, I lost my parents when I was only three. My two siblings and I became wards of the state. As orphans we were starved and beaten for no reason. The worst season at the orphanage was winter. We nearly froze to death. Christmas was our time of want and acrimony. We received no presents. There was no cheer. We stood outside in the cold in rags to beg for alms. When we returned empty handed as we often did, we were beaten and sent to bed without supper. My sister lasted two years and died from consumption. My elder brother fell down the stairs and broke both his legs. He's now a hopeless cripple and beggar in Highgate. I was the luckiest of the three. I graduated from the work house, and here you see me." He extended his arms as if to say, *Behold!*

They heard a loud moan. Islington jumped and looked around.

He told her, "That will be the ghost of Abraham Cohen, the murdered man. He's likely to appear anytime. Let's hurry and get the last of the trimmings down to the other levels." She took stock of what they still had to transport. She carried the boxes to the elevator one by one. He followed behind her doing the same. When the elevator was full, the ghost appeared before them.

As Featherwell foretold, the ghost was like a large white specter or flame as tall as a man.

"You who disturb my rest, why do you come?"

Though she was shivering from fright at the apparition, Islington screwed up her courage and replied in a quavering voice, "We've come for the Christmas decorations. We do that every year." The ghost might not have heard her.

In a deep voice, the spirit said, "I was killed in this very room on Christmas Eve. I came up the elevator and discovered creatures waiting for me as I stepped out. They had come to feast on my body, but they didn't care I was still alive while they parsed and ate the gobbets. They took delight in decorating this room with my innards. Only when I saw their cruel parody of Christmas did I faint and expire. Now I'm bound here forever or until my murderers are discovered and punished." The figure moaned frightfully as if in great pain.

"Can you describe the creatures that killed you?" Featherwell asked the ghost.

"They're in stone form along the sides of this building on the outside facing the street. They climbed the exterior walls and came down the chimney over there."

The ghost extended one arm towards the fireplace. It continued, "There was no resisting them."

"As humans did not kill you, how do you think your murderers can be overcome and punished?" Islington asked this sensible question.

The ghost let out a cry of pitiable anguish that pierced her to the soul.

The ghost hesitated, and then said, "If on Christmas Eve two came to this place and confronted the gargoyles, they might be overcome. They are the very embodiment of evil. As I was not a perfect man, I was easy prey for them. One of the two who come against them must be without blame. The other must know how to deal with weapons. With a diversion, the beasts will be defeated. Make no mistake, though, they must be killed no matter what forms they take when you attack them."

Featherwell shook his head. "If we should do as you wish, would you then be free to leave this place?"

"Yes, I would. Then I could go to Sheol where I belong. Will you do this great favor for me?" The ghost said this with such longing, Islington could not resist.

"I'll come, but who among us is blameless?" She wondered how to cut the Gordian knot of the ghost's conditions.

The ghost answered her at once in his deep voice, "The two of you are the perfect couple to achieve what must be done. He is blameless, though a complainer. You are ruthless in the face of evil and will destroy the monsters."

Featherwell laughed. "I blameless? I don't think so. I've thought evil thoughts. I've alienated myself from others. I rarely do good deeds. I spoil others' fun."

The ghost seemed to nod. "Yet you have never intentionally done anyone wrong. You are without sin. You'll do perfectly when the monsters come."

Now Islington stepped forward to object, "I'm not a killer by nature or training."

The ghost shook its head. "Yet you hate evil in your heart. You have it in you to destroy evil beings if you decide you must do it."

Featherwell was about to ask the ghost practical questions, but the apparition disappeared. Just before it vanished entirely, it said, "Avenge me. Set me free."

Their hair standing on end, Featherwell and Islington descended to distribute the remaining boxes to the second and third floors. They spent the rest of the evening orchestrating the work of the Druid's staff, going up and down the floors to be sure that everything was in order for tomorrow's opening. After their last inspection, which started on the ground floor and proceeded level by level until they reached the top floor, Islington brought out her bottle again. She took a drink and handed the bottle to Featherwell. He took a swig and passed it back to her. She followed him in doing the same, before she corked the bottle and put it back under her dress.

Islington said, "We've completed our proximate task. The store is ready for our customers to come first thing tomorrow morning. Now we have to shift our focus to our next task—freeing the ghost of Abraham Cohen."

At the mention of the slain man's name, the ghost moaned horribly. Islington put out the candles, except for ones she and Featherwell were carrying. They took the elevator to the first floor and shut up the building for the night, careful to lock the chain on the exterior door. Afterward, they stood on the street looking up the building. There were the gargoyles hanging over them and looking down with menacing looks. Featherwell thought he saw gleams of hatred in those stone figures' eyes.

He volunteered, "Miss Islington, permit me to escort you home."

She curtsied, but demurred, "It's not far, Mr. Featherwell. I can manage. I'll be all right. Good night, then. I'll see you at work tomorrow." With that she strode off determinedly into the darkness. He shrugged and walked in the opposite direction toward his apartment.

That night Featherwell had nightmares about the meeting the ghost. He envisioned the gargoyles coming to life and crawling up the sides of Druid's to the roof, then down the chimney. He saw them attack, eat, and kill a human. He awakened in a cold sweat at the thought of a human's guts festooned against the walls of the top floor. He was confused, because in his dream the guts were his own.

Islington also had nightmares about the meeting with the ghost. She saw the evil that the gargoyles represented. They came at her like the hideous, threatening spirits that came to St. Augustine in the desert. They surrounded her as if to torment and then devour her alive. She awakened abruptly in terror with her sheet in her hand as if it were a knife. She knew at that moment she could kill the evil figures with the right weapon.

After work the next day Featherwell and Islington went to a small restaurant for tea and crumpets to compare notes. They shared what they had seen in their nightmares and agreed they could do what was required to free the ghost from his snare. She told him she needed the right weapon. He volunteered his own long knife for the purpose, as he had honed it to the sharpest edge. He told her he would bring the weapon to work the next day so she could hide it until Christmas Eve.

Featherwell had an inspiration. "Miss Islington, it's high time the gargoyles were removed from Druid's. We still have two weeks before Christmas Eve. Why don't we ask Mr. Oldface to remove them as part of our Christmas theme?"

She highly approved of his suggestion. The two approached the store manager Mr. Oldface about the matter. He had a strong opinion on the matter.

"Druid's could not possibly remove the gargoyles. They are our heritage. They set us apart from places like Harrods. Our customers look forward to coming where the gargoyles are. We've been through fifty Christmases with them. I look forward to our having another fifty ahead. So the answer is categorically, no. I've been meaning to invite you to my annual Christmas party in my home. It will be three days before Christmas. I hope you'll come. A Yule Log will burn. We'll drink punch and tell stories. Fruitcake and plum pudding with whipped cream will be served."

The two employees could not refuse to attend their boss's party. Islington saw it as an opportunity to get close to Featherwell in a convivial setting. He saw it as an opportunity to drink and keep his job by doing what his employer wanted.

The night of the party was icy and snowy. Featherwell wore his greatcoat, hat, and scarf. He stumbled and fell four times walking to Mr. Oldface's home, a free standing structure off the park. Islington had already arrived. She came to greet him at the door, grabbing his arm and helping him take off his winter outer clothing. She handed him a glass of hot rum toddy and escorted him around the room to meet the others. Mrs. Oldface, an enormous woman with fierce eyes and small, grasping hands, handed each a plate with fruitcake and plum pudding slices, covered with whipped cream. They ate and drank by the fireplace where the Yule Log burned.

Over the fireplace was a large engraving of Druid's Curse on the day of the building's completion. Mr. Oldface, seeing the couple was staring at the artwork, walked over to tell them its story. He made a point of the gargoyles, which had been carved by his uncle, a master stonemason. The engraving had been done by his father, who also designed and built the structure.

"Do you understand why we cannot remove the gargoyles?"

Miss Islington nodded and seized the chance to ask, "Where did the name Druid's Curse come from?"

Oldface squinted for a moment. Then he shifted his footing and said, "On my mother's side I'm Welsh, like Henry V. My ancestors were poets and priests. You may remember the name Owen Glendower from the history books. Well, the English never conquered the Welsh. The reason for that was the druid's curse that all attempts at conquest would fail. When my father built the structure, he wanted it to have the same protection as the Welsh territory. Hence the name. So far, it's worked like a charm. I hope you'll excuse me now. I've got to make the rounds of my other guests."

Mr. Oldface bobbed off with arms open wide to hug and kiss his guests by ones and twos. Servants came to refill everyone's glass and collect their dessert plates. An old man, bowed over a cane, came to the fireplace with a twinkle in his eye.

"I'm the designer, builder, and engraver. I see you've been admiring my engraving. Ask me anything about the building. Anything at all."

Featherwell asked, "Where did you find the gargoyle designs you integrated into the building?"

"Those are taken from models on churches in the Palatinate, done after the Battle of White Mountain as the Catholics' way of fending off the Protestants whom they'd defeated. They're magical and linked to the curse in the title of the building." The old man looked at the gargoyles with a proprietary air. "Each gargoyle is unique. Somewhere I've got the sketches I did for those. If you'd like to see them, I can arrange it."

Islington asked, "Do you know about the death of Abraham Cohen on the top floor of your building and his ghost?"

The old man looked up at his inquisitor to gauge where she was going with her question. He nodded and said, "Old Abraham Cohen was my rival for ownership of the land on which the building sits. He was immensely wealthy and came from Prague originally, where his family is buried in the Jewish burial ground with headstones going every which way in the Pale. Cohen was not a very nice person. He threatened me and my family on many occasions. He initiated lawsuits to seize my property. On the night he was murdered, he was plotting to do something—I don't know what. Perhaps he planned to burn the building to the ground. So on Christmas Eve he was torn apart horribly. The murderer or murderers were never found. I've always thought his death was a vengeance for his evil ways."

"Have you encountered his ghost?" she continued.

"I've heard about the old man's ghost. I've not been on the top floor where it's supposed to reside. I don't want to speculate about it. I've got to run along now. Another glass of rum, and they'll have to wheel me home. Enjoy the rest of the party. And thank you for being part of the Druid's Curse family."

The old man hobbled along on his cane towards the drinks table and asked for another rum toddy. He laughed when he spoke with Mrs. Oldface, but she got a sour look. At her next opportunity, she came to the fireplace to talk with Miss Islington.

"My father-in-law told me you were interested in the gargoyles and the ghost of Abraham Cohen. I thought I'd let you know that the police investigated the unfortunate murder thoroughly, but found no suspects. Further, the myth of the ghost is pure rubbish, the invention of fertile minds with too little work to do. If you intend to remain with Druid's Curse, you'd best not worry yourself about folktales. Our business is selling merchandise, not ghost stories." The woman's hard eyes bore into

Islington's until the latter looked away.

Featherwell asked, "Miss Islington, shall we have one last drink and depart? While I walk you home through the weather, we should discuss what we've learned tonight."

She agreed to have a rhyton of rum. Then the two circulated to say their goodnights. They lingered for a moment with Mr. Oldface, the son, to thank him for his hospitality. Then they wrapped themselves in their thick outer garments and braved the elements.

With snow and sleet falling, she held his arm for balance as they half walked and half skated through the cobblestone streets. They were feeling warm from the liquor, but their cheeks were red as cherries. She was delighted his spirits seemed to be better than she had ever seen. She was therefore surprised at what he had to say. It was not cheery in the least.

"The plot, Miss Islington, thickens. I fear our ghost may be playing tricks on us on the one side. The Oldface family is playing another form of tricks on the other. We have tonight discovered a clear motive for murder, but humans had the motive, not gargoyles."

She mused on this observation. Then she shook her head. "Yet the gargoyles were the murderers in the ghost's account and both our dreams."

"I've been brooding on the look in Mr. Oldface's father's eyes. He clearly looked like a man who had bested his opponent. He showed no remorse for Cohen's death. Further, the way his daughter in law scurried up to us when she learned about our interest, is eloquent of both sin and defensiveness to cover it up. She has no interest in reopening an old, cold case. In fact, she actually threatened you about pursuing your line of investigation further."

Islington laughed. "Do I detect under your dour exterior, a mind of ratiocination like the American writer Edgar Allen Poe?"

"I'm afraid you've lost me, Miss Islington." As if to illustrate this, he slipped and fell on his posterior. He quickly recovered and took her arm again, being careful to keep his balance as they traversed an icy patch.

"Mr. Featherwell, do go on with your reasoning. Where does our new knowledge lead us?"

"Miss Islington, I suspect the ghost is setting a trap not only for us, but for the Oldface family."

She stopped for a moment to consider this possibility. "I understand what you're saying, but I need to know what it means. In two nights we're likely to be on the top floor of Druid's Curse. How does your theory impact our intentions?"

Featherwell took off his gloves and shook out his handkerchief. He blew a loud honk of his nose and wiped his face.

"I think we might be well advised to invite a Bobby to join us on the top floor at midnight on Christmas Eve. Do you think we can arrange that?"

"All we'll need is five quid and my bottle of liquor." Her eyes were wide, and her smile went from ear to ear. "Mr. Featherwell, you are a schemer. I catch your drift and agree we shouldn't get caught in a snare not meant for us."

Featherwell left Miss Islington at her door. When she unlocked it, he tipped his hat and began his slow way home. The weather was worsening, but the sleet had turned to fluffy snow. When he fell repeatedly, the snow cushioned his falls.

That night he had different dreams than he had before. He envisioned Mrs. Oldface butchering Cohen and cutting out his tripes. The glint in her eye showed him a murderess. He had no proof, but in his heart he was convicted. He formed a plan using the policeman. Though he was not yet in the proper Christmas spirit, Featherwell was deflected from his "Bah, Humbug" mentality because he was chasing a mystery. The excitement of the chase trumped his desire to belittle the season. Mentally, he was back in the orphanage looking for a way to survive against the odds.

Druid's Curse did a landmark Christmas business the next day. Merchandise flew off the shelves, giving the store its best seasonal performance in memory. Featherwell and Islington worked so hard wrapping gifts and making change that they were exhausted by the time they arrived at the restaurant for tea and conversation.

"I've formed a new idea. Our friend the Bobby is critical in my plan. I want to fashion a hiding place for him on the top floor. He must be able to see and hear what happens. At just the right moment, he must come forth and do what he thinks necessary. My plan also involves your telling Mr. Oldface that you and I will meet on the top floor at precisely midnight on Christmas Eve. Tell him we are superstitious. Tell him anything. But be sure he knows we'll be there then."

"Your eyes are glittering with excitement, Mr. Featherwell." She was intrigued. "I'll do as you ask. Am I still to play my role with the knife?"

"Hide the knife where you hide your bottle. You'll have to judge whether you need to reveal the one or the other." He arched his brow and shrugged.

"I take it you don't know what's really going to happen."

"That's right. We'll be feeling our way through the night's action. If we must fight gargoyles, so be it. I think, however, we'll be combating humans."

Islington did as she was told. Mr. Oldface at first objected to the idea. Then he abruptly changed his mind. His only caveat was for the couple to lock up after they had accomplished their aim. From the way he leered when he said this, she thought he must have decided a tryst was being planned under the guise of a ghost hunt.

Since there was nothing left except to design the Bobby's hide,

Featherwell went to work early enough on Christmas Eve to be the first on the elevator to the top floor. He created the hide for the Bobby out of available parts. It would, he thought, be a little cramped, but it would serve the purpose. When he took the elevator to the first floor, he buried himself in the last minute rush, keeping an eye on Mr. Oldface when he could.

At the close of business, much remained for the staff to accomplish. It was eight o'clock before Mr. Oldface told everyone to go home and have a great Christmas Eve and Christmas Day as well. Featherwell and Islington disappeared upstairs while the floors cleared and the staff departed. Mr. Oldface disappeared as well. Finally, they thought they were alone in the building; they awaited the arrival of their Bobby.

Officer Hound arrived at precisely ten o'clock, ready for action. A young bachelor who needed the five quid for a last minute gift for his girlfriend Sarah, Hound was delighted to be given a bottle of rum and ensconced in the hide on the top floor. Featherwell heard the man chuckle as he tippled behind the arras that had been created for him. Featherwell and Islington, with a bottle of their own, sat on a couple of old steamer trunks to wait for the witching hour.

At a quarter to twelve o'clock, a loud moaning filled the space. The apparition appeared. It came toward the place where the couple was seated and stood five paces away.

In a deep voice the ghost asked, "Have you come to right the wrong done against me when I lived?"

Featherwell stood and asked the ghost, "Is it true you threatened the Oldface family and tried to take their property away?"

The ghost stood silent while it considered what had been said. "The property was mine. The Oldface family stole it from me."

From the trunk on which Featherwell had been sitting, sprang Mr. Oldface, red in the face and pointing his finger at the ghost.

"You lie, Abraham Cohen. In life you plagued me and my family. You continue to do the same in death. Be gone!"

The ghost pulsated without speaking. From both sides of the apparition appeared gargoyles with fangs bared. They moved toward Mr. Oldface and Miss Islington.

The elevator door slid open and out stepped Mrs. Oldface, her face contorted into a vicious mask. She held a drawn knife and moved rapidly in front of her husband and toward the gargoyles. She slashed her knife to the left and right. Seeing this, Miss Islington imitated her actions. Neither woman struck at the ghost. They sliced at the gargoyles only. The gargoyles fell on the floor and vanished.

Now hearing the scuffling, the Bobby emerged from behind his arras, his club in one hand and his bottle of rum in the other. He saw the women slashing the air with knives. He saw the apparition turning from white to black. When he blinked, the ghost was gone.

"What ho. What's going on here?" he asked.

Mr. Oldface answered, "Officer, you see before you an ancient ritual of Christmas Eve. The evil spirits of the time are dispelled with the slashing of knives. Ghosts and goblins disappear. This happens so Christmas Day will be happy and peaceful. Welcome to our ceremony."

The women stopped their slashing, exhausted. They sheathed their knives. Featherwell slipped the Bobby his five quid and winked. He extended his arm to Miss Islington and proceeded to the elevator with her. The Bobby, knowing where his patronage lay, went with them. They took the elevator to the first floor, let Officer Hound out of the building, and waited for the Oldface couple to descend.

They watched the elevator dial go to the top floor, hesitate, and then descend to the first floor again. The Oldfaces exited arm in arm. Mr. Oldface told the women to get their coats and scarves on, then wait outside while he conferred with Mr. Featherwell.

"Mr. Featherwell, I owe you a debt of gratitude. Thank you. Your initiative has allowed us to rid ourselves of the ghost of Abraham Cohen. Of course, it never happened." He said this with a knowing wink.

"No, Sir. It never happened. Officer Hound only knew he got a bottle of rum and five quid for watching a knife slashing ritual. The women know what happened, but they'd never be believed. As for me, I only did my duty."

"I have another apology for you. My wife and I suspected you and Miss Islington were going to have a romantic assignation on the top floor. That would never have done. Even the imputation would be a blemish on Druid's Curse. You clearly had no such intention." He extended his hand. "There will be an extra bonus for you and Miss Islington, payable here on the New Year's Day."

Featherwell shook his hand. He then said, "Sir, I have two remaining questions. If you would be so kind to answer them, my Christmas would be complete."

"Ask away."

"The gargoyles seem to have been harmed in the fray. Will their power to protect Druid's be impacted by tonight's actions?"

"We'll have to see. I just don't know. It's worth their loss to have the ghost gone."

"My second question is this. Did you know that your wife was in the elevator with a knife?"

"If I answer, will you swear never to tell the truth to anyone?" Mr. Oldface's visage became deadly serious.

"Of course."

"Mrs. Oldface suspected that the romantic assignation on the top floor might involve Miss Islington and myself. She is insanely jealous. Her knife was meant for your partner. When she saw the real state of affairs, she turned the knife where it would do most good. I chalk that up to Providence. Do you have any other questions tonight? If not, let's pull on our outer clothing and get home. It's past midnight now, and Christmas Day is here."

After well-wishing and hugging all around, the Oldfaces walked home in one direction while Featherwell and Islington went in the other direction, toward her place. The snow had stopped falling and a ghostly silence had descended on the mighty, sleeping city.

"You are a genius, Mr. Featherwell," Miss Islington complimented him.

"You fight like a termagant, Miss Islington," he said in kind.

They laughed. It was their first laugh together ever. He recovered his gravitas almost immediately, looking around to see whether anyone besides her had witnessed his sign of happiness. He smiled. She patted him on the arm.

"I'll never tell," she told him, snuggling close, her breath white in the black winter air.

"Then I'll compound my mortification by wishing you a very Merry Christmas." He looked straight ahead as he said this, but his face was smiling broadly.

"This just keeps getting better and better." She looked up to see him in the darkness, a smile on her face as well.

They made their way to her doorway. She unlocked the door. He kissed her gently on the cheek and said goodnight. Then she was safely inside, and he was quietly whistling, "Silent Night."

GRAVE MISTAKE
G.H. Finn

He crouched in the darkness of the graveyard, beneath the overhanging branches of a snow-covered yew tree. He had heard something. An unexpected, discordant sound.

This was an ancient place, older than the stone church which now stood at the center of the cemetery. Once another church, made of wood, had been built here, well over a thousand years ago—the first of its kind in this area, dating from the time when Christianity began to establish itself amongst the heathen Anglo-Saxons. But before even that first wooden church, an earlier shrine had stood on this ground, a temple honoring the ancestors, the original mothers and the fathers of the tribes, and the old gods of England. Back then, this had been a small, thriving, independent hamlet. Now the ever-expanding boundaries of Greater London had swallowed the village, making it yet another borough of Britain's capital city.

The freezing midwinter air was crisp and tinged with distant chimney-smoke. It was the darkest week of the year. Soon the world would turn toward the light once more, as the days slowly lengthened and a new year began. In another week it would be 1886.

He heard the strange sound again. The clouds parted and the light of the moon lit the scene before him clearly. His large eyes opened wide in surprise. He had rarely seen anyone so eager to dig up a corpse.

In his numerous years at the cemetery he'd observed many odd things, but a young woman frantically trying to unearth a coffin in the early hours of Christmas morning was something new.

He stood up off his haunches and softly padded toward the woman, across the frozen ground, his feet leaving no mark. He shook his grizzled, shaggy head in angry disbelief. Didn't the young have any respect these days? This was *his* cemetery. He couldn't stop himself growling in anger. He wasn't about to tolerate someone appearing in the middle of the night and digging up *his* graves.

The woman spun round, shovel raised, panic written across her face.

She was clearly terrified.

He paused and considered her. This wasn't what he'd expected. He composed himself. He wanted to appear stern, authoritative but not *too* intimidating. He didn't want to scare the girl out of her wits, at least not until he knew what was going on. He stood upright, making himself look serious but not too frightening, and called out. "What are you doing here? Why are you digging up one of my graves in the middle of the night?"

The woman stood in the deep hole she'd been digging, brandishing her spade as though it were an axe. When she heard a noise in the darkness she'd nearly fainted in terror. At first she thought it was a hound, perhaps one of the spectral black dogs from the old tales her Granny had told her. It was Christmas Eve, and this was a time when spirits were known to walk the earth. Then she'd heard a voice. She'd been raised in a world full of superstition, taught that supernatural forces were always around, just out of sight. To her, an unexpected voice in a graveyard was the stuff of nightmares.

But at the moment she wasn't sure which she feared more, that a ghost might menace her, that a *revenant*, a dead body driven by a restless evil spirit, would rise from its place of interment to feed upon her in the dead of night—or that the police had somehow found out what had happened and had tracked her here.

She stared at the figure that was slowly approaching. At first she thought it was a huge hound, but it was hard to focus on the shape, just a blurry mass of shadows that might be anything. As he came closer his shadowy shape seemed to change, becoming more distinct until she could clearly see an old man, shabbily dressed and looking none too happy. She could hardly blame him considering she was, technically, desecrating a grave. She thought, for a moment, she heard another sound, far off in the graveyard, but she ignored it. She looked at the old man again. He didn't appear to be a devil or a ghost. He certainly wasn't a policeman.

Of course, her more rational side insisted, he would be a night-watchman, set to guard the graveyard from vandals or grave-robbers. For a moment she breathed a small sigh of relief, even though she realized how much trouble she would be in if the old man called the police. "Are you the guardian of this place?" she asked, "The warden of the graves?"

He nodded. She noticed his eyes never left her face as he did so. She watched as the old warden came to stand by the open grave under the pale moon. He peered down into the hole she had dug. Inside was an exposed coffin. The lid had been pried open, revealing the fresh corpse of a chubby man with a bushy moustache. The guardian looked like he was about to grow angry; she was sure he was about to accuse her of grave-robbing. She shook her head frantically, insistently saying, "No! No! You don't understand! I was trying to save his life. But I was too late! I tried! Really I did!"

The old man shouted across her protestations, "Don't lie to me! If you weren't after the body, then you wanted to steal any jewelry he was buried with, or the clothes from his back. Even with a man like him, aren't you ashamed to disturb the dead?"

The young woman almost screamed, "Of course it is! I'm a good girl, or at least I try to be, but it would be worse to let a man be buried alive and leave him without trying to help!"

The guardian glared at her and demanded, "What's that? Buried alive? Nonsense. What are you talking about?"

The woman began to sob, tears running down her dirt-streaked face. As she cried she said, "He shouldn't have been buried. He wasn't dead. I should have stopped the burial. I wanted to save him."

The old warden scratched his chin. He thought he heard a scraping sound, out there in the darkness, but for the moment he concentrated on the woman. He squatted down by the side of the grave and said, not unkindly, "You'd better have a good story to tell me. Coming to my graveyard? Digging up one of my graves? Breaking open a coffin? I should skin you alive! Tell me what happened from the beginning, and then I'll make up my mind what to do with you. To start, what is your name? Where are you from?"

The girl wiped her face, which only made it dirtier, but managed to control her sobbing enough to begin to speak. "My name's Violet. I come from Knebworth, a little village about thirty miles from here. My parents wanted me to marry Bill, the greengrocer, but he's twice my age, and I was in love with Albert, the son of our next-door neighbor. We decided to elope. About three months ago we ran away together. We came here to start a new life. We thought it would be like a fairy tale, and that we'd be happy ever-after."

"At first things went well. Then the money began to run out. Albert spent every day looking for work. Sometimes he'd find something, and he brought home a little pay. But it was never enough, and things got harder with the coming of winter. Our savings were almost gone, and I was worried about what would happen to us when we couldn't afford to pay our rent. Or buy food. It's because we're so poor that all this happened. It is my fault they buried him before he was dead. I'm so ashamed. I let a man be buried alive for the sake of five pounds, seven shillings, and tuppence. Enough to feed us for the next few months, but it could never be enough to let a man die in so terrible a way."

The caretaker shook his head. "You tell a sad tale but I don't believe you. You don't look like a grave-robber or a killer..."

Violet interrupted, "I'm not!" She hung her head as she admitted, "I did steal from him, but I didn't murder the man. At least, I never meant to...but

I'm responsible for his death..." She paused, whispering, "Is he really dead? I brought a mirror with me, to check his breath...but I can't see any..."

"He's dead. No question of that," said the guardian, "I can tell. What's all this nonsense about him being buried alive?"

Violet shook her head disconsolately, "That's just it. He *wasn't* dead. I know he wasn't. Let me explain..."

"It was the day before Christmas Eve. I'd been to the Christmas market. I didn't have enough money to buy a goose, mince pies, or any other fine fare that the stall-holders were selling for the season. I couldn't even spare enough for a bag of hot chestnuts. I used the last of our money to buy food for supper. I prayed Albert would find work, so we might eat tomorrow. It was cold in the market. I knew it would be colder that night. We'd used the last of the coal. But we had each other. Even if it didn't drive away the frost, our love kept us warm at night."

"I was walking home. I took a shortcut along a back street. That's when I saw him."

Violet pointed at the corpse and shuddered, "He was hurrying, running toward me. He looked pale and was sweating, despite the midwinter cold. He pulled a scarf away that concealed his face, gasping for breath. I thought it was because of him running."

"Then I saw him stop, put a hand to his chest and lean against a wall. He wiped the sweat from his face. All of a sudden he slumped, like he was going to sleep even though he was still standing. I watched as he slid down the wall and fell to the cobblestones. He convulsed for moment. Then became still. I didn't see him move again."

"I rushed to help, but wasn't sure what to do. No one ever taught me. I tried to feel if his heart was beating, but I didn't know how to do it properly. I managed to turn him over to see if he was breathing, but I couldn't see any sign of his chest moving. I talked to him, shook him, shouted at him. Nothing. I was sure he was dead. He just lay there, on the cobblestones, with the first flakes of the evening snow falling on him."

"I didn't know what to do. Albert and I haven't lived in London very long. We don't know anyone here. I didn't want to go to the police in case they checked up on me and told my parents where I was. I didn't know what I should do or who I should tell. I decided I should try and find out who the man was or where he lived, so I could let his relatives know what had happened."

"I felt around inside his jacket and found a wallet. I only meant to search for an address, honestly I did, it was the only reason I looked inside the wallet. But I saw it was stuffed with money. More than Albert could earn in the next few months. I knew I shouldn't take it. But what good was the money to him now he was dead? I thought perhaps my prayers had been answered..."

"I checked to see if he had something with an address on it, but I never learned to read, just recognize an odd word or two. I'd no idea what his cards and papers said, or how I could contact his family to tell them what had happened."

"I knew someone was bound to find the man's body. I thought it would be better if no one knew I'd ever seen him. So I took the wallet, said nothing and went home."

"I used some of the cash to clear our back rent and pay a few weeks in advance. The landlord looked at me strangely, wondering how I suddenly had money, but he said nothing. Why should he care? He was getting his rent. I walked back to the market by a different route and bought plenty of food. We could have a proper Christmas dinner. Our first together. It felt so good knowing we wouldn't be hungry again."

"When Albert returned in the evening, he was dejected. There'd been no work for him. When he smelled cooking his face brightened. Then he looked suspicious. And angry. 'Violet,' he demanded, 'where'd you get the money for this? Did you steal this food? You didn't...you didn't have a man here, did you?'"

"I was shocked and insulted, and we argued furiously. I was upset that he could think I'd sell myself, but I could see why he was suspicious. In the end I had to tell him. I showed him the money, and the wallet."

"Albert didn't know what to think. He was relieved to know where I'd got the money and apologized for his suggestions. But he was worried because I'd robbed the dead man, though I could tell he was glad we had enough to see us through until he got a regular job. In the end we agreed not to talk about it. We had our dinner, the best meal we'd eaten in a long time, then we went to bed."

"I woke up, hours later, racked with guilt. I kept thinking about the poor, innocent man I'd left in the back street. What if no one had found his body? Stray dogs roam the streets. Terribly hungry...and there are rats. There are *always* rats..."

"What if his family were waiting for him? Worrying where he might be? And all the while, his corpse was lying in a gutter being chewed by animals...dogs ripping out his intestines, rats chewing at fingers and toes, cockroaches eating his face, carrion-crows pecking his eyeballs..."

"I couldn't stand it. I felt so guilty, so wretched. I shook Albert to wake him."

"He wasn't pleased to be woken in the middle of the night, but when I told him what was wrong, he put a comforting arm around me and told me not to worry about it. The man was dead. Nothing we could do could change that, and even if something did eat him in the dark hours, that couldn't make him any deader than he already was."

Violet closed her eyes and continued, "I was cross with Albert. I told him it wasn't just the man's body I was thinking of, it was his family. I hadn't been able to find an address for them because I couldn't read. But he could."

"Albert grumbled but agreed to have a look in the morning. 'Why not now?' I asked. He rolled over in the bed and said it was the middle of the night. The body might have already been spotted. If not, even if we did find an address for his family, wouldn't it be better to tell them in the morning rather than to wake them with bad news? Or did I think he would become more dead if we waited until it was light?"

"I couldn't argue with the small mercy of not waking his wife to tell her she was a widow, or a child to tell them they'd lost their father, so I agreed. I lay down again. But I don't think I slept another minute."

"First thing in the morning, I got the wallet and insisted Albert read through everything to identify the man. He opened it and immediately stared fixedly at what he saw, as though he couldn't believe his eyes. He showed me a card inside. I shrugged. I couldn't read it. The wallet still held some pieces of paper, but they meant nothing to me. But Albert was pointing at what I thought was a calling card. He stared at the words again, unable to take his eyes away. He let out an incredulous sound then turned to stare at me."

"'What does it say?' I asked. He read the card again. 'What does it say? Tell me!' I insisted."

"Albert's mouth was hanging open but eventually his wits returned and he told me, 'The card reads…'I AM NOT DEAD'."

The girl broke off from her story and leaned on her shovel.

The old guardian shook his head slowly. "What on earth could that mean? What did you do next?"

Violet made an effort to pull herself together. From across the graveyard came a muffled sound, a stealthy scraping. Violet took a deep breath and explained. "Albert looked through the wallet and found the man's name."

"He was called Horace Clatterbridge. Inside the wallet was an invoice which showed he came from a place called Hull, in Yorkshire. Albert found a letter folded up, tucked at the back, and he gathered Mr. Clatterbridge was in London on a business trip."

"We couldn't think what the words on the card might mean. 'I Am Not Dead'—I was afraid it was a message from the man's ghost. Albert told me not to be so silly. If a ghost had written a message the one thing it would *not* write is 'I am not dead'."

"After finding nothing else in the wallet, it occurred to Albert there might be something on the back of the card with the message on it. He turned the card over. His eyes widened as he read."

I am not dead. I suffer from a neurological disorder, a form of catalepsy which can strike unexpectedly. If I fall into a cataleptic state I may appear comatose or seem to be dead, but I will recover, eventually. This may take days if I am not given medical treatment. If I am found after suffering a seizure please contact a doctor or the nearest hospital explaining that I am a cataleptic. Thank you.'

"I looked at Albert. I was only just taking it in and realizing what'd happened. 'No! It can't be true!' I said, 'He wasn't dead? He has some sort of sleeping sickness? What have I done?'"

"I started to think of all the terrible things that could have happened to the poor man. He might have frozen in the snow. Or worse. During the night I'd imagined dogs and rats gnawing at his corpse…What if they had started to eat him while he was still alive? What if he woke-up while being devoured? Imagine waking to discover a feral dog feasting on your liver, or crows tearing your stomach open, ripping out your organs while you watched. I imagined a rat forcing its way into the man's mouth, eager to eat him from the inside. I could picture him waking and trying to scream yet being unable to do so—because a rat had chewed off his tongue and was tunneling into his throat…"

"But what if someone *had* found his body? They'd think he was dead. What if they took him to a coroner, and he cut him open to see how he'd died? They'd kill him! He might wake up on a mortuary table, open his eyes and see the coroner slicing him apart with a scalpel, putting his kidneys in a bucket…they'd kill him while trying to find out his cause of death…"

"Then another horrible thought occurred to me…If they thought he died of natural causes, he'd probably just be buried. With no papers or money on him, they'd treat him as a vagrant. He'd be given a pauper's burial. Buried alive!"

"I thought, 'What if he wakes up, inside his coffin…All alone in the dark, trapped, with the air running out…'"

"I couldn't keep the image out of my mind. Sealed inside a coffin and buried alive. Crammed into such a small space that you can hardly move, scratching and clawing at the coffin lid to try to get it open, to try to escape. But there could be no escape. The lid would be nailed shut…the coffin would be lowered into the ground and then buried. If by some miracle you could break a hole in the lid of the casket, what then? The coffin would begin to fill with soil. Even if the grave was shallow, just a couple of feet deep, there would still be tons of earth and stones to try to dig through, with nothing more than the bloody stumps of your fingers to use as tools and no air to breathe. No one could hear a call for help from beneath the ground. You'd be trapped, you couldn't escape, scratching madly with broken nails and bleeding fingers as you choked on stale air, knowing that every breath might be your last, your lungs filling with soil…"

The old warden took an involuntary step back. Violet thought he seemed pale, and he was clearly upset. It was understandable. The idea of being buried alive was terrible. Most people were afraid of it. The rich often bought expensive coffins with bells attached to them, so they could ring if they woke up inside one…but now the old man was muttering to himself.

"They did that here. Long, long ago. It was a ritual back then. A heathen belief originally, but one the Christian converts kept alive. People believed that when a new graveyard was started, the first to be buried there would become the guardian of the cemetery, watching over the bodies and the souls of all those who came after. Most often an animal was sacrificed— sometimes a horse, or a dog, occasionally a bear, or even a human being. Their deaths were normally quick—the sacrifice was usually meant to be an honor. But…not always. Sometimes the one chosen was selected as a punishment."

Violet stared as the old man continued, "Sometimes folk were fearful that the one they sacrificed would bear a grudge. That they'd come back from the dead to take revenge on whoever struck the killing blow. So they were cunning. They wouldn't kill the sacrificial victim. Instead, they'd bury him alive. He wouldn't die by a human hand, but from lack of air and the weight of the earth upon him. Then he'd have no one upon whom to seek vengeance. His spirit would be bound to the graveyard, watching over the dead forever."

"That's horrible," said Violet, as she heard a distant sound, as of something scraping on stone. The old man nodded. He changed the subject. "What happened when you realized the man might be alive?"

"I started to scream," she replied. "Albert put his hands over my mouth. He held me close to him trying to get me to me quiet, so the neighbors wouldn't hear. 'Hush!' he said, holding me tightly. 'What's done is done. The man may have recovered in which case all is well. If not, well, we mustn't get involved. We cannot tell anyone. You would be charged with theft.'"

"I sobbed, begging Albert to go and tell someone—a doctor, the police, anyone—but he was determined. He said we must keep silent. He looked at his pocket-watch. 'I should go and look for work,' he said, 'even though the money will last us a long time, we shouldn't waste it. Besides, we mustn't do anything to arouse suspicion. If it people know we've suddenly got money, yet I'm not working, they may ask questions. We must behave as normal. I'll go and look for work. I'll be back this evening and we'll celebrate Christmas Eve together.'"

"I tried to persuade Albert not to go, but he'd made up his mind. Reluctantly, I agreed to do as he said."

"Once I was alone, I started to cry again. I kept thinking of all the terrible things that might have happened to the man."

"Around midday, I started thinking, but what if these terrible things haven't happened yet? What if he was still lying in the alleyway? Or if his body was even now on its way to hospital? What if they were only just lowering his coffin into the ground...the first few spadesful of earth being thrown down to scatter against the wooden lid of the casket? There might still be time to save him. So I went out to try to save the man's life."

"First, I went to the alleyway where I had seen Mr. Clatterbridge collapse. I hoped he'd still be there, unconscious and safe. But he wasn't. I looked around to make sure there was no sign of him. An old woman turned the corner of the street, dressed in clothes not much better than rags, carrying her meager shopping home from the Christmas Market, just as I had done. She watched me looking around."

"'Yes' she said, 'This is where they found the corpse last night.'"

"'Last night?' I repeated, 'Where did they take the body?'"

"'How should I know?' she replied, 'Why? Was he a friend of yours? A relative?'"

"'I don't know,' I lied, 'I wondered if I might know him, but I'm not sure unless I see him. How could I find out where they took the body?'"

"'The woman nodded, 'Easy enough,' she said, then shouted 'Officer! Over here!'"

"I was shocked. I turned round and coming along the back street I saw a young policeman. The woman told him I might know the dead man they'd found. She asked where his body was so that I could see if I could identify him."

"I was terrified the policeman would somehow realize I was involved, or that he might demand to know my name and contact my family, but the officer was very polite and said he hoped the man would not be one of my friends or relatives. He told me the body had been taken to the local doctor. 'I'm almost certain the gentleman has been identified already,' he said. I asked the name and address of the doctor, and he told me."

"I thanked the policeman, wished him a Merry Christmas, and hurried away to see the Doctor. When I got there it was mid-afternoon. He was still out on his rounds, visiting patients. I waited and waited. Albert would be due home now. Still the Doctor didn't come back to his surgery. The sun was setting when at last a Hansom cab drew up and the Doctor got out."

"I asked about the body. He told me that because, in his medical opinion, it was clearly a case of natural causes, the body was released for burial straight away. I asked where it would have been taken. He told me that as the man had no money and was a penniless vagrant, he'd been taken for a pauper's burial in the graveyard of the nearest church. He told me how to get here and said the body would be buried at the far side of the cemetery, where the town buries beggars, criminals, and the poor."

"By this time it was early evening. On Christmas Eve! I hurried here as fast as I could, but when I arrived the church was packed. A full mass being celebrated, and that was followed by a midnight carol service. I slipped in and joined the congregation, just another face among many. When, finally, the carols were over and the people began to go home, I hid and waited until I was sure no one remained. Then I slipped into the graveyard."

"I didn't really know what I was going to do, but I saw this shovel and took it and I searched until I found a fresh grave. There was only the one, so I knew it must be his. I started digging, even though the ground was frozen and hard. The rest you know."

The old warden looked at the girl before him and asked, "You swear to me that what you have told me is true?"

Violet nodded, "Of course, why would I make up something like this?"

The old guardian looked into the coffin and was about to speak when he was distracted by a loud scraping sound some distance away. He and Violet looked around but could see nothing. The old man frowned as he scanned the darkness. Violet began to cry again.

He turned back to her, saying gently, "Shush, shush, child. I believe you, but you're wrong to think you were responsible for this man's death. I know who this man is. He was not some traveler from the North who has come to do business here."

Violet stopped sobbing and asked, "What? Who is he then?"

The guardian turned suddenly as another scraping sound came, from the darkest part of the cemetery. Violet asked again, "What do you know about this man?"

The old man turned back to her and said, "All this man's family have been buried in this graveyard for generations. I remember when his father was buried here. And his grandfather. None of them were any good. Thieves, footpads, and cut-throats, the lot of them, and all of them buried in this corner of the cemetery reserved for criminals. This man died from natural causes. He wasn't buried alive. He suffered a heart attack. He was over-weight and no doubt running scared when you saw him. His name isn't Clatterbridge; he was called Fred Baggs, a notorious burglar, sneak-thief, and pick-pocket. He'd clearly stolen the wallet from this Mr. Clatterbridge."

Violet stared at the night-watchman, tears still streaming down her face, but now she was crying with relief. "Is it true?" she asked, "I really wasn't responsible for his death?"

The guardian shook his head, "You were tempted by the money and, took it in a moment of weakness, but that's all you did wrong. We all make mistakes and do things we are not proud of, especially when we're young. Or when we are hungry. I do not think that the gods will judge you too harshly. Go back to your husband, lead a good life and help the poor. Then you will have done more good than harm."

Violet started crying again. "You mean you'll let me go? You won't tell the police?"

"Just go home," said the old man, waving his hand in a shooing manner,

"Your husband will be worried about you, and I don't want you cluttering up my graveyard."

Violet smiled at the old man. "Go home," he said, "Go on, go away and celebrate Yule. Before I change my mind."

Violet smiled again. She turned and ran away through the graveyard, on her way home. She paused just once to wave goodbye to the old man, and call out, "Merry Christmas!" but he wasn't looking.

He stared into the open coffin, seeing the fat corpse of Fred Baggs, thief, pick-pocket, and now the latest soul under his charge.

He heard the scraping sound again. Off near the richer mausoleums. He listened carefully and this time he heard voices. Two men were in his cemetery.

"Which grave are we looking for?" asked the first voice.

"Any, as long as it's expensive." replied the second, "We'll dig them up and see if they've got anything of value. Necklaces, broaches, watches, or wedding rings. But if not, at least we can take the coffin. We can get good money selling second-hand coffins."

"You sure this is safe?" asked the first voice.

"Of course," replied the second, "Who's going to be about at this time on a Christmas morning?"

The warden could feel himself becoming angry. He was the guardian of the graves and he would not see them robbed.

"What do we do if we do see anyone? I heard there's some sort of old night-watchman in the graveyard sometimes," said the first voice.

"Kill him," said the second, "He won't put up much of a struggle."

"Good," said the first voice, "It's easier if they can't fight back."

The guardian became furious. He let the shape of a man fall from around him, slipping into the form of a huge black dog. Its eyes glowed a fiery red in the darkness.

The hound was huge, horrendously ugly, and unnaturally fierce. Enormous fangs protruded from its massive mouth. He stared at the dead body in the coffin and drooled saliva all down his misshapen chin. He felt insatiably hungry, as always. But he couldn't eat any of the bodies buried here. It was his role to protect them. And he had done, for more than twelve hundred years.

Once, he had been a priest of the old gods of England. He had honored Woden and Frigge, Thunor, Tiw, and many others. Then the Christians came, telling their stories of a new god from the East. He'd been interested to hear about their Jesus. The Christ-Priests told him that their god was born at Yule, in the deep midwinter. He was happy to listen to their tales and share bread and mead with them. He had no objection to their building a church to their god. The problems only began when they demanded he give them his temple. They told him all his gods were false, and that it was a sin to say prayers to the ancestors. They drove him from the shrine, tore down the carved wooden statues of the old gods, and set up an altar to their Christ. The missionaries wanted to baptize him, if he would renounce his faith in the old ways and accept the new religion. He refused. And so they found another use for him.

When the Christ-Priests decided to start a cemetery in the grounds around their new church, the freshly converted congregation came stealthily in the night and bound him, he who had once been their priest. They took him to the graveyard and buried him alive. They called on their new god and praised his name, but still they practiced the ways of their ancestors. As they shoveled soil down into the grave below, covering the screaming face of the man they were offering in sacrifice, many of the congregation felt they were doing the man a kindness. The Christian priests said he would be denied heaven as he refused to accept Christ, which meant his soul would be sent to a place of eternal damnation and punishment. But this ceremony would prevent that. Now he would enter neither heaven nor hell. He would be tied to the graveyard for all eternity. He became what some call a Barguest and others a Grim—the guardian of the graveyard and the warden of those who were buried there.

The Grim growled, deep in the back of its throat. It began to stalk through the silent night, prowling between the tombs, tracking the two grave-robbers. He was forbidden to eat the flesh and chew the bones of those he guarded in the graveyard, but that did not extend to those who came to disturb the dead.

Before the first rays of bleak midwinter sunlight shone upon the stillness of the snow-covered graveyard, the Christmas morning calm was pierced by sudden, terrified, agonized screams.

The cold, frosty morning glistened snow-white and blood-red.

Violet and Albert were not the only ones to enjoy a hearty Christmas dinner.

For once, the Grim ate well.

THE ORNAMENT
Mike Carey

1

The storm had raged for days, burying the city in a white chaos. Getting to the hospital had taken time, far too much time, and the hospital was filled with far too many sick and injured and far too little staff.

It was Christmas Eve, and the timing could not have been worse. Mary was coming and would not be denied.

The seasoned nurses went pale at the sound of the guttural groan as the mother expelled both child and final breath from her body simultaneously.

In the outer lobby, Arthur waited anxiously. Everything…*everything* felt wrong about how this was happening. They had planned everything about this day down to the finest detail, but the storm had mocked every bit of their plans. He could not shake the darkness that colored his every thought.

When, surprisingly soon, he heard the sounds of a baby, *his* baby, crying in the next room, he leapt to his feet, but as he rushed to the doors of the delivery room, he was blocked by an old doctor. Arthur could see what the doctor had come to say on the man's face before he said the words. Everything within Arthur felt like it had sunk into his stomach, tears burned his tightly closed eyes, and only the doctor's steadying hand kept him from falling as one of his knees buckled beneath him. In a moment, his life had gone from rigidly planned out to, in a very real way, ending. The life he had, the life he expected to have, was gone. With the departure of that one loving soul from his life, everything would be strange, new and tragically different.

Again he heard the baby cry, and the part of his mind that Arthur usually listened to was trying to convince him that the proper thing for a man to do would be to, as his father was fond of saying, keep a stiff upper lip and take care of the baby. But it this time, it was a wave of stinging emotion that enveloped him and left him quite nearly destroyed, a sobbing wretch on the waiting room floor. The stiff upper lip and the child would, for the time being, have to wait.

The light woke him from a deep slumber he had no recollection of entering. He glanced down to see that someone had draped an overly starched hospital sheet over his sleeping form. He looked towards the window to see the snow had nearly ceased, and, in a still half-asleep way, cursed the snow for not having ceased a day earlier. The pain of the day before still filled him, but the sharpness of it had been slightly dulled by sleep.

He heard the footsteps on the hard, sterile floors and turned to see a young nurse approaching with a steaming cup of tea. She passed him the tea, and Arthur managed to get an audible "thank you" from a throat that was raw from his sobs.

"Do you think you're ready to see your daughter, Mr. Whelan?" she asked, softly, with pity in her eyes.

He immediately felt pangs of shame for being so weak in a situation which demanded strength. This pretty, young nurse pitying him was more than he could bear. He climbed from the chair, placed the sheet and the tea aside and said, "Yes, please. It is past time I met my little Mary."

The nurse began leading him through the door into the delivery room, then stopped and let out a shocked gasp.

Arthur followed the line of her eyes towards the back of the room. There, against the wall, a blood soaked sheet covered a shape that he recognized as his wife. Arthur's mind swirled, and he could feel bile rising in his throat and feared that he would vomit right there. He clenched his eyes shut and turned away.

"I...I am so sorry," stuttered the nurse. "Someone should have moved...I am so sorry...we are so short-handed with the storm and..."

"Please," he cut her off, "my daughter."

Without another word, the nurse led Arthur to another corner of the room where a small cradle held a much smaller child.

Someone should have prepared Arthur.

Mary was born *wrong*.

Her tiny feet were bent, severely. The soles faced each other as if they were about to clap. Her hands resembled flippers. Her individual fingers were evident, but the skin between them had not split. And while there was nothing obviously misshapen about her face, there was something about it which disturbed anyone who looked at her, something no one could ever manage to explain.

If Arthur had been a lesser man, he thought, he could have sold the child to one of the circus freak shows that had, of late, grown so popular in

Europe. But Arthur was better than that. The poor little creature was his daughter, and he would love her and tend to her needs as a good man, a good father, should.

Mary was the last bit of his beloved wife that he had left, and he would cherish her. Regardless of her afflictions, she was a wonderful gift.

2

Arthur was a banker by trade, and adjusting his life to that of a single father was, to say the very least, challenging. Luckily he earned enough to afford nannies for the child. They arrived every day just prior to the start of his work day and stayed for as long as needed.

Despite the cruel trickery nature had played upon her features, Mary was a happy child, and the nannies had not a single complaint about their time with her. Arthur was relieved that her appearance apparently did not reflect the nature of her soul.

Try as she might, Mary could not walk. She attempted to force her feet to work with a persistence that broke Arthur's heart.

On her third birthday, Arthur and Mary boarded a train for Switzerland to consult with a young doctor who had some radical theories on amputation and reshaping bodies. It was not long, however, before Arthur was fully convinced that the man was mad and the trip had been in vain.

More doctors' consultations followed, as well as some attempts to fix Mary's feet and hands.

Many of the methods employed were barely medieval in nature and achieved nothing other than torturing a small, frightened child.

With time, they found a doctor who could fix her hands, but her feet remained twisted.

Arthur purchased the finest wheeled chair he could afford, and dedicated himself to making her life, which seemed so damned, as happy as he possibly could.

3

Mary's fourth year had been difficult. It had been hard enough when she first realized that the other little children in her school avoided and shunned her because of her uncanny face, but as they grew a bit older, Mary was subjected to the special types of cruelty that young girls reserve exclusively for those who dare to not be precisely like themselves.

The instructors did their best to shield Mary from the abuse, but they were not immune to the discomfort Mary's face caused them, and Mary was bright enough to read it in their averted glances.

Arthur ached for the loneliness he felt Mary must be experiencing, although the girl never showed any sign of it. She buried herself in books, reading with an ever growing voraciousness, and was soon reading at a level far above her peers.

One bright Saturday afternoon, Arthur lifted Mary into her chair, and they headed into the busy market section of the city to buy some fruit. As they walked, he watched Mary look longingly at the people walking about on the perfect legs and feet that they took for granted. Her usually smiling face would darken a bit as she considered all that she could never have.

As they walked past a small path between two buildings, Mary's hand suddenly rose to get her father's attention. "Father!" she gasped, "Down there, please!"

Turning the chair, it took Arthur a moment to ascertain the source of her fascination. On the front steps of a tenement, a young trio was making an impressive musical display. One lad had a near masterful hand with a fiddle. Another played along with a tin whistle, while a third kept time with a Bodhran drum. The tune they played was joyful and infectious, and Arthur soon realized that it was not the musicians who had caught his daughter's attention. It was the lovely girl with long hair and skirts who laughed and spun and contorted herself in front of the musicians.

"What is she doing?" an awed Mary whispered.

"That's called dancing, Poppet." Arthur answered, "It's a way of enjoying music, I suppose."

From that moment on, Mary would never be content again.

4

Naturally, Mary had always wanted to walk, and was actually convinced that one day she would, but from the moment she saw the dancing girl, she became obsessed with dance.

It was not unusual for Arthur to find her crying on the floor, after yet another failed attempt to force legs to function when they were not built to do so.

Every night, Mary dreamed of dancing in the streets, to the fiddle, whistle, and drum music of unseen musicians. Soon those dreams would be taken to a level her young mind could scarcely imagine.

It was a late autumn day. The leaves in the trees had become a colorful canopy on the verge of their yearly shopkeeper annoying collapse onto the streets. The first chills of winter were in the air and, as always, they set Arthur to wondering what he might do to for his daughter's upcoming birthday. This year, fate would play a hand.

The bank had closed at midday, and Arthur had decided to enjoy a brisk walk home rather than deal with the annoyance of trying to attract the attention of a carriage driver. He had always enjoyed a pleasant walk, but often felt a pang of guilt for enjoying a simple pleasure which Mary never could. The shops along the main road were bustling, and many had begun to display trinkets and decorations for the Christmas season.

A sweet smell reached out to him, and on a whim Arthur decided that he would bring some sweets home for his daughter and the nannies. He stepped into the shop of a small Russian man who was well renowned for his confectionary skills.

As Arthur perused the selection of sweets, the little Russian approached him.

"You are the father of the poor girl in the chair, yes?" he asked.

Arthur bristled a bit. He did not like to think of Mary as 'poor'. He answered simply, "Yes."

"I have heard she loves the dance," he stated.

At this, Arthur warmed a bit. "She does. She adores it."

The Russian smiled and nodded. Then, leaving Arthur confused, disappeared into a back room of the shop. Hushed voices briefly conversed, and then the Russian returned, a proud smile upon his round face.

"My wife is blind," he explained, "and this is very busy time of year here. I cannot be away."

Arthur looked at him quizzically as the man produced two small pieces of thick paper. The Russian looked down at them and continued, "My brother work at theatre. Not very far. Russian ballet will be there. Twentieth of December. Russians best dancers in world. Your little daughter will love." With a glimmer in his eyes, and a wide smile, he reached out his hand, offering the two tickets to Arthur.

Arthur was stunned and briefly uncertain how to react. Pure human kindness was a rare thing to encounter, and Arthur had always been uncomfortable with gifts, especially those tainted by any kind of pity for his child. He did, however, see the tickets as perfect birthday gift for Mary.

"I do not know what to say, sir. That is most kind of you, but please, you must allow me to pay you something for such fine tickets," Arthur offered.

"Pfft..." The Russian huffed and waved his hand. Arthur hoped he had not offended the man. "You are good customer. It does my heart good I can do this thing for you and your little girl."

A few minutes later, a beaming Arthur departed the shop, the two tickets within his suit pocket, and carrying two bundles filled with more pastry than his household and office could consume in a week. If he could not pay for the tickets one way, he would pay for them another.

5

Mary could not contain her excitement in the weeks leading up to the show. She rarely spoke of any other subject. It is a safe assumption that her school work suffered considerably those few weeks, but likely not enough to endanger her academic career.

Molly, a young Irish woman, who was Mary's favorite nanny (although Mary would never be rude enough to say so and risk hurting the feelings of Hannah, the second nanny) made Mary a lovely, long, black and green dress to wear to the theatre. Mary adored it. Arthur made a mental note to add a bit to Molly's Christmas bonus this year.

As the day of the performance grew nearer, Mary made an odd request. She wanted a veil, like those she had seen on both brides and grieving widows. She did not, as she explained to her father, wish to make anyone uncomfortable at such a special event.

There were times Arthur grew to believe that his daughter had grown mercifully oblivious to the effect her face had upon others. This reminder was painful. He was a proud man, and hoped that his daughter would also be proud and indifferent to the judgments of others. Yet this was her birthday, and Christmas time. It was not a time for forcing life lessons; it was a time for granting wishes.

And so the morning of the twentieth came. Molly helped Mary into her new dress, and Hannah pinned the veil to her hair. Mary beamed, thrilled by the unusual sensation of anonymity.

The temperature had fallen to a seasonable cold outside, and although she hated to have her dress hidden, Mary relented to the warmth of a winter coat and scarf.

There was a small bit of snow on the ground, but not enough to make pushing her chair difficult. Arthur pushed her along to the edge of their property where they met with a carriage Arthur had arranged for. With accustomed effort, Arthur got Mary out of her chair and into the carriage, and the coachman deftly loaded the chair into the luggage portion of the vehicle.

With a crack of the whip, the carriage pulled away from the curb and the adventure had begun. The carriage brought them as far as the train station. Their timing was about as close to perfect as it could be. The train chugged its way into the station just as Arthur and Mary arrived.

Once on board, they found themselves seated opposite a charming and friendly old Scotsman. Mary thought he was funny and loved his accent, while Arthur looked forward to the end of the ride when they could part company with the fellow.

The train ride was mercifully short. The Scotsman wished them good day and went on his way. Another carriage, also arranged in advance, awaited their arrival. This coachman was younger than the first, and had considerably more difficulty maneuvering the wheeled chair into a secure spot. In the end, Arthur ended up assisting the flustered lad.

Before hopping into his seat, the coachman popped his head into the window to face Mary, and, tipping his worn cap and flashing a smile, he said "I'm sorry for the delay, lass."

Mary very briefly pondered what the life of a coachman's wife would be like.

The coach made its way through the crowded streets. Pedestrians, people on horseback, carriages like their own, and even motor-cars (which stunned Mary with their speed) created a labyrinth in motion. Mary wondered how anyone could traverse it safely. Even Arthur was impressed.

When they finally pulled up in front of the theatre, all other city-inspired awe was pushed aside. Mary leaned out the coach window and took in the glorious visage of the beautifully ornate building. There was a theatre close to Mary's home where she had seen plays and moving pictures in the past, but it instantly became little more than a hovel in her thoughts compared to the marble columns and stone gargoyles which now threatened to overwhelm her eyes with grandeur.

"Oh, father..." she said, in a voice that was not much more than a whisper.

Arthur smiled and put his hand on her shoulder. This would be a perfect day.

6

The young coachman unloaded the wheeled chair far easier than he had loaded it. A line was forming at the entrance to the theatre, and Arthur and Mary took their places at the end of it.

Mary didn't mind the wait, she would've been happy looking at that building forever, or at least a very long time.

"HELLO!" an unmistakably Russian voice cried out from the theatre doors, "I have been watching for you!"

The man, tall, thin, and with a mop of black hair strode quickly towards them. "My brother told me you are coming! Welcome!" he exclaimed while shaking Arthur's hand vigorously.

Mary smiled. Her father, being a reserved sort, was not comfortable with boisterous people.

"Come. You follow me. I have special seats for you!' the Russian said, leading them ahead of the line and into a side door.

The theatre was still empty as the Russian led them down to the center of the front row, directly in front of the orchestra pit. There was a space between two chairs just large enough for Mary's chair to fit in to. To be honest, Mary would've preferred to sit in one of the luxurious looking theatre seats, but she did not want to seem ungrateful, so said nothing.

Arthur thanked the Russian with a handshake far more subdued than the one they had shared previously and made a mental note to purchase much more pastry from his brother when they returned home.

As they settled into their seats, Mary craned and twisted her neck in every direction in an attempt to take in all of the beauty around her. The architecture, the statues, the private balcony seats lining the sides of the room, the ornate chandelier which hung just in front of a large circular section of ceiling which was adorned with a mural even Michelangelo might've been envious of, it was almost more than she could process, and she feared she might faint and miss the show.

But then the main doors opened and the crowd being filing in and slowly finding their seats.

A few eyes glanced curiously their way before disregarding them and moving on. Mary noticed, with amusement, that most of the men entering seemed bored already, while the women seemed most interested in showing off their latest jewelry or young man acquisition to their peers, as if in some competition that Mary was still young enough to regard as quite silly.

As they settled into their seats, many of the women, even those also seated in the front row, pulled out small yet ornate opera glasses.

Mary leaned towards her father and whispered, "Are they blind, father?"

"No, Poppet," he responded with a grin, "they're just putting on their own performance."

Mary didn't quite understand, but everything else quickly left her thoughts as the orchestra entered and the first notes, spun like gold from violin strings, rose from the pit in front of them.

7

The volume of the music swelled, becoming almost too loud for those in the seats bordering the pit. The house lights dimmed, casting the high society crowd into shadows.

The gigantic, red velvet stage curtains opened wide, as did Mary's eyes, and neither would close for almost two hours.

Mary was transfixed and spellbound by the graceful dance that unfolded before her eyes. It would not be an exaggeration to say that she forgot to breathe several times during the performance, resulting in embarrassing yawns which she tried to stifle.

As the dancers spun and leapt, so did Mary's heart. The joy flowing through her was like nothing she had ever experienced, and she wondered if she might be glowing.

Her exuberance was not lost on her father. Arthur found himself rapidly shifting his attention back and forth between the stage and the show playing out on his daughter's joyously animated face. For every cruel trick nature had played upon the poor girl, for all the hours he spent working when he could've been home with her, for every last thing he could not give her, he could at least give her *this*, one perfect experience that she could cherish her entire life.

8

The building shook with applause as the dancers took their bows and the massive curtains began to close. Mary was clapping so furiously that she nearly slipped out of her chair. Fortunately Arthur was watching and managed to avert that minor tragedy.

Mary exhaled, feeling as if she had not done so in hours. She turned to Arthur and gasped, "Father! That was the most amazing thing I have ever seen! Did you see those dancers? Did you?"

Arthur laughed. "They were hard to miss, little one."

"Oh, father…" she continued, still wearing a look of astonishment upon her face, "should we go? I cannot wait to tell Molly all about it!"

"Molly?" he asked, one eyebrow raised in a comically quizzical manner, "What about poor Hannah?"

"Oh, I am sure she will be there when I tell Molly! Come, let's get home!"

Arthur looked behind them. The crowd was slowly working its way out of the theatre in what seemed to be an undulating ocean of flesh and expensive clothing. Attempting to enter that writhing mass with the wheeled chair seemed, to him, to be a terribly treacherous idea.

"I think we'd best wait until the crowd thins out a bit. We don't want to be running over toes."

So they sat, discussing in great detail the spectacle they had just witnessed. A few times Arthur attempted to shift the conversation towards the magnificent building, but Mary's mind was decidedly one-track. For all she cared, at that moment, they could've been sitting in a log cabin.

9

By the time they exited the theatre, the crowds had dissipated, and the streets were all but deserted. They had exchanged brief niceties with the Russian theatre owner as he escorted them out the doors, which he had rapidly chained behind them. The theatre's exterior lighting extinguishing a moment later, the street was plunged into near darkness, a lone street light keeping the night at bay.

Mary's youth and excitement from the show shielded her from the realization which had quickly dawned upon Arthur. The coach he had hired to return them to the train station after the show was nowhere to be seen, and even the cabs for hire which frequented the area had all been taken by other theatre-goers.

Just then, the noise of creaking wheels reached his ears, and for a moment, he thought a carriage was near.

His brief hope was dashed as the cart came into sight. It was of the type frequently seen at outdoor markets, but filled with a far more varied collection of wares than Arthur had ever seen piled onto one cart before. The woman pushing the cart was no less of a sight. It was doubtful that she was as old as she looked, for she looked as old as the Pyramids of Egypt, but something in her eye sparkled with cunning. Her clothing was a mish-mash of scarves which, while now faded, must've been garishly colored at one point.

"Ugh," Arthur thought to himself with unrestrained disgust, "Gypsies."

Mary looked at the woman with cautious amusement.

"Romany are an old people." The woman began to speak as if she had heard Arthur's thoughts, or perhaps merely read the disdain upon his face. "Old and wise in ways that your people have forgotten."

Mary was fascinated by the old woman, but Arthur felt uneasy.

"We are not interested in whatever it is you are selling," Arthur said curtly, attempting in vain to cut short the encounter.

The woman glared at Arthur for a moment, and then turned her attention towards Mary.

"Just come from the show, did you?" she asked. "Did you enjoy the dancers, girlie?"

"Oh yes!" Mary exclaimed, anxious for the opportunity to tell a new person about the experience. "They were wonderful! It was amazing how they-"

"I imagine anyone hopping about on two feet might be amazing to such as you," the old woman interrupted, gesturing at the chair.

"THAT IS QUITE ENOUGH!" Arthur raged at the old woman. He could feel his face growing red and hot with anger as he moved forward to get between Mary and the old Crone.

"Apologies! Apologies!" the old woman bowed and walked back a few steps "I am old and have grown accustomed to speaking my thoughts with no regard for gentle wording."

She turned to her cart and began to rifle through the varied oddities piled upon it.

"I think I have something the girl may like."

"I told you, we are not interested in buying any of your baubles." Arthur's anger had subsided but his annoyance had not.

Ignoring him, the old woman produced a small wooden box with brass hinges from under an old blanket.

Her wrinkled hands opened the box and lifted out its hidden treasure, a round glass ornament, the type often seen hanging from the branches of Christmas trees. The glass orb was transparent, and within, slowly spinning, was a small silver ballerina that glimmered and reflected every light it could catch.

Mary stared at the glass orb and the tiny dancer, eyes wide and mouth agape. Then she swung her head to look at her father with a request she did not even have to speak aloud.

The Gypsy woman had won and Arthur fumed; there was no way he was going to break his daughter's heart over the price of a simple ornament.

"How much?" he asked.

But the old woman's demeanor had changed without warning. She stared at Mary with something that resembled awe.

"Why do you wear that veil, child?" she quietly asked "Are you shy, ugly, or both?"

Taken aback, Mary merely replied, "I'm…different"

With shocking speed the old woman lunged towards Mary and, reaching out one clawed hand, lifted Mary's veil.

Mary let out a brief shriek, and Arthur moved to rush to her aid.

BE STILL! The voice echoed in Arthur's head, sounding like the old woman's voice, yet somehow younger and stronger. Arthur found that he could not move, that he could not even shake as fear gripped him. It was then that it occurred to him that the woman had not spoken the words and that for all their deafening clarity, he had only heard them within his mind.

The old woman stared into Mary's eyes, and Mary, no longer afraid and unaware of her father's plight, stared back. After a few long moments the old woman smiled and said, "I won't take a single coin for this."

She raised the ornament to her face and kissed the glass surface, leaving a stain of ancient lips, and then placed it in Mary's hand.

"This girl is very, very special," she whispered, turning towards Arthur.

With that, whatever was holding Arthur still released its grip. His relief was brief, however, as Mary began to scream.

The old woman had crumpled as if she was made of dry leaves, and she stared up at them with eyes that were quite dead.

10

Their trip home was delayed by necessary but for the most part perfunctory discussions with the local constabulary. The police did not seem overly concerned over the loss of, as one officer put it, "just another Gypsy peddler."

Mary stayed silent for most of the proceedings, answering questions when asked and nothing more. She sat, transfixed on her new prize, the little dancer lazily spinning in its glass enclosure. Arthur was understandably concerned for Mary's well-being. This was Mary's first brush with death since she was old enough to comprehend it. The shock of the old woman's sudden passing had to have been traumatic for the girl.

The police inquiries had made it impossible for Arthur and Mary to get a train home that evening, so with the assistance of a sympathetic police sergeant, they found an available room in a quaint inn close to the train station.

It did not take them long to settle in, as they had no luggage and would be forced to sleep in their clothes and wear them home the following day. Mary stretched out on the large bed while Arthur tried to determine if the old couch or the hard floor would offer more comfort.

"Thank you again, for this wondrous day, Father," said Mary, breaking the momentary silence.

Arthur thought it a bit queer that she did not mention the old woman, but perhaps it was merely her way of coping with the horror of it all.

"You're welcome, my angel. Now let's put out the lamp and get some sleep. We'll want to catch the early train in the morn."

"A few minutes more, Daddy? Please?" she asked.

Arthur lifted his head from the floor and saw that Mary was still intently examining the tiny dancer in the glass globe.

"So what is so fascinating about that little ornament, Child?"

"Oh, don't you see, father?" Mary turned to him with a smile. "She's me."

11

By the time Arthur and Mary returned home, the house had been fully decorated for the holiday. A couple of men from town had delivered an impressive tree that nearly touched the ceiling of the main hall. Hannah and Molly had worked tirelessly to assure the home was bright and festive for the Mary's return.

"We expected you much earlier, sir," Hannah said, greeting them at the door. "We were concerned."

"Couldn't be helped, I'm afraid. There was some unpleasantness," Arthur explained, his attention more upon the decorations than on the conversation.

"Oh! Are you and the young miss all right?" Hannah gasped with sincere concern.

"I believe so. I'd rather not talk about it in front of my daughter, but I will tell you and Molly what transpired after Mary has gone to bed."

Arthur looked over to see that Mary had wheeled her chair to the side of the tree. As he walked to her, she turned to him.

"It's lovely, isn't it?" she asked.

"It is. Finest tree I've seen in years. Your new ornament would look nice hanging from it," he suggested.

Mary looked shocked at the suggestion. "Oh no, father! It might fall off the tree and break."

"But what good is a Christmas ornament if it's not on a tree?"

"Not this one, father. I have to keep this one safe," she explained, lifting the ornament from its box and looking at the dancer inside. "This girl is very, very special."

Arthur felt a cold chill flash down his back as he remembered the old Gypsy's words. It was to be the final joyful Christmas the house would see for a long, long time.

12

The years had been hard.

During the winter following the encounter with the Gypsy, Hannah had been killed when she foolishly attempted to cross a not quite frozen enough lake upon a horse. The horse's corpse had been recovered, but Hannah's never was.

Mary barely seemed to notice the loss.

Being alone in the house with Mary and her father had resulted in an increased closeness between Molly and Arthur. Eventually the relationship crossed a line into territory many deemed inappropriate, and a there was a small scandal. When word of this reached Molly's parents in Killarney, they demanded that their daughter return home to Ireland.

Again, Mary seemed indifferent.

Mary had become difficult as the years passed. Her obsession with the ornament grew stronger each year. Her once hungry mind now seemed to have but one focus. Her studies suffered immensely. She spent days speaking to no one unless absolutely necessary.

Arthur had taken the ornament away from her on several occasions. Several times he tried to smash the thing, but could somehow never bring himself to strike it or dash it to the ground. And each time Mary had become so angry and so distraught, not sleeping or eating for days, that Arthur gave in and returned it to her.

While Arthur was a logical man, not given to believing in things like 'Gypsy curses,' the thought that the misfortunes which had befallen the house seemed tied to the arrival of the ornament had occasionally crossed his mind.

He had hired a new nanny. To avoid the scrutiny that had plagued him during the affair with Molly, he had hired a conservative older woman who answered only to the name Mrs. Granger.

The woman took good care of the home, and competently completed every task expected of her. There was, however, no warmth in her relationships with Arthur and Mary. To her, it was a paid position and nothing more.

Mary made no secret of her dislike for the woman, and, while Arthur missed the effect a warm and loving woman had on the house, he did respect and appreciate Mrs. Granger's professionalism.

Mary's 15th birthday arrived. A snowstorm had been raging for two days that was unlike anything the area had seen since the days surrounding Mary's birth.

Mrs. Granger had dutifully prepared a lovely birthday cake for the girl, and had then headed home to wait out the storm with the never-seen Mr. Granger.

Arthur carefully placed fifteen small candles into the frosting on top of the cake and lit them one by one.

Mary was sitting on her bed, examining her ornament for the millionth time when Arthur entered, her cake sitting on a serving tray, the fifteen small flames bringing with them a feeling of warmth that had nothing to do with physical temperature.

"Make a wish and blow out the candles, Angel," Arthur said with a smile, placing the tray over her legs.

Mary returned the smile and inhaled deeply, but when she attempted to blow out the candles, she coughed violently instead.

Speckles of red appeared across the white frosting.

13

The disease was brutal and rapid. Mary weakened. Her skin became gray. The doctors did all that they could which, in the end, amounted to nothing at all. As the sickness ravaged and weakened her, her only concern still seemed to be with the ornament.

"Please bury this with me," she would say to Arthur at least four times a day.

"No one is being burying for many years to come, Love," he would reply with feigned confidence.

Of course, that was untrue.

Mary died in mid-February.

Mrs. Granger had gone to fetch Mary for breakfast, only to find her cold and twisted on the floor by her bed. The ornament was clutched to her chest.

During the winter months, when the ground is frozen and difficult to dig in, it was common for bodies to be kept in ice-houses until the weather became more agreeable.

Arthur could not bear the thought of Mary in such a place, and paid a group of men 'whatever it took' to excavate a proper grave next to her mother.

The day of the funeral was sunny and unseasonably warm, which seemed to be somehow inappropriate to Arthur.

The gathering at the gravesite was small. There was, of course, the local vicar and a few coworkers from the bank. Mrs. Granger was there, for no reason other than duty. Most surprisingly to Arthur was the appearance of Molly (accompanied by her father to assure propriety).

And although there was grief and sympathy, and perhaps something more in the girl's eyes, Arthur was blind to it all.

His heart was as closed as the casket which held his little girl.

His little girl and her ornament.

Lowered into the dark, cold ground.

In every way that mattered, Arthur was completely and hopelessly alone.

14

Arthur's first act, upon returning home, was to hand Mrs. Granger a handful of bills and dismiss her. He could fix his own meals and desired solitude.

When he returned to work, he was not the same man. The pleasant gentleman his coworkers had enjoyed had changed to a cold and efficient shadow of a man. He continued to do his work, and in some ways his work improved, but might well have been mechanical for all the personality he demonstrated.

It was one month to the day after Mary's burial that the dreams started. Although as to whether or not Arthur thought of them as dreams or nightmares, even he was unsure.

Every night, Arthur would drift off to sleep only to find himself sitting in the front row of an enormous theatre. Some nights, he would be the only one in the audience. Others, he would be shocked to find the old Gypsy woman with eyes wide in death and a rictus grin seated behind him. Music he knew, but could never place, would begin, played by an unseen orchestra. The red velvet curtains would part and reveal a single silver dancer. Her featureless face, almost a mirror, would look down at Arthur, and then she would begin to dance. The dance would begin gracefully, even beautifully, but that would not last. In short time, the dance would become fast and frantic, and spasms would rock the silver form. Finally with a scream, the figure would leap from the stage, lunging at Arthur.

At that point, Arthur would always awake, and, if he managed to get back to sleep, the dream would begin anew.

15

The lack of sleep quickly took its toll. Arthur found it harder and harder to function each day.

His work suffered immensely, and he turned to drink in his despair. It was a costly mistake.

In short time, his attendance and errors at work forced the bank to give him notice, and while Arthur did have considerable savings, he could not afford to be jobless for long.

And still, every night, the silver dancer dominated his meager sleep.

Then one cold evening, as Arthur sat quietly in the darkness, a simple realization dawned upon him. He realized, with perfect clarity, that the dreams which had robbed him of sleep for so long were obviously a manifestation of his dismay over the loss of Mary. The silver dancer was unmistakably a reference to the ornament that Arthur so closely associated with his little girl.

Arthur needed something. If he could not have his little girl back, then he needed the thing which reminded him the most of her.

He lit a candle and descended the stairs into the vast basement of the house.

It was not long before the candlelight found the object of Arthur's search.

He reached for the shovel.

16

The moon shone brightly above the land, illuminating the small family plot enough that Arthur left his lantern behind. He walked slowly and methodically to Mary's stone, which was easily discernable, even in the dark, due to the delicate statue of an angel which topped the marker.

Arthur's head spun. There was a moment where the gravity of the actions he intended struck him. For a moment, he was sane. Then, with new resolve, he glared at the grave. The shovel bit into the cold ground. The night's dark work had begun.

Hours passed. Arthur was exhausted and his arms had gone weak.

The hole he had dug gaped around him, and he briefly wondered if anything were buried there at all.

Then his foot shifted, displacing a layer of soil and uncovering a tell-tale bit of wood.

Arthur fell to his knees and brushed the dirt from the cover of the coffin. It was in worse shape than Arthur anticipated, which he attributed to moisture getting to it.

Then, as Arthur walked in small circles, trying to determine how to get into a position to open the coffin, the lid cracked and collapsed in.

Arthur's boot landed heavily on what was once Mary's odd face, collapsing it and scattering small white worms.

Hopelessly off-balance, Arthur collapsed onto the corpse which had once been his daughter.

Fighting back nausea, he pushed himself upward and quickly glanced about, searching for the prize he had worked so hard to acquire.

There, still clutched in her thin hands, was the box containing the ornament.

With no regard for the carrion, he kneeled over, and he violently tore the box from dead hands and clutched it to his breast.

And there he sat, and then peacefully slept, next to the mangled corpse of his daughter in her cold dirt grave, until the dawn.

17

The sun reached the corner of the grave where Arthur's head was resting, gently stirring him from the best sleep he had had since Mary died. His back and arms were sore from digging, but he could not remember a time he felt better.

Placing the ornament, secure in its case, gently upon the edge of the hole, Arthur awkwardly scrambled out of the grave. He briefly considered leaving the grave uncovered until his arms felt stronger, but, fearing that, although the odds were against it, some passerby might notice the open grave, he set to work concealing his daughter, once again, beneath the soil.

It was midafternoon by the time his task was complete, but he was still in high spirits. He gathered up the ornament case and, holding it tightly to his chest, walked back to the house, whistling a tune he had only heard in his dreams.

18

Two years came and went without Arthur even setting foot outside his home. He had arranged for prepared meals to be delivered daily, and ritualistically, the person delivering the food would leave it by the door, and find payment in the same spot.

Rumors circulated throughout the town as to what Arthur was up to in his sealed off home. Everything from physical illness, to madness, to a secret lover were discussed ad nauseam. And although none were fully true, a bit of each was rather close.

For in that time, within that house, the ornament was Arthur's constant companion. He would sit for hours, watching the tiny dancer lazily spin in slow circles, or gently holding it in his hand as he gazed out one of the large windows at a world he felt he needed no part of. Sometimes he would read from his large collection of books, but always aloud, as if the dancer could hear. Perhaps she could, or perhaps Arthur was merely mad, he knew one of those possibilities must be true, but he had no idea which.

Then one morning there was a knock upon the door. The sound startled Arthur, and for a moment he was unsure what to make of this sudden unaccustomed sensory input. Then, a fog lifting from his mind, he placed the ornament lightly upon a cushion and walked towards the door. Every step he took further from the ornament, he felt weaker.

By the time he reached the door, it was all he could do to stand and open it.

It was Arthur's solicitor, and the look upon his face was all Arthur needed to know that the visit would not be a pleasant one.

As the man began to speak, Arthur turned away to get back to the ornament. Arthur barely listened, yet he got the gist of the message. Arthur had spent through his savings and was dangerously in debt. His house and lands were at risk.

The solicitor had, in a long career, been forced to deliver devastating news on many occasions. He was used to tears. He was used to rage. He was used to pleading. He was quite convinced that nothing left on this world could surprise him. And yet, Arthur did not cry, or scream, or beg. He merely smiled and held up a glass Christmas tree ornament and said, "Have I ever shown you this?"

The solicitor hastily departed the house, chilled to the bone in a way he would not have thought possible.

19

Enough of the solicitor's message had gotten through to Arthur that he knew money had become a severe problem.

Some of his old clarity returned to him as he decided on a plan of action. He would go and speak to his former employer at the bank and try to explain that his previous unacceptable behavior was due to being distraught over the loss of his daughter. He would ask, beg if needed, for his job back. If that failed he would try to get any job within the bank and work his way back up.

Arthur felt that he had established enough good will during his time there that his former employer would take him back. If it was out of friendship, kindness, or simple pity, Arthur did not care.

To prepare, Arthur lined and cushioned the satchel he formerly used for carrying bank paperwork so that the ornament case would fit safely inside. The thought of leaving the ornament at the house was so abhorrent; Arthur had not even considered it.

The next morning, he found himself filled with ambition. He had taken a hot bath and shaved the night before. He slipped on one of his finest suits and suddenly realized for the first time how much weight he had gained over the past two years of inactivity. The suit was tight, but manageable.

With the typical care he reserved solely for the object, he placed the ornament into its case, and lowered the case into the bag he had prepared for it.

Leaving the house proved more difficult than he had imagined. Stepping back into the world from the house which had been his sole sanctuary for so long sent a tremor of anxiousness through his body. He felt his face reddening and cursed as he realized he was sweating profusely.

He put his hand on the ornament case for strength and stepped out into the world.

The walk from the bank felt both comfortingly familiar and discerningly strange. Few things had changed since Arthur last walked the streets, but the things which had changed were glaring reminders of two years lost.

He stepped into the bank building. Faces glanced, looked away, and then looked back in shock and recognition. Arthur immediately wished that he had made an appointment.

"ARTHUR!" a loud voice boomed across the room, "As I live and breathe!"

Mr. Marley walked swiftly across the bank lobby and, reaching out, grasped Arthur by the shoulders.

"Good to see you, my boy! Good to see you!"

The warmth in Mr. Marley's greeting embarrassed Arthur. "Good to see you too, sir. I…I was hoping that we might talk," he stammered.

"Of course. Of course," Marley said with a smile. "Come into my office."

And with that, hours of negotiations began. In the end, friendship and no small bit of pity won out.

Once again, Arthur was employed.

20

Arthur threw himself back into his job with everything he had. For a time, that would be enough.

At first, Arthur found that his days were plagued with moments of mounting tension. Only checking the ornament case to assure that the glass globe was safe and secure would alleviate the tension. These moments grew more and more frequent, until Arthur feared they might cost him his job.

Eventually, in an attempt to alleviate his fears regarding the safety of the ornament, he moved the ornament to a spot upon his desk. Placed there,

Arthur could see it at all times.

Whenever someone would inquire about it, Arthur would merely reply that it was a memento of his deceased child.

Marley was tolerant, yet he found the presence of the ornament on Arthur's desk to be rather unprofessional.

It was not perfect, but it was working.

Then, one afternoon, a bank customer, his wife, and his very young son found themselves at Arthur's desk. They were hoping to acquire a loan, and were in deep conversation about rates and terms with Arthur when their son, a lad named Colin, snatched the ornament from the desk.

Arthur let out what could only be described as a growl, and with frightening speed he circled the desk and seized his treasured prize back from the child. When the child squealed in misplaced glee and reached for the ornament again, Arthur delivered a devastating backhand to the child's face, sending the boy sprawling across the hard bank floor.

In the chaos that followed, Arthur managed to place the ornament back into its case and pack the case into his bag. He stormed out of the bank doors. He did not need to hear the words from Marley to know that he was, once again, unemployed.

21

The months that followed were difficult. Arthur gained and lost several jobs far beneath his social status. Every job loss was directly or indirectly related to the ornament, but it was beyond Arthur's capacity to realize it.

In short time, he had lost his family home and most of his possessions. He wondered briefly what the new owners would do with the hallowed ground which held his wife and daughter, as well as several generations of his ancestors. Then he decided he really didn't care.

The ornament and the little silver dancer were all that he needed.

In time, he found a small room above a pub in one of the less reputable sections of town. In exchange for cleaning the pub every evening and running a few errands on occasion, the pub owner gave Arthur room and board.

And every free moment, every chance he got, Arthur quietly adored his precious ornament.

No matter how far he had fallen, no matter how miserable his circumstances appeared, no matter how much he had lost, as long as Arthur possessed the ornament, he was content. The dancer was all that mattered.

If not for the ornament, Arthur might have taken his own life before now, but leaving the ornament in this world while he travelled on to the next was something that Arthur could never allow to happen.

But some things are beyond anyone's control.

22

Christmas Eve. Snow was falling fiercely everywhere. Pubs across the country were filled with both the revelers and the distraught and lonely.

The pub beneath Arthur's room was no exception. Loud laughter and music floated up through the floor boards, filling Arthur's room and making any relaxation impossible.

With a sigh, Arthur sat up in his cot. Rising to his feet he picked up the ornament from its cushion beside the bed and walked down the old wooden stairs to the pub below.

The room was full. Drinks were flowing freely. The two waitresses were being run ragged. A group of intoxicated men were playing a spirited game of darts which endangered everyone around them.

After a short search of the room, Arthur found a small, out of the way table in a shadowed corner of the room. He climbed behind the table and sat, his back against the wall.

His eye was briefly drawn to a young couple kissing beneath a hanging mistletoe. He remembered love. He remembered the joy of it, and the pain it always seemed to ultimately cause

Somewhere in the back of his mind, he recalled that this would've been Mary's birthday.

"Happy Birthday, Poppet," he said quietly, to no one at all. A tear surprised him as it ran down his cheek.

But then the thoughts of his daughter drifted away like gossamer and were replaced with a glint of silver.

Arthur sat quietly, his chin resting on one hand while the other held the cherished ornament before his eyes. The lights of the pub danced across the glass orb and the silver figure inside it, creating a lively display which held Arthur fully entranced.

So entranced that he did not notice the approach of a young, rather gigantic, Irish ruffian.

"What do you have there, mate?" the big man asked.

If Arthur heard the Irishman, there was no sign of it.

"Listen. I've got a lass who loves things such as that what you're holding there. I need to get her a gift before morning. How much do you want for the little thing?" he asked, pulling pound notes from his pocket.

Arthur looked up, acknowledging the man's presence for the first time. "It's not for sale."

"Oh come on now," pleaded the red-haired giant, "I'm in a bit of a fix and you'd be doing me a right good favor. It's just a bit of Gypsy craft, iddinit? I'll pay you a fair bit more than it's worth."

Arthur could feel himself turning red, and he snapped at the man, "Is there something wrong with your ears? It is not for sale. And its worth is far more than anything you have to offer!"

But then it was the Irishman who was turning red (or more red, to be accurate). Slamming his hands onto the small table between them, he lurched over until his face was close to Arthur's.

"I asked nicely," the brute hissed from between gritted teeth. Arthur could smell the strong stench of liquor emanating from the man like a cloud. "GIVE IT!"

With that, the man grasped for the ornament only to have Arthur quickly pull it out of his reach. The table tipped over, taking the large man with it to the floor. Arthur seized the opportunity and fled, the ornament clutched to his chest.

As he navigated through the confused crowd, heading for the pub door, he could hear the Irishman bellowing as he rose to his feet and began to give chase.

Arthur exited the pub in a full run, but almost immediately lost his footing on a patch of ice and was sent crashing to the ground.

The ornament escaped his grasp.

Arthur spun around and watched in horror as the shiny ball flew in what seemed to be a slow graceful arc through the air. It landed, however, without any grace. It collided with the cobblestones and shattered. Small bits of glass flew in every direction. The silver dancer bounced once and then was still.

Arthur let out a wail, and clambered on all fours into the street. His hands bled as he frantically tried to gather the glass shards in the darkness.

The weary coach driver, too eager to get home, was pushing his horse to go faster than he should have. He saw the man on his hands and knees in the street a moment too late.

Arthur opened his eyes. He was in a familiar theatre, in a familiar chair. Familiar music rose from an empty orchestra pit. He noticed that it was a full house. Every seat was packed. The music reached a crescendo and the deep red curtains rose.

There stood the silver dancer.

She looked at Arthur.

Unlike the dreams of the past, she did not dance. She merely looked.

After a moment of silence and stillness, she leapt from the stage, lunging at Arthur.

Arthur reared back in his seat, full of fear, wondering why he had not yet woken up.

The dancer's arms wrapped around his neck, and then, like mercury, the silver flowed away.

"Father!" Mary cried, "I have been calling you for so long! You've finally come to see me dance!"

She embraced him and kissed his tear streaked cheeks.

Then she was back on the stage, twirling and jumping gracefully on strong, agile legs. She flashed a smile just for him as she continued her performance.

Arthur wept openly, without shame. It was a miracle.

It was a gift.

Epilogue

A crowd was gathering. Some grimly curious people wanted to see the aftermath of the accident. Other, kinder souls, rushed to help the distressed coachman. His horse had broken a leg, and his cart had rolled over, throwing the man a good distance. A couple of folk had gone directly to the crumpled mess that was a man.

The big Irishman wasn't interested in any of that. He scanned the scene, searching for something very specific. He likely would have missed it if a reflection of light hadn't caught his eye.

He walked across the street and there, by a sewer grate, was a shiny glass orb with a tiny silver dancer inside. Glancing around to make sure no one was watching, he scooped up the ornament and smiled. Things were going his way. He walked back into the now nearly empty pub and over to a woman seated at the bar. She had been beautiful when she was younger, but life, broken hearts, and alcohol had taken their toll. Still, she retained enough of her old charms to attract the attention of a big, dumb Irish boy.

"This is for you, Love," the boy said with a lascivious grin. "Merry Christmas."

"Merry Christmas," she replied and took the ornament from his hand and held it up to a light. The little dancer flashed with light and spun and spun.

"I love it," Molly said with a smile.

ABOUT THE WRITERS

E. W. Farnsworth lives and writes in Arizona. He is widely published online and in print, with over two hundred short stories and eleven books released during the period 2014 to 2016. For updates on his writing please visit his website: www.ewfarnsworth.com.

Brad P. Christy is the author of the short stories: *Miseryland, Angel Dust, Krampus: The Summoning, and Cape Hadel*. He is a member of the Writers' League of Texas, and holds a degree in Creative Writing and English. Brad lived in Germany for three years where he immersed himself in their folklore, and now resides in the Pacific Northwest with his wife.

Jessamy Dalton lives in rural Virginia, where she reads, writes, and helps out on her family's small farm, and somehow goes on existing despite the fact that most of society considers neither writing nor farming to be 'real' jobs.

Corinne Clark first became enchanted with gothic mysteries after reading *The Letter, The Witch and The Ring* by John Bellairs at the age of ten. Having since devoured the ghost stories of Henry James, Wilkie Collins, and Amelia Edwards, among others, she has turned her hand to writing her own works of gaslamp fantasy. She is currently working on a YA novel, which is set in Victorian London and includes ghosts, of course. You can find out more about her by visiting corinneclarkwriter.com

Brian Malachy Quinn currently teaches Physics at the University of Akron and in his free time writes and creates art. He is the author of *Astronomy: A Computational Approach*, Van-Griner 2010, and ghost writer of a book on wealth management. His gold standard for short story horror is Poe's *Fall of the House of Usher* and he enjoys writing specifically historic horror in which he has to learn about a certain by-gone period. His art can be found at: www.brianquinnstudio.com

M.R. DeLuca has short stories published in *Shadows in Salem* and After *the Happily Ever After*. In addition to the beauty of words, M.R. enjoys numbers, speleothems, and homemade whoopie pies.

Casey E. Hamilton is a writer of all things speculative, usually with a history bend. In her spare time she drinks quarts of tea, revels in her city's Lincoln obsession, and plays the ukulele—much to the chagrin of her three cats. Her home on the web is https://caseykins.com

Gabriel Barbaro grew up in Amherst, Massachusetts and attended Sarah Lawrence College. A diagnosed bibliophile, his fascinations include science fiction, fantasy, and horror. Gabriel writes dark short stories and lives in Harlem, NYC with his beautiful fiancée and their two loving cats Banana and Mochi. www.gabrielbarbaro.com

Kenneth E. Olson has authored short fiction for various anthologies including *Steamy Screams, So Long and Thanks for All the Brains, From Their Cradle to Your Grave, Cesspool,* and *In Shambles.* His first novel, *Ripples,* is available from Amazon.com, and he contributes regularly to *Bad Taste,* a horror-themed, flash-fiction newsletter available by request at thebadtasteproject@gmail.com. Kenneth lives in Minnesota with his wife, two children, and four canine fur-babies.

Larry Lefkowitz's stories, poetry and humor have been widely published. Lefkowitz's humorous literary novel, *The Novel, Kunzman, the Novel,* is available as an e-book and in print from Lulu.com and other distributors. Writers and readers with a deep interest in literature will especially enjoy the novel. Lefkowitz's humorous fantasy and science fiction collection, *Laughing into the Fourth Dimension* is available from Amazon books.

Bill Dale Grizzle, or just Dale to all who know him, was born and raised in rural Northwest Georgia; he resides there still and almost all his writings are heavily influenced by his folk surroundings. Dale is honored to have another short story selected for publication by FunDead Publications and hopes you enjoy the story. His short story, *Inspection Connection* was featured *in Shadows in Salem* in 2016. Contact him on Facebook at Dale Grizzle, or by email at billdalegrizzle@aol.com.

R.C. Mulhare is no stranger to the spookier side of Christmas/the Winter Holidays, as she moonlights in grocery retail when she isn't writing, which during the holiday season, has her wishing she could wear Krampus horns in rotation with an elf hat. Thanks to her co-author and mom, I.M. Mulhare, penfriend to dozens of people worldwide including The Land Down Under, who provided a wee R.C. with a healthy diet of the *Brothers' Grimm Faery Tales* and the poetry of Edgar Allan Poe, and her dad who's an expert at wrangling Christmas trees and telling exciting stories, she's more than well-equipped to take on any Yuletide chaos. She's delighted to have people visit her at http://www.facebook.com/rcmulhare/

Callum McSorley is a writer based in Glasgow, Scotland. He graduated from the University of Strathclyde with a degree in English, Journalism & Creative Writing. He has published journalism in magazines the world over while working for homeless charity INSP. His first collection of short stories, *Beaten to a Pulp!,* is out now. Visit him at: https://callummcsorleyauthor.wordpress.com/

A lifelong fan or horror and the macabre, since he was traumatized by an episode of *Alfred Hitchcock Presents* as a child, Mike Carey is a wee bit twisted. He's spent his years doing cool stuff, lame stuff, and all the stuff in between. He's lived his entire life in the Salem area, and plans to have his entire death there, as well. www.SalemUncommons.SmackJeeves.com

Amber Newberry is the head of FunDead Publications, and she writes as often as the muse gives her opportunity. She published her first novel, *Walls of Ash,* in 2012. Amber is working on a follow-up, if her ADHD would just allow her to stop taking on new projects and finish one of the manuscripts currently collecting dust.

DJ Tyrer is the person behind *Atlantean Publishing*, which has just released its twentieth-anniversary anthology, *A Terrible Thing* (available from Amazon). DJ has been widely published in anthologies and magazines around the world, including *Chilling Horror Short Stories* (Flame Tree), *State of Horror: Illinois* (Charon Coin Press), *Steampunk Cthulhu*(Chaosium), and *Sorcery & Sanctity: A Homage to Arthur Machen* (Hieroglyphics Press), and issues of *Black Girl Magic, Weirdbook,* and *Ravenwood Quarterly*. In addition, DJ has a novella available in paperback and on Kindle, *The Yellow House* (Dunhams Manor).
DJ Tyrer's website is at http://djtyrer.blogspot.co.uk/

Kevin Wetmore is an award-winning writer whose short fiction has appeared in such anthologies as *Midian Unmade,Whispers from the Abyss 2, Urban Temples of Cthulhu,* and *Enter at Your Own Risk: The End is the Beginning,* as well as such magazines as *Mothership Zeta, Weirdbook,* and *Devolution Z*. You can read his other holiday horror piece, *A Ghosthunter's Guide to Christmas Yet to Come* in *Winter Horror Days*. He is also the author of such books as *Post-9/11 Horror in American Cinema* and *Back from the Dead: Reading Remakes of Romero's Zombie Films as Markers of their Times*. You can check out his work at his website: www.SomethingWetmoreThisWayComes.com

Wendy Schmidt has been writing short stories, essays and poetry for the last ten years. Pieces have been published in *Verse Wisconsin, Chicago Literati, City Lake Poets, Literary Hatchet, Moon Magazine,* and *Rebelle Society*. You can read one of her stories, *The Curse Now Lifted,* in the award winning Anthology, *Shifts*. Visit her author page at: https://www.amazon.com/Wendy-L.-Schmidt/e/B014VD4A6G

Sammi Cox lives in the UK and spends her time writing and making things. Ghost stories, fairytales, folklore, and witchcraft have all played their part in firing up her imagination and inspiring her to write. You can keep up to date with whatever she is scribbling by visiting her blog: https://sammiscribbles.wordpress.com/

G. H. Finn keeps his real identity secret, possibly in the forlorn hope of one day being mistaken for a superhero. Having written non-fiction for many years, G. H. Finn decided to start submitting short-stories to publishers in 2015 and was flabbergasted when the first story he'd ever submitted was selected. Since then he has had a wide range of fiction published and especially enjoys mixing genres in his work, including mystery, horror, steampunk, dieselpunk, dark comedy, detective, fantasy, supernatural, speculative, weird, folkloric, Cthulhu mythos, sci-fi, spy-fi, crime and urban fantasy. ghfinn.orkneymagic.com

WE LOVE YOU TO DEATH

www.FunDeadPublications.com

www.FunDeadShop.com

Made in the USA
Coppell, TX
04 December 2019

12389595R00118